The Plot to Kill the Premier

A Marc LeBlanc Mystery

Jeremy Akerman

The Plot to Kill the Premier
© 2024 Jeremy Akerman

Cover art by the author
Cover design: Rebekah Wetmore
Editor: Andrew Wetmore

ISBN: 978-1-998149-44-5
First edition August, 2024

Moose House Publicatons
2475 Perotte Road
Annapolis County, NS B0S 1A0
moosehousepress.com
info@moosehousepress.com

Moose House Publications recognizes the support of the Province of Nova Scotia. We are pleased to work in partnership with the Department of Communities, Culture and Heritage to develop and promote our cultural resources for all Nova Scotians.

We live and work in Mi'kma'ki, the ancestral and unceded territory of the Mi'kmaw people. This territory is covered by the "Treaties of Peace and Friendship" which Mi'kmaw and Wolastoqiyik (Maliseet) people first signed with the British Crown in 1725. The treaties did not deal with surrender of lands and resources but in fact recognized Mi'kmaq and Wolastoqiyik (Maliseet) title and established the rules for what was to be an ongoing relationship between nations. We are all Treaty people.

Also by Jeremy Akerman

and available from Moose House Publications

Memoir
Outsider

Politics
What Have You Done for Me Lately?—revised edition

The Marc LeBlanc Mysteries
Holy Grail, Sacred Gold
Unspeakable Evil
Best Served Cold

Fiction
Black Around the Eyes—revised edition
The Affair at Lime Hill
The Premier's Daughter
In Search of Dr. Dee
Explosion

This book is dedicated to my friends Roland Thornhill and Arthur
Donahoe, former politicians of the old school who, had he existed,
would have known the young Ernest Maddingly.

And to all those occupying the office of Premier of Nova Scotia,
who have given service to this province
under trying circumstances.

This is a work of fiction. The author has created the characters, conversations, interactions, and events; and any resemblance of any of the main characters to any real person is coincidental.

The Plot to Kill the Premier

The Plot to Kill the Premier

Jeremy Akerman

1

I had never met the premier of Nova Scotia until I saw him at Ray and Rachel Bland's wedding. However, he was easy to recognize from his photographs in the media, and in any event he was a prepossessing figure. Wendell Proctor was coal black, extremely handsome and, I guessed, about six feet three inches, so he would stand out in any crowd.

I am not a political person, in the sense of being partisan, but I was aware that he had been premier for about two years, succeeding Brenton Granger, who had unfortunately died in a drowning accident.

I confess I was surprised to see the premier at the wedding. I was told that Ray had at one time been active politically, but I was not aware that his connections had been that illustrious.

When I looked around at the crowd gathered on the Blands' lawn that day, I could see that the attention of attendees was about equally divided between the newlyweds and the premier and his charming wife, a large group of admirers following each around the property in a somewhat sycophantic manner.

After performing our duties as best man and matron of honour, my wife, Rosalie, and I kept ourselves pretty much to ourselves, hovering on the fringes of the festivities. We were chatting quietly under a large maple tree when I saw Proctor detach himself from the throng and head in our direction. I looked behind me to discover who was there, thinking the premier must be heading to greet an old associate. Seeing nobody within sight in that direction, I realized that he was walking very deliberately towards us.

"Mr. and Mrs. LeBlanc?" he said, beaming and extending a hand towards Rosalie.

"Hello Premier," Rosalie said, taking his hand. Clearly, she was as amazed as I was that he had singled us out for attention.

"Ray has told me all about you."

"Oh dear," said my wife. "What did he say? Nothing bad, I hope."

"On the contrary, I'm impressed by what I heard. He has described your extraordinary efforts to establish his origins, and some of your amazing, if unpleasant, discoveries along the way."

"We did our best to help him," I mumbled. "Ray and Rachel are our best friends."

"So I understand," said Proctor. "They also told me about your search for the Holy Grail in Nova Scotia last year."

"Did they?"

"That must have been a remarkable experience."

I looked beyond the premier and, about fifteen feet away, saw a pressing ring of people who obviously felt he had spent more than enough time with us, and who wanted to extricate him from our conversation.

Seeing my eye line, Proctor turned to face them. "Not now, friends," he said. "Mr. LeBlanc and I have business to attend to. If you don't mind, we could use a little privacy."

The crowd reluctantly moved away, muttering as they went. The premier turned back to us, beaming.

"Business?" I queried.

"Well, sort of. Maybe." The premier laughed. "That depends."

"Depends on what? I don't understand."

At that moment a handsome man in his forties came rushing up and put his hand on the premier's arm. "Wendell, we must go. Something has come up. We have to get back to Halifax."

"Tom, I want you to meet Marc and Rosalie LeBlanc. This is Tom Aldridge, my Chief of Staff, sometimes referred to as my nanny."

"Hi folks," said Aldridge. "I'm sorry to drag him away, but it is important."

"Okay, Tom. Bring the car around while I say goodbye to Rachel and Ray."

Then the Premier was gone, striding across the lawn to the marquee, where the happy couple were holding court.

"We may be getting better acquainted soon," said Aldridge.

"Will we? Why?" Rosalie asked.

"What is this all about?" I said.

"You may be hearing from us. Got to go now," Aldridge said as he turned away. "And please call me Tom."

"What on earth do you make of all that?" I asked Rosalie.

"It's very mysterious."

"I'm guessing that Ray has gilded the lily in describing us and our achievements."

"When they get back from their honeymoon, we can ask him exactly what he said."

"They'll be leaving soon. We'd better go and say goodbye to them and wish them luck."

As we moved across the lawn towards the marquee, a big, black Lincoln swept down the driveway. One of the darkened rear windows was rolled down. Proctor's head appeared.

"See you soon, Marc. You too, Rosalie," he said.

The car sped off to Halifax.

"Do you think we really will hear from him?" Rosalie asked.

"Probably not. Politicians are full of bullshit. You know that. They'll say anything to a person at the moment, then quickly forget all about it."

"You're right. Let's get another glass of Champagne."

2

Before I proceed with this narrative, I should say something about my-self. I have only been living in Nova Scotia, in Grand Pre, for a little more than three years. Although born in Wolfville, I was away for over fifteen years, working for a merchant bank in London. There, due to a series of gratuitous market anomalies, I made a great deal of money.

But it was a stressful and time-consuming life, and I did not keep in touch with my father as I should have done.

Truth to tell, I did not really know him. I had remembrances of child-hood and teen years, but even then he was frequently absent from home, travelling the world. I was never told the reason for these peregrinations and, frankly, had little interest in finding out.

My mother died when I was twenty-two, and, following what seemed like only a token period of mourning, my father installed Gerald in his bookshop, and was very soon off on his travels again.

Armed with my BBA from Acadia University, I accepted an invitation from a former professor to join him at the London bank in a lowly posi-tion.

When I came home with my new found wealth, I brought my car with me. It was performing extremely well—and still does—even though it is ten years old. It is a Bugatti Veyron Grand Sport Vitesse, only one of 92 made, but the engineering by Wolfgang Schreiber is so superb that the car was not only the fastest roadster in the world, reaching an average top speed of 408.84 kph, but was also impressively reliable.

As one would expect, the asking price for one of these precision vehicles was enormous so, despite my success in the markets, I had to settle for getting mine second-hand from an Arabian sheik.

In any event, the waiting list for new Bugattis is endless and, unless you had the many millions for the one-only versions, you could be old and grey by the time you acquired one.

My dream had been to own a Bugatti Veyron L'Or Blanc, a one-of-a-kind car crafted in porcelain. The porcelain goes through impact and wear testing to make sure it doesn't break on the road. But this masterpiece is worth $2.4 million, and even if one was available—which it wasn't—that was a little too rich for my blood.

Shortly after my return, my father was murdered. In the ensuing months, I became involved in the Holy Grail affair, to which the premier alluded at the Blands' wedding. For those interested, I have documented the story in a book called *Holy Grail, Sacred Blood*.

Since our marriage, Rosalie and I have been blissfully happy and have worked as an effective team on another major investigation into Ray Bland's origins, a matter Premier Proctor also mentioned. I have recorded that investigation in my book *Unspeakable Evil*.

Rosalie has a part-time assistant professorship in history at Acadia University; but as a man of independent means, when I am not investigating there is little for me to do except cook and expand my fairly good wine cellar. About a year ago I established a wine store on the main street in Wolfville, which has been open only a few months, but is expertly managed by my highly-competent business partner Louise LeBlanc (no relation). So competent is she that I feel my presence in the shop is an imposition and a hindrance to its smooth running, so I spend little time there.

So often being at a loose end, it is of considerable interest to me when there might be an investigation in the offing. Neither Rosalie nor I are officially private investigators under the Private Investigators and Private Guards Act of 1989, as we did not want to create a company to employ us, which is what the regulations require. So we undertake investigations in our capacity as citizens and do not accept remuneration for our efforts.

Beside these considerations, soon summer would be upon us. Rosalie would not be teaching, and we would not want to spend time lounging around the house.

Consequently, any time the premier wanted to contact us, his call would be welcomed. We wondered what he had in mind and why he wanted our services, when presumably he had the entire police force at his disposal.

So, we waited.

3

Two weeks passed and we heard nothing from the premier or from his Chief of Staff, Tom Aldridge.

I know now, but did not know then, that heads of governments are a breed apart, living in a make-believe world in which they imagine their words and actions have only beneficial effects. Apart from public events, where they are cutting ribbons or speaking to crowds of adoring party supporters, they live in a cocoon populated by relatively few people, all of whom owe their position to their boss.

Once a week they will be exposed to some twenty or so of their cabinet colleagues, who also owe their positions to the premier. In a universe in which they might see, at most, forty people in an entire week, they generally hear nothing but compliments and sounds of approval.

In such a rarefied sphere, it does not occur to them that hints of rewards to come, or even encouraging words, to individuals should receive the slightest attention after they have been uttered. Still less does it ever cross their minds that some people hang on their words as if they were gold, so suffer, often dreadfully, when no follow-through occurs.

The rules are different for them: solemn confidences are broken without thought, and promises are dispensed with abandon. Never was the saying 'out of sight, out of mind' more true than with political leaders.

That is, unless and until a situation arises when *they* need favours, or they are faced with difficulties which are not easily addressed. Then firm and fond friendships are quickly recalled and some of those who have been languishing in the wings will be summoned and welcomed with open arms.

Without even knowing it, their brain tells them that if they were not better than everyone else, wiser, more intelligent and more decent, they would not have been chosen to lead. In their minds, the voice of the people is easily confused with the voice of God, and they come to believe that the King can do no wrong.

Wendell Proctor was not nearly as bad as some of his predecessors as premier of Nova Scotia, but, sooner or later, all government leaders become infected with a lack of empathy for any but those who are in a position to render immediate service to the throne.

So, Rosalie and I, rather sorrowfully because we had liked the man so much, told ourselves that Proctor was just another politician full of bluster and bullshit. We moved on with our lives.

Then, one Monday morning, our cleaning lady, Mrs. Bezanson, came to do her work, which usually took her the best part of the day. We paid her by the day, not the hour, so we could rely on her not to quit until she was satisfied that everything was spotless.

"Though, I must say, Mr. LeBlanc," she said to me as she wheeled the vacuum cleaner up the hallway, "I do wish you'd let me have a go at the dusty old cellar. It wouldn't take me long."

"Thank you, but no, Mrs. Bezanson," I said, imagining with horror what damage she could inflict on my prized wine collection if she slipped or had some other kind of accident. Besides which, it pleased me to see the bottles gathering dust as they do in the great *caves* of Bordeaux and Burgundy.

"Just as you please, Mr. LeBlanc."

Then she started up the vacuum cleaner and zoomed across the carpet. "Feet up, please!" she shouted as she pushed the machine towards me.

I lifted my feet, whereupon she spent, I thought, rather too long cleaning my particular patch of carpet.

When she had finished she switched off the cleaner and stretched. "Oooh. Have you heard?" she asked.

"Heard what, Mrs. B?"

"About that priest."

"What priest? What are you talking about?"

"That young priest who works for the Valley Catholic Churches."

"I know nothing about him. Rosalie and I don't go to church. And, in any case, she's a protestant."

"Well, he's for the high jump and no mistake!"

"Why, what did he do?"

"Sexual assault!"

"Whom is he supposed to have assaulted?"

"Oh he did it, alright." She stuck out her chin defiantly. "Mrs. Morton's daughter. You know the one, right pretty she is. Only 17 years old."

"No I don't know her...or him. Has he been charged?"

"Oh, yes."

"Well, why don't we wait for the law to take its course?"

"Who needs the law? You know what them priests are like. And her a real looker."

"I think the priests you are referring to were more interested in boys."

"What's the difference? I don't trust any of them."

"Are you a Catholic, Mrs B.?"

"Who, me? No, I am not! I am a Baptist."

"Ah. Everyone is entitled to a fair trial, Mrs. B. Do you think you might be more favourably disposed to giving him the presumption of innocence if he were a Baptist?"

"That's got nothing to do with it!" she said hotly. "We're told that women must be believed. I think it's called the Me Too movement."

"But not blindly believing in the absence of evidence?"

"You're a man. You would say that. We women *know* these things. Why would she accuse him if it didn't happen?"

"There could be any number of reasons."

"I don't see what. And I tell you, Mr. LeBlanc, that there's much more of this going on that we know about."

"Sexual assault?"

"Oh, yes."

"But, Mrs. Bezanson, if we don't know about it, how can we know about it?"

"What? You're talking in riddles."

"I think you're the one talking in riddles. You can't know something you don't know. Unless, of course, you meant to say that you *believe* there are more assaults than are recorded."

"I know what I know. Women must be believed! That priest is as guilty as sin. Now I got to do the upstairs rooms. I can't spend all day gabbing."

"I wouldn't want you to do that, Mrs B., believe me."

She went away, huffing and puffing. I usually carry the vacuum cleaner up the stairs for her, but I was annoyed with her so did not move from my chair.

Some hours later, Rosalie came home from some kind of meeting at the university. She entered the room, throwing her coat on the couch.

"So, what's for dinner, Gordon Ramsay? Thrushes in aspic, or truffled larks' tongues?"

"Neither. We are having salt cod, with pork scraps and fried onions. And potatoes."

"Oh yummy! One of my favourites. I'm surprised you have lowered yourself to cook such a common dish."

"*Au contraire,* my chickadee, it is one of the world's greatest culinary delights."

"I'll go and have a wash and get changed," she said. "Could you pour me an Aberfeldy please?"

"I'd be delighted. Ice and soda?"

"Please. Just a little."

She disappeared for a few minutes, only to re-emerge half-dressed.

"I forgot to tell you," she said, "Guess what I heard at the college?"

"Was it about a priest assaulting some girl?"

"How did you know?"

"Mrs. Bezanson. She's on the warpath."

"But did she tell you who it was?"

"Yes, Mrs. Morton's daughter."

"No, I mean who was the priest."

"No."

"It's Father Mike!"

"Father Mike who?" Then it struck me like a bold of lightening. I had almost forgotten about the man who had once done Rosalie and me a tremendous favour. "*Our* Father Mike?"

"Yes."

"I didn't know he was still around here. Where's his church?"

"Saint Francis."

"Do you believe it?"

"Frankly, no. My instincts are in the other direction, but I just can't see Father Mike doing this."

"Nor me. Mrs. Bezanson says, 'Women must be believed.'"

"A few years ago I would have said the same thing, but I see now it doesn't jibe with justice. Mark, we'll have to get involved."

"You're right. We owe that man a lot."

4

The next morning I prepared one of my favourite breakfasts: smoked haddock and eggs poached in milk, slathered with butter and served with fresh sourdough bread. Rosalie wrinkled her nose in disgust and not only made herself some scrambled eggs but ate them in another room, not being able to watch me eat.

We share most preferences and dislikes, but some things sharply separate us. My liking for black pudding, Marmite and smoked haddock drives her to distraction; while her fondness for oatmeal, parsnips and cake fills me with dread.

After she heard me washing my plate in the sink, she sauntered in with her coffee.

"What are we going to do about Father Mike?" she asked.

"What do you think we should do?"

"I don't really know. There's a public meeting tonight in town. I thought we should go to that to make sure there are at least some voices who are against lynching him."

"Yes, that makes sense. But I wonder if we should talk to Father Mike first to get his side of the story."

"That would be a good idea. Do you know where he lives?"

"I guess he still lives with Abbé Mystère in that house of horrors up on Ridge Road."

"Why do you call it a house of horrors?"

"Wait till you see it. It is almost falling down and hasn't had a coat of paint in about fifty years. Inside it's very creaky and creepy."

"Ugh. Well, I think we'd better take a run up there and see what's what."

~

We hopped into the Bugatti, taking Eye Road and Maple Avenue, so we were there in five minutes.

The house, like something out of a Stephen King movie, loomed on the horizon, black and forbidding. The driveway appeared to be in rough shape, rutted and potholed, so I left the car at the roadside and we hobbled up to the front door.

Evidently the bell was not working, as nobody appeared when I rang it, so I pounded on the door. Each time my fist knocked on the frame, it shook alarmingly, producing a small cloud of dust.

Eventually, Father Chataigre, or Abbé Mystère as we had called him when we were in college, answered the door.

"Ah, Marc LeBlanc! Do you follow bad news or does it follow you?"

"Hello, Father. This is my wife, Rosalie."

"Rosalie." He inclined his grizzled old head. "So you have thrown in your lot with an *aventurier téméraire*. My condolences to you. You had better come in. It is not very difficult to guess why you have come."

We followed him into what once must have been the 'best room', with its sparse furnishings and threadbare carpet. It was a truly depressing place, with bare walls of a brownish-grey and floorboards from which any shine had long since disappeared. The only two chairs were rickety and had holes in their upholstery, which did not appear to be very clean.

Very gingerly, Rosalie sat down on the very edge of one of the chairs.

"I'll go and tell Father Michael you are here, then I will leave you alone."

Abbé Mystère disappeared into the dark recesses of the house, his feet scraping along the passage as he went.

When he had left the room, I brushed off the dust from the other chair and sat in it, my posterior sinking well below the frame of the chair. I jumped up immediately, feeling that if I stayed there I would be trapped indefinitely.

I wandered over to the filthy window, with its rags of even filthier curtains, and peered out into the yard. Four crows were savagely tearing at something on the ground, which I made no attempt to see. Some clothes of indeterminate identity hung pathetically on a loose line strung from the house to a shed. A few barely-surviving vegetables clung to life in a patch of dirt behind the shed. I was filled with gloom.

"Rosalie, Marc. Thank you do much for coming," said Father Mike as he stepped into the room. He looked as tall, young, blond and handsome as we remembered him, but had a slightly haggard look.

"We came as soon as we heard this nonsense," said Rosalie.

"I'm glad you think it is nonsense."

"Of course we do!"

"Father Mike, could you tell us what happened and why you think it happened?"

"Certainly." He drew a large breath. "This young woman, Catherine Morton, has been coming up to me in the street for some time now, making suggestions."

"What kind of suggestions?"

"You know, saying things like, 'Wouldn't you like to get me behind that warehouse,' or, 'They say you priests are celibate, but I can fix that for you,' and a variety of other things along the same lines."

"How did you respond?"

"Always in the same way. I'd laugh and say I didn't like jokes if they could do harm, and then I walk away quickly."

"Would she follow?"

"Sometimes. More than once she would touch me."

"Touch you? In the street?"

"Not in that way, but she would put her hand behind my neck and try to stroke it."

"What did you do?"

"I pulled away, of course, and left. Lately, I've even run away, although it wasn't very dignified."

"Were there any witnesses?"

"There might have been. I didn't notice. At least none who would be on my side."

"What do you mean by that?" Rosalie asked.

"Well, they were always there. But nobody was ever with me when she pulled one of her stunts."

"What do you mean? Who are *they*?"

"The girls."

"What girls?"

"The girls she hangs around with."

"How many of them were there?"

"I'd say sometimes about six, sometimes fewer."

"Were they always there?"

"Yes. Usually at a distance, but yes, they were."

"Did they say anything at any time?"

"Sometimes they would say, 'Go on,' to her before she approached me. But usually they would just giggle."

"Did she ever threaten you?"

"Yes. One day I ran into her and her gang on the street and crossed over to get away from them, but they seemed to be pushing her in my direction."

"And?"

"Well, she came over and said, 'Look here, Michael, I'm getting sick if this. If you don't cooperate, I'm going to say you tried it on without my consent.'"

"What did you think she meant?"

"What else could she have meant? Presumably that I should go somewhere and have sex with her."

"And you said, 'No'?"

"Of course I said, 'No.'"

I decided to sit down after all, and sank into the rickety chair. For some reason I noticed that neither Father Mike nor Abbé Mystère had offered us anything to drink.

My throat was dry, but I pressed on. "Father Mike, I have to ask you this. Did you, at any time, in any way, encourage this girl and, even in jest, suggest that, under any circumstances—any circumstances at all—you might be willing to accede to her requests?"

"No. Wait…I may have said something like, 'If I ever decide to leave the priesthood, I'll give you a call.'"

"Ach. That's logical but unfortunate."

"I realize that now," he said ruefully.

"Now, and this is crucial: was anything either of you said, in any of these meetings, said within earshot of the other girls?"

"Obviously, I can't know what they heard or didn't hear, but I shouldn't have thought it at all likely."

"Thank you, Father. One last question. Will you be going to the public meeting tonight?"

"Absolutely. Will you be there, Marc?"

"No. I will give my reasons at a later date, but Rosalie will be there."

"Will I ever!" she said with energy.

"But do not let on you know each other," I said. "You will have a rough ride, Father Mike, but it is essential that you deny these accusations in front of the entire mob."

"Thanks, Marc. I know I can count on the support of both of you."

"Father Mike, you once did us an immense service and we will never forget it."

5

I went to bed early that night, so I did not get Rosalie's account of the public meeting until the next morning.

Over breakfast of lightly sautéed filets of cod served with hash browns (Rosalie likes to tease me by calling it 'fish and chips'), she told me that attendance had been around 200 and that the gathering had been notable for its noise levels and for the passion of partisans on both sides.

Apparently, Mrs. Bezanson was one of the few 'antis' over 50, most of Catherine Morton's supporters having been younger female militants wearing t-shirts bearing the slogans "Me Too!" and "We Must Believe Women!" Rosalie said most of the noise came from this cohort, which attempted to hog the microphone and shout down any who did not agree with them that Father Mike should be hung, drawn and quartered on the spot.

Father Mike's defenders, fewer in number, were older women and some men known to be active in the Catholic Church.

"Did Father Mike speak?" I asked.

"He tried, but was drowned out and gave up."

"You say Mrs. B was there?"

"With banners flying and drums beating," Rosalie said. "She was out-libbing the libbers."

"Was there anyone there who called for common sense?"

"Don't be silly, Marc. It was a public meeting."

"Was Walter Bryson there?"

"I didn't see him."

"Any other lawyers?"

"Not that I could identify."

"So nobody was there to put the simple proposition that a person is innocent until proved guilty?"

"Of course not. Apart from those who sat quietly—I don't know who they were, although I think one of them was Jane Marshall—the room was divided between those hooting, 'Guilty!' and those hollering, 'He's a nice man, leave him alone.'"

"What were the girls doing all this time?"

"Girls? What girls?"

"The Gang of Six. Catherine Morton's school chums."

"Oh them. Don't know. I'm not even sure they were present."

"That could be significant."

"Maybe their parents had forbidden them to attend."

"Yes, could be. Was a trial date mentioned?"

"Someone mentioned next Thursday for a preliminary hearing."

I poured myself another cup of Darjeeling Silver Tips Imperial tea. Sipping it appreciatively, I ruminated on what I had just been told. It sounded par for the course for public meetings, consisting of more heat than light. It did not look good for Father Mike, but I thought I could see one hopeful light at the end of the tunnel.

Suddenly, something struck me. "What about the girl?"

"What girl?"

"The girl. Catherine Morton herself. Did she say anything? Didn't she address the meeting?"

"Jesus!" said Rosalie quite uncharacteristically, "I'd quite forgotten. She wasn't even there!"

"Were either of her parents there?"

"I don't know what Mr. Morton looks like, but I didn't see the mother."

The absence of Catherine, her mother, and the Gang of Six had to be important, I thought, although I could not at the moment think how.

At that moment the telephone rang.

"Mr. LeBlanc?"

"Yes."

"This is Premier Proctor's office calling. I'm Nora Wriggs. Would you be able to come in tomorrow at 2 pm?"

"Yes, I think so," I said. "What is this about?"

"I wouldn't know, Mr. LeBlanc."

"Okay then, I'll be there."

"Excellent."

"Just one thing."

"Yes?"

"Parking downtown is murder. Is there somewhere I can park where my car will be safe?"

"Yes, we can do that. The legislature is not sitting at the moment, so why don't you park at Province House? I'll notify the attendants to expect you."

"Good. Thanks."

"What will you be driving?"

"A blue Bugatti Veyron Sports."

"Really?"

"You know cars, Mrs. Wriggs?"

"I know that one," she said.

~

"So, finally the great man has established contact," I said to Rosalie as I walked back into the kitchen.

"Who?"

"The premier."

"Haha! He took his time. I wonder what he wants."

"I'll find out tomorrow. I have to be there at 2 pm."

"Want company?"

"Wouldn't mind, but she didn't mention you."

"Marc LeBlanc," she said, narrowing her eyes, "are we a team or are we not a team?"

"Fair enough. We'll leave just after noon."

"Was it actually him who called?"

"Who?"

"The premier."

"No. It was a Nora Wriggs. Presumably his secretary."

"What did she say?"

"She said could I come in tomorrow, or words to that effect."

"Ah. That means we might not even get to see the boss. We'll probably be palmed off onto that Aldridge guy."

"I hadn't thought of that. It's not like we have a choice."

We cleared away the breakfast things and, as I was doing the dishes, Rosalie turned to me.

"What time does school get out?"

"School? How should I know? What kind of school?"

"High school."

"No clue. Why?"

"Why don't we slink down to the school gates—in my Fiat—and take a look at Catherine Morton and the Gang of Six? See if we can pick up any vibes."

"What a good idea! Clever girl!"

"I'll check out the timing on the net."

That afternoon we were unobtrusively parked opposite Horton High School, near Greenwich. We had a clear view as the students came loping out to get their buses home.

A group of six girls stood apart from the others. They were all surprisingly attractive, all remarkably mature in appearance, and all very well-dressed. From the way they carried themselves and the way they shunned other students, it seemed clear that this was a clique which considered itself to be elite.

Their leader was notable for stunning good looks and for her continual peals of laughter, which we could hear across the street. This, we guessed, was Catherine Morton.

At first, the group seemed close and supportive, but soon it appeared that there was some kind of division among the girls. Catherine, if in fact it was she, seemed to be taunting the other girls, only two of whom would take her part. The other three hung back, obviously not willing to cooperate in whatever the leader was bidding them do. They shook their heads and quickly stepped away from the others and hurried to board one of the busses.

"What do you make of that?" I asked.

"Trouble in Paradise," said Rosalie.

"Whatever the reason for discord among them, it bodes well for Father Mike. It means we might be able to get to one of the dissidents and find out the truth."

"I agree. If you want I can stay home tomorrow and track this down."

"No, I think it can wait a day or two." I sat back in the car and closed my eyes.

"Are you going to sleep?"

"No. I'm trying to think where I've seen one of those girls before."

"Which one?"

"The shorter of the dissidents. The blonde one with the pigtails."

"How do you know her?"

"I don't know...Yes, I do! She is Joyce and Walter's daughter!"

"Walter Bryson, your lawyer?"

"Yes."

"What should we do?"

"Let's come back the day after tomorrow and see if the relationship between them has changed. If it hasn't, we'll pay a visit on Joyce and Walter."

"You're on."

6

When we drove into the Province House parking lot, I noticed an elderly commissionaire peering out of one of the windows. He disappeared and instantly came through the big white doors and hobbled down the stone steps.

"Are you Mr. LeBlanc?" he asked.

"Yes."

"We've been told to expect you. Would you park in that spot over there, please?"

I pulled the Bugatti into the space by the railings that he indicated, and we got out. I paused to take in the ancient edifice where our provincial members of the legislature had met for over a hundred years.

The first MLAs convened in 1758, and moved from pillar to post around the city, often meeting in private houses, until in 1811 they passed an act to erect the present grey stone building. The Act stipulated that the building was to follow a design produced by one John Merrick, whose choice, whether for reasons of patronage or availability, was somewhat curious because he was a painter, not an architect at all.

In any event, though they spent 52,000 English pounds on its construction, and lavished on it ironwork brought all the way from Scotland, the entire building was only just over 40 metres long and 20 metres wide. Since the building had to contain a court and two chambers, of necessity the meeting place for the Members of the Lower House was relatively small, albeit with a high ceiling.

An image dated 1879 shows there were thirty-two Members at that time, and although various alterations were made over the intervening years, today's fifty-five elected Members are required to sit in essentially the same space.

Visitors to the chamber exclaim with delight that, unlike the grandiose and lofty legislatures of Ontario, Quebec and the western provinces, Nova Scotia's is "intimate" and "cozy", but for those who work there it can be crowded, if not cramped.

The building was flanked by impressive statues of Joseph Howe, the champion of freedom of the press, on the left; and an unknown soldier from the Boer War, rifle held aloft, on the right. The cornerstone for the latter was laid in 1901 by King George V when he was Prince of Wales.

"Where do we find the Premier's office?" I inquired.

"It used to be here in Province House," said the commissionaire, "but it's now across the street on the other side. You go through the building and out the other door."

Obviously I looked puzzled because he quickly added, "Don't worry, sir, I'll escort you."

In the building 'across the street' we went to the seventh floor and were confronted by a stern young woman, who asked us who we were. On being told, she came out from behind her desk, forced a smile, introduced herself as Susan Greenlough, and shook hands with us.

"You'll be seeing Mr. Aldridge," she said.

Rosalie cast a glance at me and mouthed, "I told you so."

We followed Ms. Greenlough along a corridor to an unobtrusive door in the corner. She tapped lightly, then opened the door.

"Tom, they're here," She said, then left us.

Aldridge ushered us in. He appeared to be older than had I judged him when we met at Ray and Rachel's wedding, now seeming to be closer to fifty than forty, his hair thinning and a slight paunch forming.

As he asked us to sit down, I was surprised to see a familiar face grinning at us from an armchair in the corner.

"Hello, Rosalie. Hey, Marc."

It was our old friend Frank Wilberforce from the Canadian Art Theft and Forgery Prevention Agency.

"Frank! What are you doing here?" Rosalie demanded.

"Well you might ask. As a matter of fact, I'm here to suggest a little job for you two."

"A job?"

"For us?"

"Explain, will you, Tom?"

"Sure," said Aldridge, sitting on the edge of his desk. "There are a couple of paintings in the province's possession which Frank's people believe are forgeries. But since they think they may have been done many years ago, they cannot be investigated by CATFPA, which is confined to crimes committed within the last ten years".

"Yeah," said Frank. "If we did take on old crimes, we'd be swamped. So

Tom asked me if I knew any private investigators and naturally I thought of you two."

"But we know very little about paintings. How could we possibly help?" I said.

"We thought you could snoop around, talk to people from the past, to see if you could sniff out anything."

"And we are not registered private investigators," Rosalie said.

"I can fix that with a phone call," said Aldridge. "Will you do it?"

"What do you think, Rosalie?" I asked my wife.

"We can try, Marc. But I wouldn't hold out too much hope."

"What are the paintings in question?"

"We have one definite forgery and one which is likely a forgery," said Frank. "The doubtful one is a portrait of General Sir Fenwick Williams of Kars, who was Lieutenant Governor of Nova Scotia from 1865 to 1867, by William Gush, supposedly painted 1866."

"And the other? The definite forgery?"

"That is a painting by Arthur Lismer, who was a prominent member of the Group of Seven. It's a lake scene. I'm told it used to be a great favourite of a former premier, Gerald Regan."

"Yes," said Aldridge. "It hung on his office wall the whole time he was premier."

"When was that?" Rosalie asked.

"From 1970 to 1978."

"I doubt there wouldn't be many around from that time," I said.

"No, not many," said Aldridge.

"One who was is an old friend of yours," said Frank.

"Of mine?"

"Yes your archaeologist *cum* mystery weekend guy who helped you out on your previous mysteries."

"Him?"

"Yes, after he was an archaeologist, he was a member of the legislature from 1970 to 1980. I understand he was a great friend of Premier Regan."

"Good God! I had no idea."

"Well, this is where I butt out," Frank said, as he raised his considerable bulk from the chair. "I've brought you good people together, so I can get back to my work."

"Drop by for dinner sometime, Frank."

"Thanks, that's an invitation I cannot and will not refuse."

Frank lumbered out of the office and we heard his heavy footfall down the corridor.

When Frank was gone, Aldridge closed the door. "Come with me," he said, opening a door in another wall. There was a further padded door beyond that one. He pushed this open and propelled us forward.

Suddenly we found ourselves face to face with Premier Wendell Proctor.

"Welcome, Rosalie. Hello, Marc." He got up from his desk, beaming at us. "Take a seat, friends. You stay, Tom."

We sat down on a huge chesterfield, where the premier joined us. Aldridge sat at the premier's desk.

"Premier, as I told them in the other office, we don't know much about art and—"

"Forget that," the premier interrupted me. "You can go through the motions on that matter, but you won't find anything—not after all this time."

"Then why—?"

"I want you to help me with something else. Something which could be important."

"Vitally important," said Aldridge.

"What is it?" Rosalie asked.

"Tell them, Tom."

"You must agree to keep this strictly to yourselves. Do you agree?"

"Yes, of course."

"Okay. Here's the thing. Wendell has been getting death threats."

"Don't all public figures get them?"

"These are different. We're convinced these are genuine and from the same person or persons."

"What do the police say?" I asked.

"We haven't taken this to the police."

"Why on earth not?"

"Think about it for a minute. What would happen if we did that?"

"This place, the legislature and your home would be crawling with cops."

"Exactly. If that happened we wouldn't be able to get any work done, and it would make Wendell look like some kind of cowardly baby."

"Less of the cowardly," admonished the premier with a grin.

"I see that," said Rosalie. "But how would it be done?"

"I'd appoint one of you—I couldn't swing both—as a special consultant with a roving commission on, say, 'making government relevant to the people', or something like that. You'd have authority to go anywhere in government and talk to anyone. I'd make sure the cabinet understood that they and their deputies would have to comply."

"I guess at least one of us would have to live in Halifax."

"It would look better if you were here three days a week."

"We'd have to get an apartment," said Rosalie.

"No need." The premier was firm. "Cynthia and I have all kinds of rooms. Besides, it will strengthen your authority if people know you are staying with us."

"If you're sure."

"Sure I'm sure. I already discussed it with the real premier."

"The real premier?"

"Hell, that's Cynthia!" The premier laughed as he stood up. He seemed even taller than I remembered.

"We have to get back to Grand Pre now. When do you want us to start? We'll need a thorough briefing as soon as possible."

"How about the day after tomorrow?"

"I think we can do that. Rosalie?"

"Yes, we can, premier. Some days I have to be at the university, but there's no reason why Marc can't be here the whole time if necessary."

"Tom, set it up. Day after tomorrow. Ten o'clock. Here."

"Leave it to me, Wendell."

7

The next morning, over a breakfast of home-made sausages and free-range duck eggs, Rosalie and I discussed the previous day's encounter. We also had our favourite Jamaican Blue Mountain coffee, together with fresh croissants and lavender honey from our neighbours at Tangled Garden in Grand Pre.

"Assassination threats are a bit out of our league, don't you think?" Rosalie asked me. "Were we a bit hasty in accepting the job?"

"I was wondering that too," I said. "But it's my guess they're the usual empty threats. There must be thousands of emails and letters sent to politicians saying that unless they do this or that they will die a miserable death."

"The premier and Aldridge seemed sure the threats were genuine."

"We'll take a close look at them tomorrow. Without police involvement, I doubt the source of the emails can be traced; and even then, if the perpetrators are serious they would have covered their tracks well. Apparently, it's not that hard to do."

"I think we'll get some idea from the tone of the threats. I tend to think that if they're long and windy, they'll be hollow nonsense, but if they are terse and to the point, they might be the real thing."

"Yes, I agree," I said, "and it will be interesting to find out from the premier and Aldridge from whom they might be coming."

Rosalie poured more coffee and slathered honey on a croissant. It ran down her fingers, which she sucked dry. "You got any plans for today?"

"Yes, I have to spend most of the day with Louise at the wine shop. And don't forget we have to be at Horton High at 3.20."

"Oh right. To see if they are developments with the Gang of Six."

"Yes."

"Marc, I've got an idea. Why don't we just happen to be passing and give the Bryson girl a lift home? That way we could grill her about Catherine Morton."

"Good God, no! She's a minor, and we shouldn't be asking her anything without Walter or Joyce's consent. We'll call in at the Brysons after dinner."

"Yes, I see that now I've thought about it. Shall you come back here and pick me up?"

"Yes, about 3:00."

Truth to tell, I am very proud of the wine store, though my contribution to its success has been minimal compared with Louise's. She has worked day and night and has made the place a rather magical oasis on Main Street, with a beautiful layout, a wonderful presentation of the products and a lighting ambience designed to make the reds seem redder and whites richer.

From the outset we agreed not to try to please everyone by carrying a few bottles from every country and every price. Also, we avoided acquiring wines from places like Bordeaux, Burgundy and Napa, largely because the best of them are horrendously expensive, and due to the fact that they need long aging before being ready to drink. Few people understand this about most high quality wine, so will pay out a lot of money, drink the wine too early and be very disappointed. I grieve for those diners I see in restaurants who order a recent Bordeaux for well over $100, then grit their teeth because the wine is bitter, tannic and unforgiving. I think it is something approaching a crime for restaurants to carry wines which need ten years or more to be drinkable.

We also avoided carrying cheap "plonk", which could be easily obtained anywhere else, and wines with ridiculously high levels of alcohol. These latter, while they might give the drinker a quick buzz, would not be pleasant because they are severely unbalanced.

So, with a few exceptions, Louise and I opted for areas around the world where the wine is very good but not too pricey, and may be approached relatively soon. The exceptions are wines like Champagne, which is expensive but ready to drink, and New World Pinot Noir, which is generally charming and approachable in its youth.

At 2:45 I left Louise to finish up the monthly accounts, and headed back to Grand Pre. There I parked, sounded the horn, left the Bugatti and transferred to Rosalie's Fiat.

To employ a well-worn cliché, the difference between the two cars is like night and day, or chalk and cheese, but the Fiat has its uses. Indeed, it would be difficult to spy on anyone in the Bugatti because it is so noticeable in both appearance and sound.

Rosalie climbed in beside me and we drove to the school, taking the same advantageous position we had assumed previously.

Soon the students poured out, but the Gang of Six were not in formation when they straggled out. Catherine Morton, still laughing and tossing her head, now had only one acolyte in tow. Two others were walking separately from Catherine and her friend. Then came another sauntering on her own. Finally, the Bryson girl, somewhat shyly, it seemed, made her way to the bus and boarded.

"What do you think is going on?" I asked Rosalie.

"It looks as if the Gang of Six is no longer a gang."

"It is too much to suppose that Catherine's allegations about Father Mike are responsible for the schism?"

"I'd say it was highly likely."

"Right. So we're going to the Brysons' tonight?"

"I think so, yes, but Marc…"

"What?"

"I think we need to know the girl's name before we go."

"Yes, you're right. Let me think."

"Start at the beginning of the alphabet and it may come to you."

"I'll try."

I did as Rosalie suggested and when I came to the 'J's, I remembered.

"Jennifer! It's Jennifer."

~

About eight that evening we drove over to Prospect Street, where the Brysons owned a large house with a sprawling lawn and garden. Rosalie went past so we could see if they were still at dinner, and, seeing they were not at the dining room table, pulled in and parked.

"Rosalie, Marc! What are you doing here?" Joyce answered the door in some surprise.

"Hello, Joyce. Is Walter home?"

"Yes, he's in the den. Come in. Is something wrong?"

"We wondered if we could have a quiet word with both of you."

"I don't see why not. What's it all about?"

"Let's wait till Walter is with us."

"Very mysterious! He's right in here."

She opened the door and ushered us in. Walter was reading the paper. "Walter, we have visitors."

"Good heavens. What can we do for you?" he asked, rising.

Slowly, carefully, we explained the situation as we understood it, stated our belief in Father Mike, and said we thought that Jennifer might have some crucial information on the matter.

"I'm sorry," Walter said quickly. "I can't be a party to any discussion, whatever Jennifer may decide. Arthur Aston, the prosecutor, is very ill and Jill Sanderson, the magistrate, is out of town for some time, so there is a good chance I may be asked to fill in. I'm going to leave the room now. Joyce will go up and ask Jennifer if she wants to talk to you. If she says 'no', that'll be that. You understand?"

"Certainly we do, Walter."

"Wait here. I'll go up and see her now," Joyce said as Walter left.

Joyce was gone for less than five minutes. When she returned, she shook her head. "No, I'm sorry. Jennifer's not ready to talk about it. I can tell she's very upset but she can't talk now."

"Okay. We'll get out of your hair," I said.

"Marc....I have a feeling that if you give her a few days, she might be able to tell you something."

"I see."

"Yes, try again in a few days."

"We will. Good night, Joyce. And thanks."

8

Rosalie and I had an early breakfast of scrambled eggs, toast and coffee, then got on the road. There was less traffic than expected, and the Bugatti made it to downtown Halifax in 49 minutes. We repeated yesterday's routine with the commissionaire at Province House.

As we went through the main hall of Province House and before we mounted the steps to the west door, I noticed that the security system was fairly thorough, but not foolproof. Visitors were required to pass by a desk manned by a commissionaire and walk through a metal detector, but MLAs and their staff, and those who worked in the building, had passes and did not have to go through the detector. I saw that they either assumed they would be recognized by the commissionaires or just waved their passes as they walked on through. I imagined that if a diversion were created it would not take much for a would-be assassin to get up to the public galleries.

On the seventh floor, this time Susan Greenlough was much friendlier when she greeted us and whisked us along to Tom Aldridge's office. As soon as she had gone back to her desk, Tom again ushered through the double doors into Premier Proctor's room. After formalities and offers of tea or coffee, we sat down and the premier got to business.

"I've had a Report and Recommendation prepared for the cabinet, which will meet in an hour. You'll come in with me, Marc, because you are named in the R and R. You won't be staying. You'll be in there just long enough to be introduced, and for me to impress upon them that their full cooperation is demanded. Okay with that?"

"Yes, Premier."

"Alright. Tom will show you the death threats when we are finished here. They are short and to the point, basically saying that unless I change course within the near future, I am a dead man."

"Change what course?" I asked.

"Ah, that's a problem. We don't know."

"Then how can you change it?"

"Obviously we can't. But we have a pretty good idea that they are talking about one of two things. The first is the very serious person trafficking which is taking place in the province. I recently stirred up a lot of bitter resentment by stating that the criminal action in this despicable trade was significantly, but not exclusively, being conducted by members of my own community."

"You mean the North End of Halifax?"

"No." The premier smiled. "I mean people who are the same colour as me."

"Oh." I felt foolish to have missed his meaning, so I quickly moved the discussion on. "What's the second possibility?"

"That these threats are coming from extremists within the so-called 'environmental movement'. I have enraged these people by speaking out against the headlong scramble for electric cars."

"Why have you done that?"

"Because very little black boys and girls are slaving day in and day out in the Congo for small or no wages, digging the lithium, cobalt, graphite, nickel, and manganese which is needed for the batteries of these vehicles."

"It's a disgusting racket in which children are suffering," Tom Aldridge intervened. "To reduce their reliance on Chinese imports for their materials, North America and Europe companies want direct access to these minerals. So, instead of relying on middlemen for raw materials, they're investing in the mines themselves, or are getting the minerals straight from the mines."

"Yes," said the premier, "and that makes them responsible for the working conditions of those mines, for child and slave labour, and the considerable pollution associated with the mining."

"I drive a ten-year-old Bugatti, so I know very little about electric cars. Do they really need all those semi-precious minerals?"

"Pretty much," said Tom. "Each kilogram of EV battery cell needs about 72 g of lithium. Each battery needs 200 grams per kilogram of cobalt. The experts are telling us that demand for electric battery production by 2030 will need as much as 450,000 tons of lithium, as much as 420,000 tons of cobalt, and about 2 million tons of nickel."

"So, you see, Marc and Rosalie, it is not nearly as simple as the well-to-do, middle-class, virtue signallers would have you believe. There are thousands of young, black lives at stake."

"Quite apart from the fact that, for the foreseeable future, only the wealthier people will be able to afford electric cars. The average price for an electric car in Canada is now \$83,500," Tom said. "So if we push electric cars and phase out gasoline cars too fast, the poorer people will have to walk."

"Or use public transit," Rosalie said.

"Much of that in the rural areas, is there?" The premier asked.

"I take your point, Premier," she said. "I wasn't thinking."

"So, which of the extreme environmental groups do you suspect?" I said "It's my impression there are a lot of them."

"It's our assessment that none of the home-grown organizations would ever stoop to death threats," Tom said, "so either this is the work of a single lunatic or of a group based outside the province, and quite likely outside the country."

"It's your job to find out which of them might be behind this," the Premier said with a grin.

"Of the two alternatives, which do you think is the more likely?" I asked.

"We have no idea." Tom said. "The human traffickers are utterly ruthless people with no conscience and no morals, so they would have no reservations about killing. On the other hand—and don't quote me on this—the environmental crowd contains so many loonies, it would only take one to flip and go rogue."

"Do you have go-to people I can consult on either of these?"

"Not on the environmental side. Your guess is as good as ours," Tom said. "But our contact for human trafficking is Superintendent Kennedy at the RCMP."

I smiled broadly. Rosalie and I exchanged knowing glances, something the premier noticed.

"You've heard of Kennedy, have you?"

"He's an old friend," said Rosalie.

"He's come up in the world since I first met him a few years ago," I said. "Then he was a humble sergeant with HRMP and now you tell me he is a superintendent."

"Well, there you go," the Premier said, standing up to indicate that the meeting was over. "See him and he'll fill you in on the overall scene, and who the local villains are. But don't tell him why you are asking. Say I asked for a fresh opinion on the situation. If you want, I'll give him a call and let him know you're coming."

"Yes, please, Premier. That would be very helpful."

"Okay. Let's go and meet the cabinet. The R and R says you are Special

Advisor to the Premier on Government and all matters pertaining thereto. Did I understand correctly that you don't want remuneration?"

"Yes, Premier."

"I think we have to give you a nominal sum to make it legal. How about ten dollars a day, plus out of pocket expenses?"

"Thank you, Premier. That would be fine."

I walked with Proctor to the cabinet room and stood beside him as he took his seat. As I looked around the table I could see that everyone was surprised to see a stranger in their midst.

I recognized some of the cabinet members from their photographs in the newspapers or on television news. I noticed Mark Gardiner, Minister of Tourism and Culture at the end of the table; and Bill Clark, Minister of Transport and Public Works, half way along. Closer to the premier was Angus MacKinnon, Minister of Economic Development; and on either side of Proctor were the Finance Minister, Chester MacCormack, and the beautiful Joan Howard, a sometime movie star who was Deputy Premier with responsibilities for the Cabinet Office and Intergovernmental Affairs.

"Colleagues, this is my very good friend Marc LeBlanc," announced the premier as he settled in his seat. "Today we will be appointing him to a special job as personal assistant and advisor to me on all matters."

There was a slight gasp around the table. One or two members stole glances at each other. Angus MacKinnon leaned forward, his face creased by a frown. Joan Howard, who had clearly been briefed ahead of time, smiled and shouted, "Welcome, Marc!"

"You are to give him full co-operation on anything he wants, anything he asks for. Tell your deputies they must cooperate or else they will be hearing from me." Proctor turned to Adrian MacIsaac, the Clerk of the Executive Council. "Adrian, circulate the R and R and we'll vote on it. I presume nobody wants to debate it."

"Premier." Angus MacKinnon cleared his throat.

"Yes, Angus?"

"I don't wish to debate the matter, merely to inquire as to the term of the appointment."

"The Report and Recommendation says one year," said the premier, surprising me, as I had no intention of spending an entire year on this project. "But we hope and anticipate I can dispense with his services long before that."

Adrian MacIsaac read out the document. It took no more than a few minutes.

"In favour?" Proctor called and then, without looking around, "Carried unanimously. Thank you, Marc. You may go now."

As I left the cabinet room there was thunderous applause from the members, who were thumping the table. Somewhat dazed, I stumbled into the corridor, not having the slightest idea how to proceed with this commission, and wondering how on earth I had allowed Rosalie and me to become involved.

9

Wendell and Cynthia Proctor lived in a large, old house on upper Gottingen Street, in the heart of the premier's constituency. They had no children, so there was plenty of room for themselves and for guests. I gathered that sometimes some of Wendell's relatives from Truro came to stay, and occasionally Cynthia's parents visited from Ontario.

However, this did not mean that the house was very often empty, because, Cynthia told us, Wendell's parents dropped in frequently, and so did his sister Grace and her husband, Matthew, together with various uncles and aunts, most of whom lived in the city's north end.

Laughing, Cynthia said that when the Proctor family did descend, the women loudly occupied the kitchen, while the men sat around in the living room, speaking in undertones.

Grace, who she said was a large, sometimes bullying, big-bosomed woman, made her presence felt in no uncertain terms. She made it clear that she took credit for Wendell's becoming premier and for his marrying Cynthia, on whom she now doted, having conveniently forgotten that initially she had been violently opposed to the match.

In contrast, Cynthia said Grace's husband was 'a darling', a man of very few words and an extraordinarily good and generous nature. Despite Wendell's exalted status, apparently, they all treated his house as if it were a community centre, coming and going pretty much as they pleased.

However, Cynthia told us, the premier had put his foot down now that we were coming to stay. He had instructed the family to keep their visits to a minimum, and on no account to come unannounced. He had told his mother, Blossom, and Grace that since he would need to have many confidential discussions with me, it would not be proper to have them dropping by at all hours of the day and night. In the interests of the province, they had grudgingly agreed.

Cynthia had arranged it so that we had a bedroom and bathroom on the top floor of the house so we might have some privacy, but, unless we preferred otherwise, that we should eat with her and her husband. This involved a certain adjustment for us, at least for me, as we had become used to a somewhat rarefied diet and to particularly good wine with our meals. Simple food was to be the order of the day, but we agreed we would be none the worse for that.

Until now neither Rosalie nor I had any first-hand experience of inter-racial marriages, unless Ray and Rachel were counted, and then one got into the debate about whether Jews were a race or members of a religion. To us, Wendell and Cynthia seemed the ideal couple, very much in love and coping well with the difficulties of the premier being on call day and night.

Cynthia intimated to us that originally her whiteness had been the cause of Grace's opposition to their relationship, but she had relented when she felt that it might advance his political career. That was in the past, and it was clear from the way she spoke of her sister-in-law that now they were the very best of friends. From everything we heard about her, Grace was a phenomenon whom we looked forward to meeting.

Our first night there was cozy and quiet, just Cynthia and ourselves present as Wendell had to be out of town at a party function on the South Shore. We heard him returning home long after Rosalie and I had gone to bed, and when we came down for breakfast, he was already heading out to his office.

As Cynthia cooked us some bacon and beans, we discussed what we should do that day.

"I guess if we're to make the painting problem seem more important than it really is, we had better do something about that," I said.

"Yes. 'Go through the motions', as Wendell put it."

"I suppose we should talk to my old archaeological friend, Akerman, and—I hate to say this—also with Gerry Swift at the provincial Art Gallery."

"Doctor Gerry Swift," Rosalie corrected me with a laugh. We made fun of the man because when I had seen him before he had haughtily insisted on my using his title. "But I'll bet he treats you differently when he finds out you are making inquiries at the behest of the premier."

"I wouldn't bet on it. He's so arrogant, I imagine he feels even premiers are way below him."

"And we should have lunch with Frank Wilberforce. I gather he is staying in Halifax for a day or two."

"Lunch with Frank will be an experience. I wonder how many courses he will order."

"A lot! What then?"

"Then a meeting with Patrick Kennedy would seem to be imperative."

"Alright," said Rosalie," I'll do some calling and set things up."

Our meeting with Dr. Gerry Swift at the Art Gallery of Nova Scotia was almost a non-event. It was though every word had to be dragged out of him, most of his communicating being done by shrugs and nods.

"We understand that the Lismer is almost certainly a forgery," Rosalie said.

"Hmm."

"Do you agree?"

"Who knows? That seems to be the accepted view."

"And the Gush?"

"Shouldn't think so. But then, nineteenth-century pictorial imperial hagiography is not my specialty. Thank God."

"Are there any other paintings in the province which might be forgeries?"

"Aren't there always?"

"Anything specific?"

"Not that I know of."

"Well, thank you Dr. Swift, you've been most…"

But he had turned and just walked away from us. Contrary to Rosalie's expectations, he had been even more arrogant and obnoxious than he had been in my previous encounter with him.

"Let's go and see your archaeologist/politician friend," said Rosalie. "At least we should get a better reception there."

"But not anything which would help us. This is strictly a 'going through the motions' visit."

I parked in the spot I had been given at Province House, crossed the Grand Parade and walked up the hill to Brunswick Street. As before, we walked down the street and were heartily hailed from a flowery balcony by a man dressed in shorts and a T-shirt, holding a watering can.

"Marc LeBlanc! My favourite sleuth," he called. "Come on up!"

He greeted us at the door in bare feet, and with inescapable handshakes. His apartment was crowded and the walls were covered with paintings done by himself. Some of them I recognized as being depictions of various scenes around the province.

We cleared papers and documents from the couch and sat down, while he put on the kettle for coffee.

"My wife is at work, but I've told her all about you," he said from the kitchen.

"It's too bad we can't meet her," said Rosalie.

"I should tell you from the outset that this time we are working for Premier Proctor on a number of projects," I said.

"Are you, indeed? How did that come about?"

"It's a long story."

"Go ahead. I've got time."

This gave me no choice but to relive some of the history of our relationship with Rachel and Ray Bland, our investigation into his supposed grandfather's origins, and how we had met the premier at their wedding.

"So how can I help you this time?" he asked.

"We've been told you were a member of the legislature in the time of Premier Gerald Regan."

"That's right. I was elected in 1970, the same year he became the premier, and I was there for the whole of his administration."

"Do you remember his office?"

"Very well. I was in that office many times. The Premier's office was then in the southeast ground floor corner of Province House. Later they moved it across the street."

"Do you recall a painting by Lismer?"

"Oh, yes. It was a lake scene. Regan loved that painting. I liked it a lot, too."

"Did he ever indicate that it was a copy?"

"A copy? Good heavens, no. Why should he have?"

"There's reason to believe it is a forgery. Or, at least, the one the province has now could be a fake."

"I'm no expert on the Group of Seven, but I always thought it was the real thing, and so did Premier Regan."

"So there was no mystery attached to it?"

"Not that I ever heard. But if you are looking for a real mystery, you should ask what happened to the portrait of Regan which the party commissioned a very famous artist to paint."

"Why, what *did* happen to it?"

"Nobody knows. The money was raised, the artist was paid, but the painting never saw the light of day."

"Extraordinary."

"Isn't it just?"

"Do you know what happened to the Lismer after Mr. Regan left office?"

"No, I don't. I am sure Premier Buchanan, who succeeded Regan, didn't have it on the wall in his time, and he was there for twelve years. After Regan, presumably it was repossessed by the Art Gallery of Nova Scotia and disappeared into the catacombs."

"What catacombs, Mr. Akerman?" asked Rosalie.

"It was just a figure of speech. But we do have catacombs of a sort."

"What do you mean?"

"Tunnels underneath Halifax. Supposedly, the city is riddled with them."

"Surely, this is just hearsay?" I was frankly skeptical.

"No, at least not entirely. When I first became an MLA I was given a tiny office in the basement of Province House, and when I got bored I used to nose around. One day I discovered a small door to a below-street-level space which extended under almost the entire building, in which piles of old furniture had been left to gather dust. At one end, I found a partly-concealed entrance to a tunnel."

"Really? Did you go in?"

"I only went a short distance because it was filthy and dripping with water. I meant to return at a later date, but in the meantime they moved my office to a building across the street and I never thought much about it again."

"We've taken up too much of your time," I said, thinking we were getting way off point. "Besides, we have a lunch appointment. Thank you for your help."

"Okay. I'll see you next time."

"Next time?"

"On your next mystery." He grinned broadly.

We had arranged to meet Frank Wilberforce at the Bluenose Restaurant, and when we got there we saw him installed at a table in the centre of the room. Most people who go there try to obtain one of the eight booths by the window so they can watch the world go by, but for Frank that was not a sensible option. His immense girth meant that if he managed to squeeze into a booth, he would likely never get out.

Rosalie ordered the chicken Caesar salad while I had a plain omelet. Frank had chowder to start, with crackers, followed by 14-ounce prime rib with fries and vegetables, and then Dulce Leche cheesecake, which was described as 'light and creamy, laced with dulce de leche filling, with a graham crumb base topped with toffee crunch'.

Rosalie and I had finished our meals long before Frank, so we watched and waited while he ploughed his way through. When he had finally finished eating, he wiped his face with a huge, bright red handkerchief and settled back in his chair with a loud sigh.

"That should keep me going until dinner," he said with a big grin.

"Now Frank," said Rosalie, "tell us more about this forged painting business and why you went to see Tom Aldridge the other day."

"Okay. My visit to Aldridge was a very small, not very significant, part of a massive world-wide operation being coordinated by Interpol."

"Why? What happened?"

"Suddenly—I mean within the last three weeks—we've seen across the world what looks like an upsurge not only in apparent thefts of works of art, but also in their replacement by excellent—I could say superb—forgeries. The two paintings here in Nova Scotia are not likely part of it, but we had to check them out."

"How serious is it? What kinds of art are being affected?"

"A wide variety of items, from the Mappa Mundi in Hereford Cathedral in England to the Voynich manuscript."

"I've seen the Mappa Mundi," I said. "It's supposed to be an early medieval map of the world. It's quite beautiful in its own way. But, if I recall correctly, it is literally under lock and chain. It would take precise planning and a lot of nerve to steal that and replace it with a fake."

"That's what I'm told," said Frank. "I've not seen it myself."

"This other thing, the Voynich manuscript. What's that?"

"The Voynich manuscript is an illustrated, hand-written document at Yale University in Connecticut. The text is in an unknown language, on vellum which has been carbon-dated to the early 1400s."

"Who wrote it?"

"Nobody knows, but they think it was originally from Italy during the Renaissance."

"What was it for? What was its purpose?" I asked. I was intrigued because I had never heard of this manuscript.

"Again, nobody really knows. The manuscript consists of around 240 pages. Most of them are full of weird illustrations showing people, fictitious plants, and astrological symbols."

"Extraordinary! How did it get its name?"

"It was bought by Wilfrid Voynich, a Polish book dealer, in 1912. They named it after him."

"Is it worth a lot?" Rosalie asked.

"It is impossible to value until someone comes along to translate it and show it isn't a hoax. In this case, and a few others, it seems the crimes have been committed to satisfy vanity instead of monetary gain."

When Frank mentioned vanity as a motive, I immediately thought of my older brother, Lawrence. I knew he was head of an international crime ring involving art, and I knew he was arrogant enough to perpetrate something like this. But Larry was a subject I could not mention to anyone, not even Rosalie.

Since we had been led to believe that the painting matter was not Premier Proctor's priority, I considered that there was not much to be gained by listening to Frank for much longer, even though his information was fascinating.

"Well, Frank, this has been a real eye-opener," I said, taking the bill and standing up. "Thank you very much."

"You're quite welcome. Don't forget the dinner invitation."

"How about the Saturday after next?" Rosalie said. "We should both be back in Grand Pre then."

"Fine. I'll see you then," he said, again mopping his face with his red hankie.

Out on the street, I checked my phone and saw there was a message from RCMP "H" Division headquarters, so I called them back immediately. The woman who answered told me that Superintendent Kenney could not see us that afternoon after all, but could see us the next morning at ten-thirty.

"That's too bad," Rosalie said. "What shall we do now?"

"We are hearing all kinds of interesting stuff, but I'm getting a feeling this investigation is not really focused," I said. "I think we should go back to see Aldridge and look at the threats."

10

I awoke early the next day and, after washing and shaving, I quietly tip-toed down the creaky stairs, hoping not to wake anyone else.

However, when I got to the kitchen I discovered that the premier was already up and munching cereal at the table. He was dressed ready for work and had his huge briefcase by his side, from which he had extracted some documents to read while eating.

"Good morning, Premier," I said.

"Look, Marc, if you're going to be living in this house for a while, it's going to be a bit silly if you carry on calling me 'premier'. Wendell is my name."

"Okay...Wendell."

"Help yourself to"—he looked at the cereal box with a grimace —"Wheatypuffs, but I don't recommend them. Make yourself some toast, or cook yourself some eggs."

"Thanks. I think I know where the pan is."

"Under the stove. Eggs should be in the fridge. Go ahead. Usually I just grab a bowl of this stuff to tide me over for a couple of hours, 'til Susan comes into the office. She brings me a fried egg sandwich from the café on the corner, which I eat at my desk."

He finished his cereal, wrinkled his nose, and then took a swig of tea. "Are you making any progress?"

"To be honest, I don't think so. We don't know yet where we should be concentrating. We saw Swift, Akerman and Wilberforce yesterday, but didn't get very much. We're seeing Kennedy today."

"Is there anything I can do to move things along?"

"Actually, there is," I said as I put slices of bread into the toaster. "If you could say something publicly to further inflame the would-be assassin, it might provoke a response which could provide us with a clue."

"Smart thinking. Consider it done. I'll say something on both subjects at my press conference at noon. I'll double down on the environmental stuff and use some strong language to characterize the bastards in the trafficking trade."

"Sounds good. If we get anything back which gets specific, we'll know what to home in on."

"I gotta go. Good luck."

He shoved the papers into his case, grabbed his coat and went out to the yard, where his driver was waiting for him.

I was eating my eggs when Cynthia came down. She said nothing about my having cooked my own breakfast, which I took as consent to my doing so whenever I wanted. She made herself some fresh tea and sat down.

"Did you and my hubby have a good talk while I was asleep?"

"Yes, we did, but I hope you didn't think we were talking secretly behind your back."

"No, I didn't mean that." She laughed heartily. Then she looked at me with a soft smile. "He's quite something, isn't he?"

"He certainly is." I was strangely moved by the warmth of her loyalty and the depth of her love for this immensely tall black man. "He seems to take his job very seriously."

"Yes. Sometimes I think he takes it too seriously. I wish he'd take a little time to relax now and then."

"I know little about politics, but I can imagine it is a grueling business."

"It is if you're in government. But I'm not complaining. My eyes were wide open and I knew what I was getting into."

At that moment Rosalie wandered in. She and Cynthia discussed what they would have for breakfast, then she turned to me.

"Marc, I've had a message on my phone. It's from Rachel Bland. She says Father Mike was remanded for trial yesterday at the preliminary hearing. He has bail."

"Does she say when the trial will be?"

"It will be much quicker than expected, she said. It'll be in two months' time."

"That is quick."

"The magistrate said that, in view of the stress to the girl and her family, it should be heard as quickly as possible."

"Very intelligent decision. Who was the magistrate?"

"Guess."

"Walter!"

"You got it."

"But I hope he won't hear the case. If he does, we won't have a chance of getting Jennifer to tell what she knows."

"No, Rachel said Walter indicated someone would be named by the Chief Judge of the Provincial and Family Courts."

"Well, I hope it'll be a sensible judge. If it's a die-hard Protestant feminist, Father Mike could be in trouble."

"Do you really think that? Judges are unbiased, aren't they?"

"Supposed to be, but unless they make it obvious, they can get away with all kinds of tricks to assist one side or the other."

"Not like in the United States, I hope. Some of those judges overseeing Trump's cases were horrendous."

"No, we're not as bad as that yet, thank God. But, sweetheart, you'd better not dawdle. We have to be in Dartmouth at 'H' Division at ten-thirty."

"I think I'll stay and keep Cynthia company, if you don't mind going on your own."

"No, I don't mind. I don't know how long the meeting will go, and I might go out to lunch with Kennedy. Then I must go to see Tom Aldridge after that. So I don't know what time I'll be back."

"I imagine Cynthia and I will find something to occupy us."

When I finally threaded my way through the bureaucracy and security at RCMP headquarters, my meeting with Patrick Kennedy started out on an extremely embarrassing note.

"Marc, look: I'm so sorry the way things turned out the last time we met." Patrick was referring to the way in which our last investigation was summarily stymied by the Mounties in what I thought was a high-handed manner.

"It wasn't your fault."

"I know, but I felt really bad about it. I wasn't even allowed to be in with you when they gave you the treatment."

"Please, Patrick, don't mention it."

"Those NSCI people can be real bastards, although don't quote me on that. Even my Chief Super had no say in the matter. They just descend on people and completely take over."

"Patrick, please! I understand."

"I'm glad you do. You know that I still can't find out what happened or why, and I'm a Superintendent now."

"So I heard. Congratulations from me and Rosalie."

"How is she?"

"Fine. She preferred to spend the day with Cynthia Proctor rather than us."

"Yes, I heard you were tight with the premier now. I had a call from Tom Aldridge to say you were coming. I gotta say, I was surprised that the premier of Nova Scotia had hired my old buddy Marc as a consultant."

"Advisor. I was also surprised, Patrick, but here we are. Tell me all about the human trafficking in the province. I'd no idea it even existed."

"Where do I start? It is a very, very serious problem. This may take some time. Do you have to be anywhere?"

"No, go ahead."

"To one extent or another, the trade in humans has revolved around North Preston. Not that it doesn't happen elsewhere in the province, but it has been recurring there, it being the hub of a major gang that deals in modern day slavery, together with drugs and arms trafficking. The gang is called North Preston's Finest, though there is nothing fine about them, believe me.

"It's hard to be exact at any one time, but there are as many as a dozen gangs in the area, NPF being the most important. Most of the gang members are black. We can't be sure of the numbers, but some say we are dealing with not less than 50 and not more than 100 young men."

"Do these gang members wear any kind of distinctive clothing, like some of the gangs in the US?"

"The NPF guys have tattoos, usually on the neck."

"How far back do they go?"

"As far as we can tell, sometime in the 1980s. Maybe much longer."

"Who are they?"

"Mostly they are related in some way and membership seems to be inherited. These bastards are very dangerous, have no morals or scruples and are often armed to the teeth."

"Do they have links with other gangs across the country, or are they purely home-grown?"

"As far as we can tell they are at least in touch with other gangs, particularly in Quebec and Ontario, and there actually may be an affiliation of some kind."

"Tell me something about what they do and how they go about it."

"Well, I guess you could say that their major businesses are prostitution and other forms of sexual exploitation. They procure girls and force them into prostitution, and run girls who work for strip clubs and escort agencies. They use strong-arm tactics if anyone gets out of line, but initially they use psychology and manipulations on young girls who are not too smart or are easily dazzled by promises.

"They groom the girls, sometimes by becoming the girls' boyfriends, and when they have wormed their way into a girl's confidence they start getting her to do all kinds of things by threatening to leave her or spread lies about her in the community. Some of these men will often have three or four girls on the string at the same time.

"A typical ploy is to get a girl to travel to someplace in Quebec or Ontario and live in a motel. Then he tells her they are going to get a house or condo to live in, but that to get the money for that, she will have to work in a strip club. She agrees, but then he tells her she has to make $1,000 a night and better not come home until she has.

"Of course, the only way she can do this is to sell her body. The girls are also forced into prostitution with intimidation or threats of violence against her or her family."

"Is it ever possible for a girl to escape from these men, Patrick?"

"Very seldom. In fact, I'm not aware of any. If she tries to get out of prostitution, her pimp says 'sure', but that it will cost her $5,000 or more, which is impossible."

"Don't any of the girls go to the police?"

"Sometimes, but these men have them watched around the clock, and if they make a statement to the police, they have to be kept under wraps twenty four seven, which is not often possible. If the pimps get to them, they force them to retract their statements."

"So, it's a form of slavery?"

"No, it *is* slavery." Patrick said forcefully.

"Isn't there anything anybody can do to stop this? How about their parents?"

"Sometimes the parents are conned, too. The new boyfriend comes over for supper, bringing flowers or gifts for the mother. After a while the daughter has mood changes, becomes difficult to reach, and next they know she moves away. Then she's lost to them for good.

"You see, Marc, sex trafficking is not just sex work, because it's exploitative and robs the victim of choice and free will through manipulation, force, coercion, and threats."

"Is there a lot of money involved in human trafficking?"

"Around the world, Interpol tells us it's worth about $160 billion."

"And how does Nova Scotia stack up against the rest of the country?"

"We're one of the very worst provinces."

"If I wanted to see any of this first hand, where would I go, Patrick?"

"North Preston, but it would be insane for you to go there. Besides, they would see you coming. If you did stick your nose in and they caught you, you would probably end up dead."

"That's not very encouraging."

"Nor should it be," said Patrick gravely. "With all due respect, Marc, this is not something for an amateur detective. I'd advise you not to meddle in it."

"I appreciate that," I said. "But, with all due respect, Patrick, is there someone other than yourself I could speak to? Someone who, maybe, was once a gang member?"

"As a matter of fact there is," Patrick said with a grin. "A man called Edison Thomas, but he's wary about saying something which could get him into trouble with us and with the NPF. If you do see him, you had better stick to one topic and not take too long about it."

"Where do I find him?"

"He lives in Mulgrave Square," Patrick said, writing the address on a piece of notepaper. "I can't go into the details, but he owes me a big favour, so I'll give him a call and let him know you're coming."

"Thanks a million, Patrick."

"And, Marc: park your car a long way from the Square and on a main street."

"Why?"

"It looks too much like something a gangster would drive. Besides, it might get scratched."

It was a lovely day, with high, wispy clouds in a deep, cobalt blue sky. As I drove over the MacKay Bridge, though my spirits were high, I still felt I had not yet got my teeth into the case, and was still wandering about in the wilderness.

I did as Patrick advised and parked the car at the premier's house, then walked from there, Uniacke Square being only four streets away.

Bearing in mind Patrick's other piece of advice, I decided that the best approach to Mr. Thomas was to be relatively indirect. I would not question him on his past or on the NPF's activities, but instead would find my answers by asking about the premier's popularity in the black community.

Edison Thomas was a big man in his early sixties who had, Patrick had told me, spent over thirteen years in prison, under two different sentences. He had a barrel chest, a grey beard and elaborate tattoos on his arms and neck. Mr. Thomas was a dusky, medium shade of brown, rather than the gleaming ebony of the premier.

He said he was alone in the small house, although I gathered he was married and I could hear sounds of human activity in another room. He told me to sit down in a big cane chair and thrust a beer into my hand.

"So, you a friend of Superintendent Kennedy?"

"I guess so. I've known him for several years."

"Me, too. He used to be on the city force. He helped me out once, after I quit the rackets."

"He told me."

"So, what you looking for?"

"I'm a friend of the premier. You know him?"

"Sure. Who doesn't? I know the Proctor family for a lot of years."

"Is he well respected in the black community?"

"Depends on who you ask, but I guess he has the backing of the majority."

"So, he'd be re-elected here okay?"

"Hell, yes. He gonna walk it. No trouble."

"Who are the people who don't like him?"

"Couple of bitches and complainers didn't get what they wanted. Not many of them. Most belong to the Burlington family. There's been bad blood between them and the Proctors forever."

"Why? What's it about?"

"It was so long ago, ain't nobody can remember."

"Any of them hate him badly enough to want to do him harm?"

"Hell,, no." He gave me a puzzled look. "They all talk, them people."

"You heard what he said about your former line of business?"

"Yeah. I heard."

"And?"

"And what?"

"What was the reaction to it in the community?"

"Most folk know what he said is true. Everybody knows it's a shitty line of work, and some families are protecting the worst of the gang members. If the cops come around people, clam up. They're scared, so you can understand it, but until the community stands up to the NPF, things is gonna go on as usual."

"Were the gangs upset over the premier's comments?"

"Hell, no. They don't give a shit about him or what he says. Politics is a foreign country to them. Some of those bozos wouldn't even know he was premier of the province."

I felt the fog was lifting from my mind as I left Uniacke Square and walked back to get the car. I started the engine and switched on the radio.

As I settled in my seat, I heard a reporter relaying what Wendell had said at his press conference. Following my suggestion, he really laid it on the line in no uncertain terms. He strongly condemned what he called the 'wall of silence' protecting the NPF, saying they were an indelible stain on the character of the black community.

His comments relative to the environment were even more provocative. He reiterated his opinion of electric cars, said the movement against fossil fuels was "hasty and ill-considered" and said that eco-extremists were "loony, middle class elitists, wearing their hearts on their sleeves to make themselves appear virtuous."

I was confident that the strength of the premier's comments would flush out a quick response from the hater, and I had a pretty good idea from which camp it would come.

When I got to Tom Aldridge's office, he was in a slight panic because he thought his boss had gone too far, but he did see the logic of my argument that it needed a strong statement to elicit another death threat, this time with specifics which might help us pin down where the danger lay. He showed me the original messages. At first glance they could have been from any one.

There were three of them. The first said:

Idiot! If you don't reverse your position, you are a dead man.

The second read:

You have really lost the plot. Better call the undertaker.

And the final note:

In the countdown. Measure your coffin, moron.

All three messages were to the point, with no superfluous language which might identify the sender.

"Not much to go on, is there?" Tom said

"No, you're right," I said. "Brusque and incisive, yet..."

"What?"

"I'm not sure. There's something, but I can't put my finger on it."

"There might be something in the next one, which, unless I'm very much mistaken we should be getting very soon."

We idled away the time, drinking coffee and looking out of the windows.

After about forty minutes, there was a tap on the door, and Susan Greenlaugh entered bearing a print-out.

Tom grabbed and read it aloud. "'Right. You want a cock-up. You'll get one that will really have you hopping. Next time it will be you.'"

"What the hell does that mean?" he said.

"It sounds as if he somehow wants to demonstrate that he's serious."

"By doing what?"

"I guess we won't know 'til it happens."

11

I awoke early the next morning also, but when I came downstairs there was no sign of the premier. Instead there was a note on the table, weighted down with the pepper shaker.

> Marc: Don't go off anywhere today. Tom has appointments lined up for you. Be in by 7.15. Wendell

I had no idea what this meant. Tom had not mentioned any appointments when we last saw each other. I racked my brain but could not imagine who these people might be.

So I scrambled some eggs, made some toast and coffee and was on the road just before seven o'clock.

After I had parked the Bugatti in the spot assigned to me, I went directly to the premier's office, gave a perfunctory 'good morning' to Susan, and headed down to Tom's room.

"Ah, there you are. At last," he said as if he expected me much earlier. "Take a pew."

He was in his shirtsleeves, and was behind his desk, which was strewn with files. He pushed them towards me.

I glanced at the cover of each, noting the names:

> Chester MacCormack, Angus MacKinnon, Stephanie Gilmour, Joan Howard, Mark Gardiner, Chretien Cormier, Bill Clark, Kesegoo'e Sillyboy, Leona Beals, Fiona MacPherson, Angela Staples, and Ernest Maddingly, Harold Waybrett, Gloria MacPhee, Benoit LeBrun

"But these are all members of cabinet."

"Most of them will prove to be waste of time. The ones you need to treat very carefully are MacKinnon and Gardiner."

"I have to see them all?"

"Precisely," said Tom. "I've lined up interviews with each of them today and tomorrow. You'll have about forty minutes with each if you need it."

"*I'm* interviewing *them*?"

"Yes."

"But why? Why would they want to be interviewed by me?"

"Because they've been told to cooperate with you."

"What will I say? What questions will I ask?"

"That's up to you, but give them some bullshit about reinventing government."

"Why are MacKinnon and Gardiner special?"

"Because they ran against Wendell for the party leadership. So be thorough with them, as long as you don't give the game away."

"What game?"

"I thought you were an investigator, Marc," Tom said, frowning. "Don't you get it? This would-be assassin could have someone working for him on the inside."

"Inside the *cabinet*?"

"You never know."

"Jesus!"

"Old wounds can fester. Hard feelings can last forever. Don't forget that both these men were publicly humiliated."

"That's putting it too strongly, isn't it?"

"Well, Gardiner was thrashed. He only got a hundred votes. MacKinnon thought he had it in the bag, but we beat him by 284."

"But aren't you all on the same side?" I asked, knowing as I did so that I sounded naive.

"Marc, do you know the difference between a cactus and a caucus?"

"No. What is the difference?"

"With a cactus, all the pricks are on the outside!" He laughed, but without humour.

"You make it sound like a jungle. If you feel like this about your own people, how must you feel about the opposition parties?"

"It pays to be on your toes," Tom said seriously. "You know the old saying: 'Uneasy lies the head that wears the crown.'"

"I do, but you don't wear the crown. Wendell does."

"I'm here to do the worrying. I'm here to take the crap. I try to steer the knucklehead stuff away from Wendell so he can concentrate on running the province."

"I can see you do a good job of that."

"Thanks."

"Wait a minute," I said. "Wasn't Joan Howard also beaten by Wendell for the leadership?"

"Yes, but she's as good as gold."

"How can you be sure?"

"Because she was our stalking horse in the race. We put her up so the contest would go to more ballots."

"Now I'm lost. Politics is a foreign country for me. I'll take your word for it. Why do I have to interview her if you know she's safe?"

"For appearances. Might look suspicious if she was left out."

"Okay. I'll get started."

"And, Marc…"

"Yes?"

"Don't overlook Ernie."

"Ernie? Who's Ernie?"

"Maddingly. He's as old as Methuselah and as useless as tits on a bull, but he was bitterly hurt when he was forced out of the premiership, and might be nurturing his grievances to keep them warm."

As I left Tom's office, with arms full of files, my mind was reeling. I felt as if I were in a madhouse and not able to find the way out. The height of Tom's paranoia struck me as almost insane, and I wondered if the premier knew of his suspicions, and, if so, if he approved of the methods I was instructed to follow.

Then I remembered the note he had left for me, which strongly suggested that he had at least some knowledge of it.

Just how Tom thought I might be able to discover if a member of the cabinet were secretly hatching a plot to assassinate the boss escaped me. The culprit—if there was actually one—was hardly going to confess to me, a stranger, or even give me the slightest hint of their involvement. The whole thing seemed utterly foolish to me, and I resented having to waste time talking to fifteen boring politicians who would likely spend the entire time boasting about their accomplishments.

So I set about my task in a dispirited mood, wondering how Rosalie and I had got into this quagmire in the first place. Still, it had to be done.

I decided to start by reminding them of the general, if not sweeping, nature of the mandate given by cabinet when they appointed me, then to ask them for the general view of the way the government was operating, and finally to ask if they had specific suggestions for improvements.

Only if criticisms reflected on the premier, or if there were any slighting references to him, would I then innocently inquire why they felt that way. Frankly, I did not expect to get many suggestions which were concrete, and almost no comments which were not fully supportive of their boss.

I started with Stephanie Gilmour, Minister of Community Services, who was a friendly, attractive, cultured woman who said everything she should have and nothing she should not have.

Then I saw Kesegoo'e Sillyboy, Minister of Lands, Forests and Native Affairs. Her interview reflected the bitterness she felt over her colleagues' alleged inattention to her opinions, although, after hacking at several of her fellow ministers, she did finally have some kind words for the premier.

Minister of Finance Chester MacCormack was the model of a diplomat and managed to say absolutely nothing about anything. He smiled, frequently rearranged his ample posterior on his padded leather chair, and made sure I did all the talking. However, I could not detect in him the slightest animus towards the premier.

Justice Minister Angela Staples clearly resented my being there and as good as said I was wasting her time, a charge with which I could not, in all conscience, have argued. I found her to be very cold, and I imagined she would be ruthlessly efficient, but because she seemed more like a machine than a woman, I thought her an unlikely suspect to harbour strong feelings about any human being.

I saw the other ministers throughout the rest of the day and most of the next one. A few sat me down, then paced up and down in front of me, expounding on their own virtues. One insisted on telling me five disgusting jokes in a row.

But most of them either used me as a sounding board to ascertain the premier's feelings towards them and whether they might expect promotion, or tried to use me to talk him into approving pet projects they had not been able to persuade cabinet to adopt.

So, as I expected, most of the interviews yielded nothing of consequence; at least nothing which I thought was consequential at the time. However, three, of the encounters were very different and for very different reasons.

Meeting Joan Howard was literally a stunning experience. She was so beautiful, so magnetic and prepossessing, that I was stumbling over my words like an embarrassed little boy. She was completely forthcoming and made no attempt to avoid or hide anything. That she was totally supportive of Wendell Proctor as premier was abundantly clear, and she spoke of him as if he were a very dear brother.

That brought me to Mark Gardiner, whose opening words were of barely concealed hostility. "So what's this really all about, LeBlanc?"

"I'm sorry?"

"Oh, come on! Why are you really here?"

"The premier explained it to you at the cabinet meeting."

"You don't expect me to believe that baloney, do you?"

"Minister, I can't help what you believe. All I know is that I've been asked to do a job—"

"A job on me! You're out to get me, that's what!"

"No, no, not at all."

"Go ahead then, ask your questions, but don't expect me to incriminate myself, if that's what you're hoping for!"

"Nobody is trying to *incriminate* you, Minister."

"Of course you would say that."

"Under the circumstances, I think it might be better if I left now."

"So you could tell Proctor that I refused to cooperate? I'm not falling for that one. No, go on, ask your questions."

Our interview only lasted about fifteen minutes, but it felt like an hour of wrestling with a python. He constantly seethed with contempt and derision, but I could not tell if it was for me, the premier or the world in general. At the door he almost spat at me as he curtly said his goodbyes.

I was immensely glad to escape and devoutly hoped I would never have to repeat the experience.

The last minister I saw was Angus MacKinnon, a tallish, handsome man in his late forties. I had heard he was a marvellous speaker and a skilled politician who was regarded as something of a god in the eastern end of the province, from which he hailed. I found him to be extremely friendly and cooperative. He treated my visit as if it were a great honour for him, and made it clear that I could have the entire day with him if I wished.

He made a great flourish of going to the door and loudly calling to his secretary, "Mrs. Hawkins, please cancel all my appointments. And make sure we are not disturbed. Mr. LeBlanc is here on very important business."

"I understand you ran for the party leadership at the same time as Mr. Proctor," I said. Since beating about the bush had got me nowhere with the others, I thought I should get straight to the point.

"Oh yes," he said with a chuckle. "You should have been there. It was a real spectacle. Wendell and Joan stitched me up properly. It was a work of art."

"Were you very disappointed?"

"For about three days, yes. Then I realized I'd had a merciful release."

"How do you mean?"

"You're staying with the boss, aren't you?"

"Yes. He and Cynthia have been very kind to us."

"Us?"

"My wife is with me."

"Oh, right. Well, you know what it's like. I doubt Wendell gets home before eleven at night and then he's gone again before seven."

"Sometimes before six."

"Well, there you go. I thought I would like the pomp of it, and being called 'premier', but when I thought about it, I understood that in that position you may be the master but you're everybody's servant, too."

"I think that's rather well put, sir."

"Do you? Thanks. I think we make a good team, you know. I have more political skills and governmental experience than he does, but he has more charisma and stamina than I do."

"That sounds like an ideal match."

"Do you know much about politics, Mr. LeBlanc?"

"Almost nothing."

"It's a rough, tough, cut-throat, take-no-prisoners sort of life, but it can also be strangely rewarding."

As we talked I became very comfortable in his presence and found him to be a charming man with a winning smile. But when he thought I wasn't looking, I imagined I detected a glint of steel in his eyes.

Had he really lost the ruthlessness for which he was once renowned? Was he really satisfied with being one of the guys rather than the man at the top? I was not sure.

When I tried to see Ernest Maddingly I was told by his secretary that he was 'unavailable' on either day. I asked for an alternative date for an appointment and was informed that they would get back to me. Clearly, this was one which would need the premier's muscle.

12

When I went down the next morning, the premier was making tea.

"Want some?"

"No thanks, I prefer coffee."

"We've got lots of that, too. Help yourself."

"Thanks."

"How'd you make out?"

"You knew about those interviews?"

"Sure did."

"Don't you think it was a tad paranoid to suspect a member of the cabinet plotting to kill you?"

"A tad, maybe. But Tom wanted to be thorough."

"I guess I can see that, but was I the right person to do it? Some of them were damned unhappy to see me."

"Who were the unhappy ones?"

"Staples, for one."

"Frigid bitch," said the premier with uncharacteristic venom, "but she's the most competent minister I've got and she knows the law inside out."

"Gardiner was the worst. He was hopping mad."

"Fuck him," said the premier, who was showing a side of him I had never seen before. "He always was a wuss. Who else?"

"Those were the only ones who were openly hostile. Most didn't say anything about anything. Played their cards close to the chest."

"Sounds like Chester," he said with a laugh.

"Yes, he was one."

"Who were the most helpful?"

"Howard..."

"Wonderful woman. She's an absolute angel."

"And MacKinnon. Couldn't do enough to cooperate with me."

"Angus? That's interesting."

"He said you and he made the perfect team."

"Did he, by God? Well, well. I'd never exactly thought of us like two oxen pulling a plough, but he's not far wrong."

"One refused to see me."

"*What*?"

"Well, I shouldn't say refused. Just wasn't available."

"Who was the motherfucker?"

"Maddingly."

"That fussy old asshole! I'll give him 'unavailable'! You'll see him first thing. Go to his office as soon as you get into town. If they won't let you in to see him, tell them to call me."

"Are you sure?"

"Sure I'm sure. I only keep him in the cabinet because the old people in the party love him. He's neither use nor ornament, and if he wants to leave, I'd be happy to oblige him. You can tell him I said that."

"I'd rather not.'"

"Alright." He flashed me an enormous grin.

Just then a car horn blew three times.

"There's Jack. I'm out of here. See you, Marc."

I did as I was instructed and duly showed up in Maddingly's outer office.

Ernest Maddingly was Provincial Secretary, a position which at one time had been the second most important post in the province. Now it was a shadow of its former self, being a ragbag collection of bits and pieces of government which other departments didn't want. Its most important functions were to keep and guard The Great Seal and administer marriages, births and deaths.

"I'm here to see Mr. Maddingly," I said to the elderly, blue-haired lady at the desk.

"I'm sorry, he can't see anyone without an appointment."

"I tried several times yesterday to get one, but was told he was unavailable."

"Well, there you are," she said primly, as if that closed the matter once and for all.

"I spoke to the premier an hour ago and he said I should tell you that if you have a problem you should call him now."

Her eyes nearly popped out her head and her body bristled with resentment and offence. She tossed her blue head about for a few seconds, then she pressed the intercom.

"Yes?" A tired old voice said.

"I have a Mr. LeBlanc to see you, Minister."

"I thought we'd settled that foolishness yesterday," said the voice.

"He says if you have a problem you are to call the premier right away."

There was a long, painful silence, during which the only sounds were Maddingly's laboured breathing through the intercom, and the restless rustling of his secretary's bombazine dress.

Finally, he mumbled something which the secretary interpreted as assent.

"You can go in," she said curtly.

I went through a set of double doors into what seemed like another era. Apart from the intercom and a telephone, the office could have been something out of Dickens. Maddingly must have deliberately asked the Public Works Department to comb the cellars for old furniture and, it would seem, the older the better. Had the minister been dressed in a wing tip collar I would not have been surprised. Instead, he wore a top-quality, dark grey suit which I could see had been made many years ago.

He did not get up from the desk or offer me a seat, so I looked around and, spying an elegant Victorian chair, dragged it closer to the desk and sat down.

"Yes, what is it?" he asked in a pained manner.

Ernest Maddingly must have been close to, or past, eighty. He was thin, sallow and had a few bad teeth which made him appear more sinister than I suspected he really was. He constantly rubbed and fiddled with his very bony, white hands, on which the veins stood out, rather like a relief map of the Andes.

"You know the task I have been given by the premier."

"I may have known something about it." He spoke impatiently, as if to a child who was asking for a larger allowance. "I can't be expected to remember everything."

"Why don't we start with your ideas on how to improve government," I said as cheerfully as I could.

"Well, *really*!" He snorted. "How utterly trite. Good heavens above!"

"I understand, Mr. Maddingly, that you were once premier yourself."

Suddenly, everything changed. His face lit up, he edged forward on his seat and actually smiled. When he spoke, his tone was entirely different.

"Ah, yes indeed," he said with a satisfied sigh, "and a very good premier I was too, by all accounts. Of course I wasn't given the opportunity to occupy that office for long. Had I been treated properly—as I rightly deserved—and permitted a decent term, I'm confident I could have achieved much, much more. In fact, I think it's fair to say that I could have gone down in the history books as one of the best, if not *the* best, premiers in modern times."

I was astonished by this outburst and by its energy. Maddingly had become a different, rejuvenated man, his former listlessness transformed. I sat back and let him ramble on.

Proudly, he told me how his constituency had been re-electing him for nearly fifty years, how he had served in the cabinets of five premiers, and how honoured he had been to be able to contribute to the political life of the province over such a long time. He held the record, he repeated "*the record*", for service in the history of the legislature.

Then, just as suddenly as he had become young and spirited, he now became harsh, bitter and sneering as he relayed the story of how, when a former premier had drowned and he had stepped into his shoes, 'they' conspired against him and denied him the chance to govern for what he called a 'decent length of time'.

He never specified who 'they' were, but he repeatedly referred to 'them' as *a jumped up cabal*. No names were mentioned, but it was clear to me that one of those he felt had cheated him out of his rightful place in the sun was Wendell Proctor.

As I left his office and walked slowly over to see Tom Aldridge, I wondered if an eighty-year-old man possessed the motive, the strength and the wherewithal to conspire with an assassin. How would someone like Maddingly even know how to get in touch with an assassin? And even if he could, would a man who prided himself on his rectitude and sense of justice descend to such depths?

On balance, I thought it unlikely, but the vehemence with which he had denounced the *jumped up cabal* nagged at the back of my mind.

13

The next day, before going to see Tom Aldridge, I decided to reject Patrick Kennedy's advice and go to North Preston. I do not know what I expected to learn from a mere drive-through, but I felt I needed to see the community for myself. If I was anticipating an obviously murky place with evil lurking round each corner, I was completely disabused of the idea.

The first thing that struck me about the place was that, quite contrary to any notions of its being a densely populated slum, the community was a very pleasant one in an almost-rural setting. There were a few dilapidated buildings, some old car bodies and some scruffy driveways, but no more than in any other Nova Scotia village or town.

I saw a few people going about what seemed to be their legitimate business, but no hoodlums hanging out on street corners, no sinister-looking men in large cars in the act of seducing young girls.

I slowly coasted up North Preston Road onto Simmonds Road, past a very smart and extensive community centre, then looped back and soon came upon the Johnson Road, and eventually got back to where I had started. One or two kids ran out to stare at the Bugatti, a few old men smiled and waved, and only one young man wearing a woollen hat scowled as I passed by.

If this was the hub of the NPF's despicable criminal activities, it certainly did a good job of hiding them from prying eyes. I wished I could have talked to some of the inhabitants, but I remembered Patrick Kennedy's cautionary words and resisted the temptation to stop.

The more I looked around here, the more convinced I was that this was not the source of the threats on the premier's life, and searching here for the would-be assassin would be a wild goose chase.

I got back to Tom's office just before noon and found him having a sandwich at his desk.

"Hey," he said, taking a bite. "Where've you been?"

"North Preston, having a look around?"

"Are you crazy? That was risky."

"Have *you* ever been there, Tom?"

"No. I haven't."

"Maybe you should reserve judgment until you do."

"Ouch! Point made. Wendell goes there from time to time, but he likes to go with Senator Carvery or his brother-in-law, Matt."

"Tom, I'm convinced that the NPF route is a blind alley. It just doesn't feel right."

"I was tending in that direction myself," he said. "So, we think we're dealing with an environmental fruit cake."

"I hope he or she is only a fruitcake and not a terrorist," I said. "Could you pull those death threats again, please? Something about them is bugging me."

"Sure." He went over to a filing cabinet, unlocked it and took out a file. "Here you go."

"Read them to me, will you?"

"Okay. Here goes."

Idiot!
If you don't reverse your position, you are a dead man.

"Next."

You have really lost the plot. Better call the undertaker.

"And the next, please."

In the countdown. Measure your coffin, moron.

"And the final one."

Right. You want a cock-up.
You'll get one that will really have you hopping.
Next time it will be you.

I sat there racking my brain. I knew there was something distinctive about these threats, but I could not put my finger on what it was.

Tom watched me, frowning with frustration. "What is it?"

"I don't know. I can't pin it down."

"When you're trying to think, you look like Boris Johnson," Tom said with a laugh.

"What did you say?"

"I said when you're trying to think, you look like Boris Johnson."

"That's *it*! Of course that's it!" I cried.

"What? What are you talking about?"

"Tom, who in this country says things like 'cock-up', 'moron' and 'lost the plot'?"

"Not too many, now you come to mention it. Who *does* say things like that?"

"The Brits. I lived there for eighteen years. Our suspect is a Brit!"

"Nice work, Sherlock. That narrows the field down a bit."

"For a start, it confirms our feeling that the suspect is not a human trafficker from North Preston."

"That's for sure. But where do we go from here?"

"I think I may have to go over there."

"Go where?"

"To London."

"Right, that makes sense, I guess, but even if you did, where would you start looking?"

"I'll need a contact who really knows their stuff. Someone who has specialized in environmental fringe groups."

"If such a person exists, my guess is it would be a journalist."

"Tom, go on the net, look up the main newspapers and TV channels—BBC, ITV, Sky, the *Times, Daily Mail, Telegraph*, *et cetera*—and see what comes up."

"Okay. You're going to have to give me some time. Why don't you go get a coffee or gossip with Susan? Half an hour should do it."

When I returned Tom looked triumphant. "I've got your man," he said. "Robson Callister."

"Sounds like a hero from a Jeffery Archer novel."

"Never read one, so I wouldn't know. But this guy has been working on the environmental file for over thirty years. He was a regular for the *Times* and *Sunday Times* for years, but is now freelance. He's written hundreds of articles on the subject and has contacts in high and low places."

"How would we get in touch with him?"

"Already done."

"What?"

"Using Wendell's name, I contacted the editor of the *Times* and asked him for Callister's email address. So, again using Wendell's moniker, I sent him a message asking if he could meet with the premiers' chief advisor."

"That's a bit of a stretch. Did he reply?"

"Not yet."

"He may not."

"Then I'll try again, this time offering him a fee."

"Can you do that? With taxpayer's money?"

"Marc, the premier of Nova Scotia can authorize any expenditure he likes. You should see some of the things previous premiers okayed. You wouldn't believe some of the schemes and stunts Premier Buchanan approved. And he made sure the potentially most embarrassing items just disappeared."

"How on earth did he do that?"

"He simply told the deputy minister of finance to take care of it. So the amount was broken down into a dozen categories, each one being assigned to items in different departments."

"I had no idea such things happened, or were even possible!"

"Marc, anything is possible. You just have to make sure it's hidden if it could be troublesome."

"And if Robson Callister wants a hefty fee, where will you put that? Just fold it into the Office of the Premier?"

"Good God, no! Are you insane? We would never do that. In fact, the reverse."

"What do you mean, the reverse?"

"It doesn't look good to the voters if the Premier's Office costs too much. So, to make it look like he is a bargain, we move some expenses incurred here to other departments, particularly the big spenders like Health and Education."

"*I'm* getting an education today," I said. "I thought your administration was a government of honesty and reform."

"Compared with previous governments, we are," said Tom with a huge grin. Then he looked at his monitor. "Here we go. Mr. Callister has replied."

"What does he say?"

"He says he would be glad to be of assistance and estimates you would need to spend two days with him, but he would want to be compensated for his time."

"What's his daily rate?"

"Two hundred and fifty pounds."

"What's that in our money?"

"Let me see." Tom typed on his keyboard. "The exchange is $1.66 to the pound. That would be $414.29 a day, so we are looking at $828.58 total."

"Will that be a problem?"

"That's chicken feed. We'll put it in *Public Works Provincial Building Security*."

"Just like that?"

"Just like that."

"When does Callister want to see me?"

"Let me look. He says he'll be tied up on a story in Glasgow for four more days, but he can meet you the day after that. The 17th."

"That can work. I'll have to take the Bugatti back to Grand Pre and get Rosalie to drive me to the airport. Maybe she'll be able to come with me. Tell him I'll see him then. Where will we meet?"

"Just a minute....he says you'd better come to his home, but you must keep it a secret. He has problems with fanatics."

"Okay, mum's the word. What's the address?"

"3, Yarmouth Place. He says it's on the corner with Brick Street. You know it?"

"London is a big place."

"He says it's in Mayfair."

"Wow. He must be a high flyer."

"He says it's behind Shepherd's Market."

"Ah, the only *un*fashionable part of Mayfair! Tell him I'll find him."

"Come at 10 am, he says."

"Okay, I'll be there. If I can get a room I'll stay at Fleming's Hotel on Half Moon Street. It's in the same area. It'll only be a ten minute walk to his place."

"Right. That's done."

"Tom," I said, "If it's all the same to you, I'd like to pay for the flights and accommodation myself."

"Are you crazy? We can easily squirrel it away under *Miscellaneous Unclassified and Unforeseen Expenses*."

"No. I can easily afford it. And it might be useful if there were any awkward questions."

"Good point. If someone makes a fuss we can say you are donating your time and expenses to the province out of the goodness of your heart. That should shut them up."

"Do you never stop thinking in terms of scoring political points?"

"No, never," he said. "Not when I'm working. When I'm home, it's a different matter."

"I'm glad to hear it."

"Say, why don't you and Rosalie come and have dinner with Heidi and me the day after tomorrow?"

"We'd like that. Shouldn't you ask her?"

"Yes, you're right. I'll call her now."

I went over to the window and looked out while Tom telephoned his wife. The trees were in full leaf, green and luxurious, and the sun shone down through the branches, causing dark, dancing shadows on the grass.

"I got her at the bank. She says she's not much of a cook but she'll be glad to meet you both. About seven alright?"

"Yes, fine."

14

The day Rosalie and I were due to dine with the Aldridges was a Sunday, so the premier did not go into his office and we all had breakfast together, along with his sister, Grace, and her husband, Matthew. Cynthia and Grace did all the preparation and cooking, leaving the rest of us to chat around the table. Matthew, a large, amiable man, said little, mostly grunting his assent or dissent.

Wendell was in an ebullient mood and, replete with jokes, gestures and impersonations, related stories about his previous day's meetings with constituents. Neither Rosalie nor I knew the people to whom he was referring, but we found it highly amusing nonetheless.

From time to time Grace would loudly butt in with her opinion, usually unflattering, of the person being discussed.

Soon there were dishes and plates on the table, loaded with eggs, bacon, ham, pancakes, stacks of toast, jugs of maple syrup, mounds of butter and enormous pots of coffee and tea. We attacked the food with relish.

Matthew, rather pithily, commented, "Dropping a loaf of bread on the table around here is like dropping the puck at Madison Square Gardens," and we all laughed heartily. Matthew may have been a man of few words, but those few were good ones.

"Tom tells me you think you've narrowed it down," Wendell said to me, speaking cryptically, indicating I should do likewise.

"Yes. We think so. We don't think it's the local problem."

"Uh huh. And nothing to do with paintings?"

"No. That was a non-starter."

"I thought so. I think I said so at the time. So what next?"

"Didn't Tom tell you?"

"What?"

"I'm off to London."

"Oh yes, he did. I hope it turns up the answers."

At the mention of London, Rosalie and Cynthia perked up.

"What's this?" Cynthia asked. "How lovely!"

"Why didn't you tell me?" Rosalie demanded. "Can I come?"

"Of course you can come if you can get time off from the University."

"How long would we be gone?"

"Four days at most. Still want to come?"

"Yes. I call in after breakfast to see if I can rearrange some tutorials."

"Why don't we all go?" Grace asked.

I noticed Matthew rolling his eyes.

"What a good idea!" Cynthia said.

"No," Wendell said decisively. "This is business."

"But if Rosalie is going—"

"No!" Wendell's tone suddenly changed.

His womenfolk immediately fell silent. He went on eating.

Nobody felt like saying anything after that, so Rosalie gave me a nod in the direction of the bedroom. We thanked Grace and Cynthia for a lovely breakfast and retreated to our room.

"Boy!" she said when we had closed the door. "When he says 'no', he really means 'no'."

"I've heard Tom say that, when they're deliberating a particular subject and Wendell says 'next', it means they must move on and that nobody should try to continue the discussion. Besides, you're in on the secret. We couldn't possibly have Cynthia, Grace and Matthew following us around in London. Wendell was right."

"Yes, I see that. I'll call Acadia right now and see if I can get away. When would we be leaving?"

"The day after tomorrow. And return four or five days later."

"Okay."

"And I'll see if they have a room at Flemings Hotel."

It transpired that Rosalie could get the time off and that Flemings had an executive room available. It would cost me $770 a night, but that would not present a problem to my financial resources, and we would be very centrally located.

I got flights via Toronto to enable us to fly business class and have "lie down" seats for the overnight journey. Wendell told me he had an extra garage which could be made secure, so I would not have to drive the Bugatti back to Grand Pre.

That settled, I arranged a taxi to take us to the Aldridges' house that evening.

Tom and Heidi lived in a modest, modern house in the City's west end.

It seemed to be a quiet neighbourhood, with the street lined with trees and not much traffic.

The taxi dropped us off and, as we walked up the driveway, Tom appeared at the front door with a young woman who, at first, we took to be his daughter.

However, when we got inside, Tom introduced her as his wife, Heidi. She must have been twenty years younger than Tom and was extremely beautiful; tall and shapely, with big blue eyes and bouncy blonde hair. Rosalie later told me that Heidi possessed what she called "poise". I would have called it "grace".

As the evening progressed we learned that Heidi was the daughter of a former premier of the province and was the youngest manager of a head branch of a national bank in Halifax.

When we were escorted into the living room, we were surprised to see, ensconced in a deep, high armchair, the very elderly Jewish lady we had met at Ray and Rachel's wedding. She must have been well into her nineties, but still had a twinkle in her eyes.

When she saw us, she beamed. "*Shalom Aleichem.* Forgive me," she said, "for not getting up. When I get settled in this chair, I can't get out of it without help."

"I see you know Chedva Bensaid," Tom said. "She has been my *Bubbe* for years."

"I am the nosy next-door neighbour," said Chedva.

"Yes, I used to live in this house many years ago until my first wife, Iris, died," said Tom. "Then when my son moved back to Cape Breton, I sold the house and got an apartment."

"That's right," said Chedva, "then, just after Tom and Heidi were married, I looked out my window and saw the *For Sale* sign. So I called Tom right away and he went straight to the real estate agent and made an offer. So here we are, together again. Though for how long, who can say?"

"You'll be here for a long time yet, Chedva," said Heidi, going to her and wrapping her arms around the old woman.

"*B'ezrat HaShem,*" she said with a sigh.

Rosalie and I both commented later that this was a household totally enveloped in warmth, fondness and affection. Tom was a completely different person in his own house, the tough, the cynical, the opportunistic sides of him having fallen away, and in their place were kindness, consideration and a certain softness.

We attributed this to Heidi's proximity, because there was no doubt they were utterly in love. We noticed that, at the table, he constantly had his hand on hers or on her back, and occasionally on her knee.

Heidi offered us a drink, and Rosalie asked for a white wine.

"Have the Scotch, Marc!" Chedva called out. "It's not as good as some of the single malts I have at my house, but it's not bad. It's Johnnie Walker Gold Label."

"Okay, if you recommend it, I shall take a small glass."

"Take a big one. I did!"

"Why not?" I said to Tom. "Fill 'er up."

"So, Tom, I didn't know you had a son," Rosalie said.

"Yes, he's 26 now."

"What line is he in?"

"Mostly sanctimony and other people's business," Tom said with a laugh.

"Tom!" Heidi immediately rushed to her step-son's defence. "Andrew and Tom don't see eye to eye on many things. He's a lawyer with Legal Aid."

"He almost stole you away from me."

"He did no such thing! I dated him briefly, then decided I preferred his dad."

Rosalie and I exchanged furtive glances while Chedva chuckled away like an old hen. By the time dinner was ready, she had fallen asleep and had to be gently awakened.

"Time to eat, Bubbe." Tom said, offering his arm to help her up.

"Oh Good," she said, coming alive. "I'm starving."

We sat in a rather cramped dining room off the main living area, Chedva at the head, and Tom poured a serviceable wine to go with a vegetable soup.

"I gather Marc is a good chef and wine expert," Tom said to Rosalie.

"He thinks he is," She replied, getting an appreciative laugh from the others.

"Why are you here, Rosalie?" Heidi asked.

"How do you mean?"

"I mean what are you doing in Halifax? Don't you live in the Annapolis Valley?"

"Yes, in Grand Pre."

"But Tom says you've been here for some days and that you're staying with Wendell and Cynthia."

"Yes we are."

"Then..."

"Sweetheart." Tom came to our rescue. "Rosalie and Marc are helping

Wendell with a special project."

"Sounds interesting. How special?"

"We can't really talk about it," Tom said, giving her a strange look.

"Ah cloak and dagger stuff!"

"Hardly." I said. "The premier asked me to see and talk to a variety of people to find out their opinions on a variety of topics."

"You should be in politics, Marc. If ever there was a non-answer that was it!"

"Sorry."

"Don't apologize. I recognize the signs. When Tom goes quiet or changes the subject I know a cabinet secret is involved." Heidi was enjoying herself and her eyes were laughing gaily. "Let's serve the main course."

Chedva, who had fallen asleep again, had to be re-awakened for the rare roast prime rib of beef with potatoes, mashed turnips and Yorkshire pudding. It looked very inviting, especially with a bottle of New Zealand Pinot Noir.

"Don't you abide by *Kashrut*?" I asked Chedva.

"Certainly I do. How do you know about such things?"

"Rachel Bland is our best friend."

"Ah, of course. What a treasure that dear woman is! But why do you ask me about *Kashrut*?"

"The Yorkshire pudding and the mashed turnip."

"No milk, only water in the pudding," sang out Heidi, "and no cream, only kosher butter in the turnips!"

"Heidi knows me well by now." Said Chedva, then: "*Barukh ata Adonai Eloheinu, melekh ha'olam, hamotzi lehem min ha'aretz.*"

"*Baruch Hu, u'varuch Sh'mo.*" Tom said.

I found myself automatically saying *ahmein* along with the others, then tucked into the excellent food.

"Have you encountered many characters on your quest, Marc?" Heidi asked.

"Quite a few. Some old friends, some new enemies. One is a very officious curator who treats me as if I had bubonic plague, and another eats absolutely mountains of food at every meal. Another actually told me that Halifax has underground tunnels under the peninsula."

"Good God!" Heidi cried.

"Why? What's wrong Darling?" Tom was solicitous.

"What an extraordinary coincidence," she said, "because I have just discovered a tunnel under my bank.'

"You *what*?" I think we all spoke at the same time.

"Yes, yesterday. I had some men remove a false wall which was getting very dilapidated and there it was, the entrance to a tunnel."

"Someone trying to rob the bank?" Chedva asked?

"No. This wall is nowhere near the vault. It's in a different section entirely. This is on the harbour side. The vault is actually on another, higher level of bedrock on the street side. The tunnel—if it is a tunnel, it could be a cave—looks like it has been there for a hundred years or more."

"Did you go in?" Rosalie asked.

"Just into the entrance which was kind of partly blocked. It looked dark and damp inside."

"What will you do with it, Sweetheart?"

"I guess that, at some point, I'll have to get some contractors to concrete it over, purely from a liability standpoint in case someone gets hurt."

"Heidi…"

"Yes, Marc?"

"Where is your bank?"

"It's on Hollis Street."

"Anywhere near the legislature?"

"Yes, a few blocks further south."

"I wonder if I could ask you for a very big favour."

"Sure, Marc, if I can."

"Heidi, before you get your contractors in, could I see this tunnel?"

"I'm not sure…."

"Please, darling, do as he asks," Tom pleaded.

"Alright," she said, looking a little mystified. "I guess it won't do any harm if everyone keeps quiet about it. I don't want a crowd of sight-seers milling around and asking to go down to it."

"Tomorrow?"

"Okay, why not? But it will have to be before we open."

"That would be fine. Thank you."

15

The premier was having his cereal when I went down the next morning, so I took the opportunity of asking him if he had any coveralls we could borrow. He pointed to the door of the basement with his spoon, so I opened it and descended into a room crowded with paraphernalia, including several sets of coveralls and several pairs of rubber boots.

I called Rosalie to come down, and together we tried on clothing and footwear until we found sizes which fitted us. We also took a couple of very large flashlights.

"Why do you want that stuff?" asked Wendell, who was now gathering his things to leave for the office.

"Heidi mentioned last night that she found a cave or tunnel in the cellar of her bank, so we're going to take a look at it."

"I hope you won't forget the main reason you're here," he said seriously.

"No, don't worry, we won't. We're just taking a peak out of curiosity, because when we spoke to him, Akerman mentioned tunnels, too."

"That guy! I wouldn't put too much faith in anything he tells you." He grabbed his briefcase from a chair. "When do you leave for London?"

"Later today. So we won't see you for at least four or five days."

"Did you lock up your car alright?"

"No, but we will before we go."

"Okay. Well, good luck."

"Wendell..."

"What?"

"I hope you're taking extra special care these days. We still don't know if this guy is serious, but if he is he could strike at any time. So it's imperative you stay on your guard."

"Yeah. I know. Thanks, Marc. I'd better get going."

Heidi was waiting for us on the sidewalk outside the bank. When I had parked the Bugatti, I could see Province House a few blocks away to the north.

"Thanks for a lovely dinner last night," said Rosalie.

"It was our pleasure. I think Tom quite likes Marc."

"The feeling is mutual," I said.

"And Mark was certainly a hit with Chedva."

"They have a mutual friend in Johnnie Walker."

"Haha! Let's go in. It'll be a few hours before the staff arrive."

We were ushered into the now quiet and rather tomb-like space, and then through a door which led to the various levels below the street. When we had reached the lowest level, we could see remnants of the false wall lying scattered around, and a gaping hole in the old stone wall.

Rosalie and I dressed in the coveralls, pulled on our boots, then gingerly probed beyond the jagged entrance.

"How long will you be?" Heidi asked.

"We don't know what we're going to find, but if you tell us what time you want us to be back, we'll make sure we're back by then."

"Can you be back by eight-thirty?"

"Okay." I looked at my watch. "It's six-thirty now, so wherever we are in an hour we'll turn around and head back."

"I won't go to my office. I'll just potter around here until you return."

Once we had negotiated our way through the remains of what had previously served to block the entrance, we started to penetrate the gloom ahead. It was totally dark and our flashlights made eerie flicker-ings on the low roof and narrow sides.

It became quickly clear that this was indeed a passage, measuring about three feet wide and about five feet five inches high, which meant that I had to constantly keep my head down. Underfoot, the floor was rough and slippery, making for very slow going.

After we had been moving for about 20 minutes the tunnel came to an end as it joined another, slightly wider, one running north-south. We dir-ected our flashlights in both ways, but could not see the tunnel coming to an end in either direction, or any features which might warrant further investigation. Nonetheless, we decided to explore, Rosalie taking one way and I the other, agreeing to call out at two minute intervals to assure the other that we were still safe.

We proceeded in this fashion until our voices grew so faint we de-cided it might not be safe to continue. We returned to the junction with the tunnel to the bank.

"Anything?" She asked. "Any other tunnels or strange features?"

"Nothing to the south. You?"

"Just before we turned around, I saw what could have been another tunnel—a smaller one—ahead, but my flashlight was waning. I think the batteries are on the blink."

"Was it on the harbour side, or the street side?"

"The left side. The street."

"We'll have to leave it. We'd better get back and get ready to go out to the airport."

When we emerged, Heidi was waiting for us, anxiously looking at her watch.

"How did you get along?" she asked. "I have to go and let my staff in now."

"This tunnel joins another tunnel. We couldn't go too far because of the time," I said.

"Heidi, you go on. We'll wait here until you've let your staff settle."

While Heidi scurried away, Rosalie and I stripped off our coveralls and boots and put them into a bag. They were very damp and quite dirty.

"We'll have to clean this stuff before we return it to the Proctors."

"We won't have time today. It will have to be when we get back from London. I don't imagine they will need them in the next few days."

When Heidi returned, she noticed the bag and, on being told what it contained, offered to take them to her house and get them cleaned.

"Thanks, Heidi. We owe you," I said. "But I have two more favours to ask."

"What are they?"

"The first is that you don't block off the tunnel until we have time to come back and have a real look at it."

"Okay. I haven't called the contractors yet. I'll leave it for a few weeks."

"Oh, thanks,"

"What's the other favour?"

"May we have a quick peek at the vault?"

"Sure," she said with a laugh. "Follow me."

We had gone about eighty feet from the harbour side of the bank to the Hollis Street side, and as we went up to the next level, the steepness of the slope in the bedrock of the Halifax peninsula became apparent. Heidi led us to a discreet door in the wall, unlocked it and let us in.

I was immediately disappointed not to see masses of steel bars and, behind them, a huge, circular door with wheels and levers. Instead, there was a wall of reinforced concrete in which was embedded a keypad about fifteen inches long, containing two keyholes, twelve digits and a dial.

"That's it?"

"Yup! What did you expect? Something out of a movie?"

"I guess I did. I thought it would be a massive steel thing with a giant wheel on it."

"There's a little more to it than meets the eye, but unfortunately I can't show it to you," Heidi said. "Let's go back up."

We drove from the bank to the Proctor house, firmly ensconced the Bugatti in the spare garage, then went in to pick up our baggage and say goodbye to Cynthia.

Then we got a taxi to the airport and took our flight to Toronto, where we had a two-hour wait before boarding Flight 854 for London Heathrow. We refused Champagne and all other offers of refreshment, and immediately put our seats into the horizontal position and went to sleep.

16

Seven hours later we landed at Heathrow to a grey and seemingly-bleak morning. It was 6.35 London time.

Even when it is grey and cloudy, there is always a slight *frisson* of excitement when landing in London, no matter how many times one has done it; but should the sun be shining it is like coming to demi-Paradise. The air promises good things.

In the terminal, despite the throng of humanity wearing every conceivable costume in every colour under the sun, our Business Class tickets gave us access to the Fast Line and we nipped through without any human contact, merely showing our passports to a camera.

I looked over at the immense rows of people from Africa, India and elsewhere, sweating in the lengthy line-ups to have their papers examined by Immigration Officers, and reflected, as I often have before, that if money does not actually buy happiness, there are occasions when it certainly makes a difference.

We went outside, where the air was cool, having that *je ne sais quoi* smell that helps to make London special, and hailed a cab.

There is an eternal debate as to whether it is better to go into central London on the Heathrow Express, an underground train which does the distance to Paddington in fifteen minutes and costs twenty-five pounds, or to take a taxi, which might take as much as fifty minutes and cost almost a hundred pounds. The problem with the Heathrow Express is that it takes twenty minutes walking in the terminal and along tunnels to get to the station, and when you arrive at Paddington, you have to wait in line to get a taxi (costing about forty pounds) to take you to your hotel.

Having used both methods many times, I much prefer to take a taxi. It might cost a little more, but you get door-to-door service and it takes approximately the same amount of time with none of the hassle.

Fleming's Hotel, on Half Moon Street, could not check us in for several hours because it was only 7.30 in the morning. So we went to the concierge's station and introduced ourselves to Andrew Sturge and his assistant, Ryan Alden, asking them to put our cases in their little room behind the desk. I gave them each fifty pounds, because we would be here for four days and would need their services again. Now they knew we were "serious" guests they would make sure we received prompt attention, anticipating an equally-generous amount when we departed.

The side streets off Piccadilly to the north, such as Bolton, Clarges, Stratton and Half Moon, have a peculiar quality in that they are only yards from one of the longest, widest, busiest streets in the world, but are somehow shielded from the noise of its traffic. A person could be walking down Piccadilly amid the raucous hustle and bustle, turn into Half Moon Street and, within a few steps, be in a different universe. This is largely because the many tall, stone, early nineteenth century buildings of which the area is still mainly comprised act as a buffer or muffle. At Fleming's Hotel, for example, as soon as you step into the lobby, you become aware of the luxurious silence

Rosalie and I had opted not to be disturbed for breakfast on the plane, as the attendants wake passengers almost two hours before landing, thus preventing valuable sleep, so when we stepped out into the street from the hotel we were ravenous. I knew exactly what we needed, and that was an old-fashioned full English breakfast, and I also knew just the place to get it.

I guided Rosalie on to Piccadilly, down one block, then right onto White Horse Street. Within minutes we were in a different world, a tiny corner of swanky Mayfair more like a working class area than the haunt of millionaires. This was Shepherd's Market, an urban oasis. Here is a charming warren of small streets with quaint shops, pubs and cafes, while a few blocks away a one bedroom flat costs about six and a half million dollars.

We turned on to Shepherd Street and went to the Piccolo Bar. It is so popular that it was packed with office and shop workers grabbing breakfast before work, so we had to wait some minutes to get a table. But it was worth the wait.

We asked for the Special, and when it arrived the appearance and aroma were so tempting, and we were so hungry, we almost dived into it. There were eggs, bacon, black pudding, baked beans, chips or hash browns, toast and coffee.

Of course, Rosalie declined to take the black pudding and ordered fried tomatoes and mushrooms instead.

The bill was a little over $25 in our money, a bargain if ever there was one.

After we had greedily satisfied our appetites, we wandered aimlessly through the market, and when Rosalie said she had absorbed enough of the atmosphere, I took her around by Hertford Street and Down Street until we came to Brick Street. I then sauntered up to the corner where it joined Yarmouth Place and stopped.

"What? Why have you stopped?"

"This is it."

"This is what?"

"Where Robson Callister lives. We have to meet him here tomorrow morning."

"You're joking."

"No. This is the address he gave."

"But this is a scruffy place. It looks like old warehouses and building sites. Does anybody actually live here?"

"Apparently, they do."

"It's kind of sinister."

"Yes, it is a bit."

"What's that green I can see at the end of the street? Trees, I think."

"That's Green Park. It's the other side of Piccadilly."

"Ooh, let's go there. It's drab and depressing here. Creepy."

"Sure. We can be there in five minutes. It's a beautiful park. I think it's London's best, although it's all grass and trees. No lakes, flowers or animals...unless you count the squirrels. There're hundreds of them."

"Let's go."

We spent almost half an hour wandering around Green Park, moving towards its southern entrance where we came upon massive, gold-painted railings.

Rosalie gasped and pointed through the gates. "What's that big building?"

"Buckingham Palace."

"You're kidding?"

"No. Let's go closer. We may see a troop of guardsmen ride past."

The crowds were not particularly dense at that hour so we managed to walk right up to the Palace entrance and peer in. The guards, each in his little sentry box, stared stolidly back at us.

Never having been to London before, Rosalie was like a little girl, excited and curious. "Is King Charles inside?"

"No."

"How do you know?"

"The Union Jack is flying above Buckingham Palace instead of the Royal Standard. That means the King is not in residence."

"Oh. And what's across the square?"

"St. James's Park. That's where we're heading now."

We sauntered along the lake, watching the pelicans, swans, geese, and ducks splashing about, until we came to the eastern end of the park. Then we went up The Mall and through the Admiralty Arch to encounter a loud buzz of traffic and people.

"Who's that guy way up there on top of the column?"

"That's Lord Nelson."

"So this is Trafalgar Square?"

"It is. Let's go walk around it. They say if you wait long enough, you will always see someone you know in Trafalgar Square."

"I imagine you could—if you waited long enough." She flashed me a beautiful smile, and it reminded me why I loved her so much.

There were already several hundred people in the square and twice as many pigeons, but we saw nobody we knew, so we walked past the National Gallery then up the Haymarket back to Piccadilly.

By this time we were exhausted, so returned to the hotel, checked in properly and went to our room, where we noticed that Ryan had installed our luggage.

I called down to thank him and to ask if he could get us a reservation for dinner at the Ritz. He said it would be difficult at such short notice, but he would try. Five minutes later he called back to say he had been able to secure us a table, and that it was a good one near the window, but it would have to be at 6.30. I said that was fine with us, and with that we went to bed and slept.

We woke at 5.30, so we just had time for a quick wash and change and a stroll four blocks up Piccadilly to the Ritz. Sweeping through the hotel to the dining room is a feeling like no other, as everywhere you are surrounded by the opulence of a bygone era.

That is even truer of the dining room itself because, although it only dates from 1906, it has the feeling of French courts of earlier centuries. The space is large, with five huge floor-to-ceiling windows and an enormous mirror at one end which gives the impression of there being another dining room beyond. There are chandeliers everywhere and ornaments decorated with gold leaf. The carpet is vast and elegant in gold, pale blue and rose. The chairs, each with arms, have rose-red upholstery, the circular tables are covered with crisp, spotless white tablecloths, and the waiters are dressed in black tailcoats.

Needless to say, the service is impeccable, which you would expect in an establishment charging a minimum of $200 a meal for one, excluding wine.

It is hard to dine at the Ritz without being impressed by its history. It was a great favourite of King Edward VII in the years before he took the throne, and its list of notable clients includes the late Queen Elizabeth and The Queen Mother, each having her favourite table. There are almost as many famous stories about the Ritz—scandals, love affairs, fortunes won and lost, cabinets made and governments defeated—as there have been luxurious meals served on the premises.

To start, Rosalie chose dressed Dorset crab with almond and fennel, while I opted for a ballotine of duck liver with damsons and pistachio. Both were absolutely delicious.

For the main course, I was going to order the hay-aged duck with apricot and lavender, but Rosalie really wanted beef Wellington, which is a dish for two, so we had that with assorted fresh vegetables.

The wine list at the Ritz is almost a mile long, with dozens of fine, rare and exquisite older bottles, many costing thousands of dollars. We ordered a bottle of Perrier *Jouet Belle Epoque* 2011 Champagne to sip on while we examined the very large menu, and to have with our appetizer.

To drink with our main course, I had the sommelier bring us a bottle of *Chambolle-Musigny Premier Cru* 2011 from Domaine Comte de Vogue. Both wines were excellent, especially the Chambolle-Musigny, which had intensity, delicacy and great complexity. The bouquet reminded me of violets and raspberries with a hint of vanilla. It was a very rich, silky and fragrant wine, which lined the palate and gave a long-lasting finish.

After the main course, Rosalie went to the ladies' room and I was just sitting, soaking up the atmosphere and looking around to see if anyone famous was dining at the Ritz that night. Suddenly an all-too-familiar but unwelcome voice came from behind me. The last time I had heard it was two years ago, at my house in Grand Pre.

"Fancy meeting you here, little brother."

"Larry?" I whirled around in a panic. I didn't want Rosalie to see him, to even know he existed. How could she, when he was officially dead?

"Sure is."

"Get out of here. Leave me a message at Fleming's Hotel. No, on second thoughts, don't."

"Worried about wifie, are we?"

"You bet I'm worried. She can't know about you."

"Okay, okay. But I see you took my advice and married the right one.

That other one was a cow."

"You were right about that, Larry. But you must go. Tomorrow night, I'll meet you in the Rivoli Bar."

"What time?"

"Make it at 10. I can say I'm going for a walk. Now go!"

"Whatever you say, little bro."

Then he melted into the crowd of diners.

"Who was that you were talking to?" Rosalie asked when she came back.

"Some guy wanted to know if the beef Wellington was good."

"What did you tell him?"

"That ours was excellent."

"It was, wasn't it? Oh, here's the waiter with the desert menu."

For dessert, Rosalie ordered English cherries with almonds and Kirsch ice cream, while I had an old favourite, chocolate soufflé with vanilla Chantilly. With that we each had a glass of *Chateau D'Yquem* 1990.

We strolled back along Piccadilly in what, under other conditions, would have been a holiday mood. The knowledge that Larry was in London unsettled me. Seeing him so unexpectedly had almost ruined a perfect evening. I knew that wherever Larry was, trouble was not far behind, and I guessed that, as usual, he was up to no good.

17

We had been so jet-lagged and exhausted the night before that we slept like the dead, and woke the next morning at 7:00 reinvigorated, and ravenous.

We had an excellent breakfast in the hotel restaurant, Rosalie having an Arnold Bennett omelette with mushrooms, ham and *parmigiano*, and I the baked eggs *en cocotte* with smoked salmon, tomato dressing and soda bread. We were so hungry we each added side orders of hash browns and baked beans.

After breakfast we went up to our room and freshened up, and then at 9:45 we wandered down to Brick Street.

At the corner of the street with Yarmouth Place we stopped and started looking at doorways to see if they had nameplates and doorbells, but none did.

"How are we supposed to find Callister if we can't get into the building?" Rosalie asked.

"This building is Number Three," I said, pointing, "But there is no door at all."

"I think you've been conned, Darling."

"Damn!"

At that moment a dark blue sports car zoomed around the corner and stopped with a screech. I looked appreciatively at a beautiful Aston Martin Rapide purring by the sidewalk.

The driver gave three toots on the horn, so I walked over to the now open window.

"Mr. and Mrs. LeBlanc?" The driver inquired.

"Yes. Mr. Callister?"

"Yes. Hop in the back, and be a good chap. Don't take too long about it."

We did as we were instructed and soon we were tearing down Piccadilly and out past the Natural History Museum to Hammersmith. As I struggled to get my bearings, I saw we were already on the Great West Road heading for Chiswick.

Pretty soon we were out on the M4 motorway and still heading west at about 120 miles per hour. Although not in the same league as my Bugatti, this Aston could certainly move, and without undue noise beyond the throaty roar from the six-litre V-12 engine.

Just past Maidenhead we left the M4, went through the quaintly named village of Hurley Bottom, back over the Thames at Henley and off into a warren of richly-wooded, narrow lanes until we got to a place called Fawley.

Halfway along what a sign told us was Roundhouse Lane, the Aston suddenly swerved off onto a tiny track overhung by ancient trees, which formed a tunnel. After some minutes we pulled onto an even smaller track and finally stopped in the middle of what seemed like a vast deciduous wood.

Ahead was an enormous oak tree, which I imagined must have been several hundred years old, and beyond that, in a small glade, were several fallow deer grazing. Off to the right was a clearing in which stood a large, half timbered, thatched cottage, with diamond-shaped leaded windows. Alongside the building a gurgling stream, adorned by bulrushes, irises, moorhens and duckweed, meandered by.

"This is it," said Callister, the first words he had spoken since leaving London.

He jumped out and came round to open the rear door. Gingerly, we stepped out and looked around.

"Mr. Callister—" I started.

"Call me Robbie, old chap, everyone does." He was grinning from ear to ear. "Sorry about the theatrics, but I have to take security precautions. I'm on about six death lists."

"Six?"

"It might only be five now. I forget."

"So, you don't live on Brick Street in London," Rosalie said, a little bewildered by it all.

"Good heavens, no! This is where I live."

"It looks beautiful."

"Do you think you could find it again if you wanted to?"

"No, not a chance."

"Good. That's how I like it. Let's go in."

We followed Callister into the cottage, he and I having to stoop to avoid knocking our heads on the door jamb, and found ourselves in a quintessentially English upper-middle-class homestead, complete with oak beams in the ceilings, tall grandfather clocks, polished wood panelling, gleaming tables and big, comfortable chairs covered with a variety of twill, ticking and damask.

By a large, stone fireplace lay a border collie, fast asleep, and running from the back of the house came a golden Labrador.

"Hello, old chap," said Callister to the dog; then, to the deeper recesses of the building, "Dolly! You home, darling?"

"Yes, I'm here, Robbie," a woman's voice called out.

She came into the room and gave him a kiss on the cheek. Like her husband, she was in her middle or late sixties, but better preserved, her hair not yet grey, and her cheeks like two shiny red apples. She wore a tweed skirt, fastened with a large safety pin, and a peach-coloured silk blouse adorned with rows of pearls.

"These are our guests from Canada, dear. Is the attic available?"

"He knows it is," Dolly said to us. "He pretends it belongs to both of us, but he doesn't even let me in there."

"For your own safety, my dear, for your own safety."

"Yes, I know. Go on up. I'll bring some lunch in a while."

"Wonderful! What a marvellous old girl you are!"

Callister led us up a loudly-creaking staircase to a landing where, again, he and I had to stoop to avoid injury. At a thick, heavy, wooden door, he stopped, searched through a key ring and opened it.

"Watch your step," he said, "there's a drop to the floor of about six inches."

We carefully stepped down into a surprisingly-large and well-lighted room, with even more surprisingly-adequate headroom. The walls were covered with charts, maps and lists. By the window was a desk and one of the most up-to-date computer systems I had ever seen, with every conceivable attachment and accoutrement.

Callister opened his desk drawer and drew out a bottle of Lagavulin 20-year-old single malt, and some glasses.

"I'm not supposed to drink whisky these days. I pretend I don't, and Dolly pretends not to know I do. It's a perfect arrangement. Do sit down, if you can find anywhere to sit."

Rosalie and I both declined a drink, she because she did not like whisky and I because it was far too early in the day. In view of the fact that we needed Callister to drive us back into London, I was nervous about how much he would drink. However, he poured himself only small one, and put the bottle away.

When he sat down again, I took a good look at him. He was a heavy-set man, about six feet tall and with a ruddy complexion. His hair was dark, but only on top where it was receding, and at the sides he had grey, almost white, swept-back wings.

I had looked him up on Google before leaving home, and discovered that he had been a colonel in the army and had been injured at Port Stanley in the Falklands War. Not being able to continue for physical reasons, he had turned his hand to journalism, first writing about the war and later specializing in the then-budding environmental movement. It was said that no one on earth knew more that he on the subject, and that the *Times* of London, for whom he was a regular contributor, now paid him as much as five thousand pounds an article.

"Let me be clear," he said. "You represent the premier of Nova Scotia. That would be like the First Minister of Scotland or Wales, wouldn't it?"

"Yes, something like that," I said, "but more like the premier of one of the Australian states."

"Ah, yes, I see. Thank you for correcting me. And what is it you want to know?"

"We want an overview of environmental organizations with particular reference to those which could be considered extreme."

"Hmm. That's a bit of a tall order, but I shall do my best."

"Why is it a tall order?"

"Well, how many environmentally-related organizations do you suppose are operating in the world today?"

"I don't know. I guess about two hundred."

"Twenty-two thousand," said Callister.

"*What?*"

"Think about it. There are 193 countries in the world. All of them have government bodies or agencies that touch on the environment, usually several of them, at the national, state or provincial, and municipal levels. And in each country there are as many as 50 to 100 NGOs, or private organizations. And then you have a hundred or more international organizations."

"Good God. These are all environmentally related?"

"In one way or another. The animal-rights groups are included, along with the vegan groups, the climate change pushers, the Green parties, the marine protection groups, the conservationists, the biodiversity advocates, the mountain people, the rainforest people, the wetland people, the bird people... are you getting the idea?"

"Yes, I am."

"Environmentalism and Climate Change are big business, Mr. LeBlanc. Very big business. Mr. Al Gore, for example, is worth approximately $300 million. After he was defeated by Mr. Bush in his attempt to become the US President, the Former Vice President made a fortune by setting up a green investment firm which is now worth $36 billion. That company pays him $2 million a month."

"Wow! I never thought of it like that," I said. "Just how big a business is it?"

"It's impossible to estimate with any degree of accuracy, but you see that, when hundreds of thousands of individuals are dependent upon the industry for their livelihoods, we must be talking in terms of several trillion dollars."

"Surely not?" Rosalie asked.

"Oh, yes. In your own country, one of your iconic environmental leaders has accumulated over $25 million and owns four homes, including one which is, ironically, co-owned with a fossil fuels company. Just one of his houses in Western Canada has been valued at over $8 million."

"So, it's a big scam?"

"Not all of it, of course, but to a large extent the 'environmental movement' is a giant gravy train. Those who don't get an actual paycheque from the industry get trips to exotic locations, research grants, commissions, publishing concessions and the like. And none of this would be possible without the media relentlessly pushing the notion that the world is ending. The journalists, too, are kept sweet one way or another."

"But isn't it?" Rosalie asked.

"Isn't it what?"

"Isn't it true that the world is coming to an end?"

"Well yes, the world is coming to an end one day, but when that day will be nobody can say, and those who say they know do not act like they do."

"How do you mean?"

"There is no shortage of hypocrites who tell us to live a certain way when they themselves are living entirely in another way."

"Like who?"

"Well, take Mr. Obama. He has spoken most eloquently about the dangers of climate change and rising sea levels, but he lives in an $11 million mansion which is only a matter of yards from the seashore. I ask you, Mrs. LeBlanc: if he really thought that rising sea levels constituted an imminent danger don't you think he would get rid of the property?"

"I take your point," I said. "Robbie, could you give me a list of these organizations?"

"It would only be a partial list of the main ones, but it will serve as an indication, a guide."

Callister went over to a filing cabinet against the far wall and fished inside. He brought out a sheaf of papers which he handed to me.

"These are just some of the main organizations," he said. "If you really want, I can get you more, but it will take time."

I looked at the list, hardly believing my eyes. Rosalie pulled up her chair and looked over my shoulder.

Global Alliance on Health and
  Pollution
Earth System Governance Project
School strike for climate
Global Green Growth Institute
Intergovernmental Panel on Climate
  Change
International Union for Conservation
  of Nature
United Nations Environment
  Programme
European Environment Agency
Partnerships in Environmental
  Management for the Seas of East Asia
350.org
African Conservation Foundation
African Wildlife Foundation
A Rocha
Anti-nuclear movement
Arab Forum for Environment and
  Development
American Forests
Bioversity International
BirdLife International
CEE Bankwatch Network
Center for Development and Strategy
Citizens' Climate Lobby
Climate Action Network
Community Forests International
Confederation of European
  Environmental Engineering Societies
Conservation International

International Rivers
International Tree Foundation
International Union for
  Conservation of Nature
Let's Do It! World
Marine Stewardship Council
Miss Earth
Mountain Wilderness
NatureServe
Oceana
Panthera Corporation
Partners in Population and
  Development
Plant A Tree Today Foundation
Pragya
Programme for the Endorsement of
  Forest Certification
Project AWARE
Rainforest Action Network
Rainforest Alliance
Rainforest Foundation Fund
Rainforest Foundation UK
Rainforest Foundation US
Rainforest Trust
Rewilding Europe
Sandwatch
Sea Shepherd
Seeds of Survival
Society for the Environment
Surfrider Foundation
The Climate Reality Project
The Mountain Institute

Jeremy Akerman

Dancing Star Foundation
Deep Green Resistance
Earth Charter Initiative
EARTHDAY.ORG
Earthwatch
Environmental Defense Fund
Fauna and Flora International
Fondation Pacifique
Foundation for Environmental
  Education
Forest Stewardship Council
Forests and the European Union
  Resource Network
Frankfurt Zoological Society
Friends of Nature
Friends of the Earth
Global Footprint Network
Global Landscapes Forum
Global Witness
GoodPlanet Foundation
Great Transition Initiative
Green Actors of West Africa
Green Africa Youth Organization
Green Cross International
Greenpeace
Green Belt Movement
IDEAS For Us
Interamerican Association for
  Environmental Defense
International Analog Forestry
  Network
International Institute for
  Environment and Development
Center for Development and Strategy
Citizens' Climate Lobby
Climate Action Network
Community Forests International
Confederation of European
  Environmental Engineering Societies
Conservation International
Dancing Star Foundation
Deep Green Resistance
Earth Charter Initiative

The Nature Conservancy
The Earth Organization
This is My Earth
Traffic (conservation programme)
Tree Aid
Wetlands International
WILD Foundation
Wildlife Conservation Society
World Business Council for
  Sustainable Development
World Land Trust
World Resources Institute
World Union for Protection of Life
World Wide Fund for Nature
Worldwatch Institute
Xerces Society
Yellowstone to Yukon Conservation
  Initiative
Young Friends of the Earth
Zoological Society of London
African Conservation Foundation
African Wildlife Foundation
A Rocha
Anti-nuclear movement
Arab Forum for Environment and
  Development
American Forests
Bioversity International
BirdLife International
CEE Bankwatch Network
Green Cross International
Greenpeace
Green Belt Movement
IDEAS For Us
Interamerican Association for
  Environmental Defense
International Analog Forestry
  Network
International Institute for
  Environment and Development
International Rivers
International Tree Foundation
International Union for

Earthday.org
Earthwatch
Environmental Defense Fund
Fauna and Flora International
Fondation Pacifique
Foundation for Environmental
  Education
Forest Stewardship Council
Forests and the European Union
  Resource Network
Frankfurt Zoological Society
Friends of Nature
Friends of the Earth
Global Footprint Network
Global Landscapes Forum
Global Witness
GoodPlanet Foundation
Great Transition Initiative
Green Actors of West Africa
Green Africa Youth Organization

Conservation of Nature
Let's Do It! World
Marine Stewardship Council
Miss Earth
Mountain Wilderness
NatureServe
Oceana
Panthera Corporation
Partners in Population and
  Development
Plant A Tree Today Foundation
Pragya
Programme for the Endorsement of
  Forest Certification
Project AWARE
Rainforest Action Network
Rainforest Alliance
Rainforest Foundation Fund
Rainforest Foundation UK

"Good grief!" I put the list down.

"Impressive, isn't it, that so many people are being fed and nourished by the idea that the world is going to end?"

"How do you account for the phenomenon...apart from personal gain? I mean, not everybody is on the take."

"No, of course not," said Callister. "There are many sincere people who are involved who do not get a penny from it."

"What motivates them? Apart from altruism?"

"I fear it is a mixture of ignorance and arrogance. They talk about 'saving the planet', when the planet doesn't need saving. It is quite capable of taking care of itself. It always has, and there is a strong possibility it always will."

"Go on."

"Well, look at it this way. The earth is approximately 4.6 billion years old. Humanoids, however, have only been on the planet for about six million years. Even the dinosaurs were here for 27 times longer than us. That means that we have been here for only"—he snapped his fingers —"that long. Scarcely a blip on the radar screen. So what gives us the right to righteously speak for the planet, on which we have only been very, very short term visitors?"

"When you put it like that, it does make one think," Rosalie conceded.

"Robbie," called a voice from outside the door, "Open up. I have your lunch."

"Okay, Dolly. Leave it by the door. Thank you."

Callister fetched a tray from just outside the door, and placed it on a small table in the centre of the room. There was a pot of tea, cups, a plate of sandwiches, and a bowl of biscuits.

"Tuck in."

While we ate, he adumbrated the history and development of the environmental industry. He asserted that its foundation could be traced to the nineteenth century and the rise of the industrial revolution, when increasing levels of from large factories, all burning coal, led to high levels of air pollution. By the turn of the century, the inadequate sewage systems were further burdened by chemical and other waste from industry.

"I think the first environmental legislation, at least here in Britain, was in 1863, when regulations on air emissions were introduced," he said. "And that was when environmentalism became 'respectable', and therefore popular with groups and some politicians."

Callister explained that, while this was his take on the subject, others suggested that the movement arose centuries earlier, in fact, shortly after the coming into existence of the human race, since human beings would always have been concerned about clean air and water.

"Of course, most of us think of Greenpeace as a forerunner, or trend setter, in the environmental business, because they used direct action in the 1970s to confront whaling ships and those who tested nuclear weapons." Callister sipped his tea and reached for another biscuit. "And most say it is from there that most other forms of direct action came into being."

"This is where we come in, I think," I said.

"Precisely. But I do have to ask why."

"Why what?"

"Why is your premier's primary interest in the—what shall I call it?—the more radical sections of the industry."

"I'm sorry, Robbie, I'm not at liberty to say."

"It makes my job more difficult. If I don't know what you are looking for, I can't very well help you find it."

"Let me think about that for a bit. In the meantime, can you talk about the more radical groups?"

"Certainly. To start with, don't overlook the various Green parties that have been elected in parliaments around the world. Some of them are frankly Marxist, and most are substantially to the left of the socialist parties."

"Really?" Rosalie interjected. "I wasn't aware of that."

"It depends upon where you are, of course, but here in the UK, for example, the party has espoused very left-wing economic policies, including vastly increasing corporation tax, a so-called 'Robin Hood' tax on banks and a 60% tax on those earning over £150,000, a four day week and the abolition of the monarchy.

"And what about the more 'hands-on' organizations?"

"Yes, well, there are literally dozens of them, including the Just Stop Oil people—"

"Are they the ones who throw paint on pictures in art galleries and block major highways?"

"Yes, that's them. Then you have Earth First, the Earth Liberation Front, and the Animal Liberation Front, all of which are more or less described by their names. Then there is a miscellany of groups which, one could say, represent a kind of iconoclastic, uncompromising, discontented, querulous, unstable environmental activism. These indulge in activities like ecotage, monkeywrenching and tree spiking."

"Good god, what are those?" Rosalie asked.

"Ecotage is environmentally-justified sabotage, monkeywrenching is also sabotage, and tree spiking is the driving of steel spikes into tree trunks so that cutting equipment will seize up."

"I imagine that could be dangerous."

"Indeed, it often is. Then you have host of outfits such as the Earth Liberation Army, anarcho-primitivists, animal liberationists, bioregionalists, deep ecologists, eco-nationalists, ecopsychologists, green anarchists, anti globalizationists and anti-capitalist protesters, ecofeminists, neo-Pagans, Third Positionists, and Wiccans."

"Why so many?"

"They may differ on minute points of ideology, they may have different goals, or they may just have sprung up in different places. And we shouldn't forget the bombers such as Mr. John Hanna, who put incendiary devices on seven crop-dusters at the Salinas, California airport on May Day, 1977. This form of guerrilla warfare later resurfaced with the Earth Liberation Front. Their claim to fame earned them the label of eco-terrorists when they burned a ski resort in Colorado, an SUV dealership in Oregon, and the rail depots in Washington, causing $12 million in damages. The FBI called them America's greatest domestic terrorist threat."

"Not very pleasant people," Rosalie said.

"Indeed not," said Callister, "and then you have groups like Plain Stupid, which was launched to stop airport expansions, and those designed to close power stations around the world. They have a variety of names."

"Are there more?"

"Good heavens, yes. Many, many more. For example, there are also eco-fascists on the right."

"On the *right*?"

"Oh, yes, they are led by a rising deep ecologist called Pentii Linkola, who is regarded as the founder of eco-fascism. He wrote a book called *Can Life Prevail?* I don't recommend it for bedtime reading, or, indeed, for the beach."

"What else?"

"Ecofeminism, of course, social ecologists, bioregionalists, enviro anarchists, vegan archists, Deep Green Resistance (who think mainstream environmental activists are ineffective and advocate sabotage against infrastructure), enviro arsonists, et cetera, et cetera. Which brings us to Extinction Rebellion."

"I've certainly heard of them," I said.

"Yes, they've been in the news quite a lot in recent times," said Callister. "They have a stated aim of using non-violent civil disobedience to compel government action, but it hasn't quite worked out that way. You may remember they blocked all the bridges across the Thames and have shut down various other routes and functions. In 2019 their protests cost the Metropolitan Police an extra £7.5 million. They keep saying they're non-violent but their activities and supporters belie this. Their activists defend causing property damage, such as smashing windows."

"You mentioned Just Stop Oil a little while ago. Could you tell us more about them?"

"Certainly. Their goal is to end fossil fuel licensing and production. Their methods have included vandalism and obstructing traffic. The group says it is non-hierarchical, with activists operating in autonomous groups, and has no formal leadership. This makes it more difficult to keep tabs on them, which is the general idea. Its people have been arrested over 2,000 times and about 140 of them have done jail time. Some of my journalist colleagues think Just Stop Oil is a bunch of empty-headed nincompoops with nothing better to do."

"But you don't?"

"I don't."

"Why not?"

"I have no firm proof, but I believe there are some within this group who are committed to very serious acts."

"Like…"

"Like assault, bodily harm, extreme property damage. Beyond that I can't say at present."

"Are they the worst?"

"Hell, no. I would have to give that award to Envirocomm."

"Envirocomm?"

"Short for Environmental Commandos."

"Are they dangerous?"

"Extremely. In my judgment, they will stop at nothing to cause mayhem. The identity of their leader is not known, but he goes by the name Vindex."

"Vindex? It sounds like a soap powder."

"It's Latin. It means Avenger."

Callister got up, dusted crumbs off his trousers and went to the door. "I must get you back into London. We'll meet again tomorrow, but not here. I'll drop by your hotel around ten—I'll be on foot—and I'll try to introduce you to some of the people in the movement."

"Will that be dangerous?"

"It could be. Let's hope not. But if we are going to poke the nest, we must expect the wasps to attack."

18

After Robson Callister dropped us at our hotel that evening, we did not much feel like going out again, so decided to have dinner in the hotel. In earlier days when I frequented Fleming's, the dining, though good, was not particularly exciting; but now it was getting a reputation for high quality since taking on a new chef in the person of Sofian Msetfi, a young and extremely talented Moroccan. I was not familiar with his food, but I had heard that he had learned much of his trade from Chef Tom Kerridge, a man for whom I had immense respect.

The restaurant, called Ormer, is quite beautiful if you like Art Deco, and when you step in, it makes you feel as if you are back in the 1920s or 30s. You have to get to it by means of a special elevator which takes you down to the basement, where there are sparkling white tablecloths, heaps of fresh flowers, wood-panelling, and large mirrors.

Rosalie and I were in the mood for fish tonight, so we chose Msetfi's Pescatarian Market menu, consisting of various canapés, a Waldorf salad, a Jerusalem artichoke velouté, pickled trompette mushrooms, and cured Cornish mackerel. The main course was braised West Coast turbot *vin jaune* with globe asparagus. Then, a sumptuous cheese trolley followed by Tahitian vanilla ice cream.

With the introductory courses we drank a rather lovely 2007 *Nicolas Francois Billecart Salmon* Champagne, which was deliciously fresh and invigorating but with underlying power, then proceeded to a stunning 2010 *Chevalier Montrachet*. The depth and complexity of this wine was most impressive, giving whiffs of apricot, lemons and summer flowers. It was a perfect match for the turbot, which many, including me, regard as the king of fish.

We finished up the Champagne with our desserts. I found the ice cream too much for my palate so I concentrated on the cheeses.

When we got to the room, we kicked off our shoes, lay on the bed and watched television, something which convinced us that, apart from their made-for-TV movies, television in England is almost as vapid and worth-less as it is in Canada and the United States.

We had watched the BBC news that morning and remembered what our friend Rachel Bland told us about the BBC being anti -Semitic in its news coverage. Within moments, what she said was borne out by what we saw and heard.

Our own CBC in Canada, and PBS in America, suffer from a similar virus, but are not nearly as bad as the BBC. What was it, we asked ourselves, about publicly-owned networks that brought out this anti-Semitic streak? We found it to be a sad phenomenon that people who had suffered so much for centuries should still be the gratuitous targets for abuse and libels.

About nine thirty, I got up, put my shoes back on and grabbed my jacket from the chair.

"Going somewhere?" Rosalie asked as she gave a big yawn.

"Just going for a walk around Mayfair to take a look at some of the old haunts I knew when I lived here."

"Shall I come with you?"

"Nah, you rest and watch the telly."

"What are you up to?"

"Nothing."

"Yes, you are. I can tell."

"It's nothing."

"What is it?"

"Look Rosalie, if I tell you something—a secret—will you promise not to question me further?"

"I don't know. You've got me worried now. What's this all about?"

"I can tell you so much, but no more. Will you be satisfied with that?"

"How can I possibly say until I know what it is?"

"Please!"

"Alright, alright."

"I have to see somebody I knew long ago. Meeting this person could trigger a criminal inquiry. If you knew the details you could be implic-ated. That's all I can say."

"Wow! I'm supposed to accept that and go back to watching televi-sion?"

"Yes, if you trust me."

"Come on, Marc. You were going to go off without saying anything. How can I trust you now?"

"Please leave it, I beg you."

"No way. Who are you going to meet?"

"Don't ask me."

"I *am* asking you!"

"Can't say."

"*Tell me!*" she shouted. "Who are you going to see?!"

"My brother," I said quietly.

"You brother is dead."

"No, he isn't."

"Yes he is. You got the death certificate, which Walter Bryson gave to the court to settle your father's estate."

"It was a fake."

"*A fake!*"

"It's a long story. You'll have to wait until I get back to hear the rest of it. Because now you *are* implicated!"

I shut the door behind me, feeling like the world had collapsed. I loathed arguing with Rosalie. This was only the second time we had fallen out, and it made me feel utterly miserable. At that moment I absolutely *hated* Larry.

I walked up Piccadilly in a towering rage. Why could not Larry have just disappeared for good after he had shown up in Grand Pre, and after having scared the daylights out of all of us? He had said I would never see him again. Why the hell did he not keep his word?

I crossed over and walked along by the railings of Green Park, now dark and ominous, reminiscent of children's books of goblins and trolls.

By the time I reached the Ritz, I had cooled down. After all, I thought, Larry did not come to London deliberately to annoy me. Surely, it was a coincidence that we were both there at the same time.

I went through the world famous colonnade and into the hotel, then turned into the Rivoli Bar. I looked around, but could not see Larry and, relieved, was about to leave when the barman coughed theatrically and nodded towards the corner.

There, at a tiny table tucked away to the bar's right, was Larry, dressed to the nines in evening dress and happily devouring a large serving of Beluga Caviar. At the side of the table stood an ice bucket containing a half empty bottle of Krug *Grande Cuvee* Champagne.

"Sit down, little brother," he said as condescendingly as ever. "Have some bubble. I just got orders of oysters and lobster rolls before the cut-off time, so if you're peckish we'll be well supplied."

I took a glass of the Krug and wondered yet again if it was the best Champagne on earth. There were many more expensive brands, mostly vintages, but few came close to the perfection of this masterpiece.

Larry was the picture of confident hubris, and of rude good health. I knew his fancy silk dinner suit concealed a body as trained and as fit as a paratrooper's in an assault platoon.

The waiter brought the food and, with difficulty, managed to manoeuvre space for the plates. The oysters and the lobster rolls looked superb, and although I had already eaten well earlier, I could not resist trying them. Both were exquisite.

"So, Larry, what are you doing in London? Or maybe I shouldn't ask."

"I am here on business and pleasure," he replied in that arrogant tone I had come to dislike so heartily.

"I imagine you're in the same line of work."

"Yes, the family business is still ticking over quite nicely." Larry frowned. "I guess there's no further word on the guy who killed Dad?"

"No. The only suspect is back in the Russian Federation, where Canadian law can't reach him."

"I can."

"Can what?"

"I can reach the bastard."

"Oh."

"It's just that I have a lot of irons in the fire right now and I don't want to divert resources. But the day will come, believe me."

"I don't want to hear another word on what you might be planning."

"Fair enough. You won't."

"I've been hearing a lot about paintings and forgeries. Certain works being copied and planted in place of the originals. Your organization have anything to do with that, Larry?"

"Rather!" He grinned from ear to ear, then waved his hand to attract the barman, who swiftly appeared before us. "Same again, please, Jack."

"Certainly, Sir Leonard," said the barman, and disappeared.

"What the hell! What is this *Sir* business? And your name's not Leonard!"

"I'm dead. Remember? So the new me can have whatever name he wants. Besides, have you forgotten that I'm in the forgery business?"

"You mean that there's a *real* Sir Leonard somewhere?"

"Sure. He's a very nice old gentleman of eighty-four who lives in Lanarkshire in Scotland."

"Jesus! While we're on the subject of forgery, can you tell me if the Lismer in Nova Scotia is one of yours?"

"Of course it is, dear boy. And a few more in Halifax. I couldn't ignore my home and native land. Naturally, they aren't worth much, but that was more for fun than profit."

"What else does your gang do for fun?"

"Please, don't call it a *gang*. That is most insulting. We are an international organization employing over 2,000 people full-time and a great many more part-time."

"I'm sorry. What else does your *organization* do for fun, or am I not allowed to know?"

"Well, for laughs we forge stories, narratives, and explanations."

"I don't follow."

"We get a tremendous kick out of disseminating misinformation about things people want to believe."

"I'm still not with you. What do you mean?"

"We have dozens of 'experts' on the part-time payroll whom we can call upon to stir the cauldron from time to time, to get people all worked up."

"Like what?"

"Everything from the loony idea of Maritime Union to UFOs."

"You're joking?"

"That's the point. It's a huge joke—on the public, who just love to swallow all kinds of nonsense from crop circles to Jimmy Hoffa being murdered and hidden in concrete."

"He wasn't?"

"God, no. He worked for us for years before he died of old age."

"That's preposterous!"

"Is it? Or is that you *want* to believe the story we invented? I guess you believe all that crap about Sasquatch and about the Bermuda Triangle?"

"I don't know about Sasquatch, but the Bermuda Triangle is real."

"*Is* it? Sure a few aircraft and vessels have disappeared in the general area, but have you actually checked out every report which claims a disappearance?"

"Well...no."

"There you go. Just like in Nova Scotia, for example, the nonsense about an ancient Chinese civilization in Cape Breton or a strange legless, dumb man being washed up down in Digby County. We started those stories, and every so often we'll have one of our 'experts' freshen the pot with a new 'interpretation'. The public is so gullible they just lap it up."

"This is ridiculous. You're lying."

"*Am* I Little Brother? Do you know that, or just *think* you know that?"

"Do you claim responsibility for the Voynich manuscript, too?"

"Don't make it sound like a terrorist act. You know about Voynich, do you? Since you ask, we *did* do a forgery of that, but do you know what is absolutely hilarious?"

"What?"

"The original was a forgery itself, done by one of the earliest craftsmen to join the organization, back in the 1900s." Larry laughed uproariously.

"Now I know you're lying, Larry. This is all bullshit."

"*Is* it? Wait a few weeks and you'll see something we'll manufacture about finding the body of Amelia Earhart."

"The flyer who went missing in the 1930s?"

"In 1937, to be precise. Of course we shall call her an *aviatrix*."

"You're nuts. Certifiably insane!"

"Go on believing that, if it makes you feel good about yourself."

"I shall. You can count on it."

"So why are *you* here in London, little brother?"

"I'm doing some research for our premier."

"What premier?" He sounded surprised.

"Premier Proctor of Nova Scotia."

"I had no idea you moved in such exalted circles." He seemed put out.

"I haven't known him long, but he asked me to do him a favour and I agreed."

"Agreed to do what?"

"I can't talk about that."

"Oh come on. If it is to do with anything shady, I might be able to help. After all, I do know a large assortment of unsavoury characters."

"I guess there's something in what you say," I said, seeing the possible advantages of having Larry on my side. If anyone knew the shadowy underworld, it was him. "It's just that my premier may be having some trouble with what you would call 'eco freaks'."

"Oh, those loonies!"

"You know many?"

"Some, but as you know, my *forte* is not championing social causes."

"I sure do."

"But we use them from time to time if we need cover for an operation."

"How do you mean?"

"Well, supposing we want to steal, or borrow, something from a gallery in Croatia, we'll spread a few *cuna* about and next thing you know there'll be an enormous, noisy demonstration against fossil fuels around the gallery, during which there'll be complete chaos to distract the docents."

"Does that happen often?"

"All the time. Standard practice. If enough money changes hands in the right places, anyone can rent a crowd. Most of the crowd don't know they're being rented. All they need is for the so-called 'leaders' to spout the usual rhetoric and inflame emotions, and they're away to the races."

"What a dreadful cynic you are."

"No, Marc. A *realist*. Well, this has been fun, but I have to be somewhere. Maybe we'll meet again."

"We might. I had to tell Rosalie about you."

"Was that wise? You could endanger her."

"I thought of that but there was no other way."

"I understand. If you ever need my help—for anything—place a personal ad in *The Times*."

"What would it say?"

"'*Sir Leonard, please call home*.'"

As Larry drained his Champagne glass, I asked him one last question. "Larry, are any of these environmental types dangerous? You know, really dangerous."

"Some of them, yes."

"Have you ever heard of someone called Vindex?"

"For Christ's sake, stay away from him whatever you do! He's a total mental case. Former SAS warrior gone wrong in the head. From what I've heard, he'd skin his own mother alive if she didn't recycle."

As I watched Larry leave, I wondered how this supremely self-confident, not to say bumptious, creature could possibly be my brother. Then, with considerable regret, I reflected that I too had some of these characteristics, though not as pronounced as he.

He was several years older than me, so my memories of our childhood were more or less limited to mealtimes because most of the time he was away with his friends. Even then he moved with a gang of which he was the undoubted leader. He simply disappeared from our lives some twenty years ago, when I was finishing up in college.

What I did not know then was that Larry was working closely with my father, and that he left on Dad's instructions to develop 'the business' abroad, making himself known to the many contacts Dad had established over time. Having lived in London so long during my banking days, I also hardly knew my father and never dreamt he was a criminal, let alone the head of an international organization.

I related much of this to Rosalie when I got back to the hotel. For the most part, she just sat silent on the bed, her eyes wide with amazement. She had few questions, shaking her head in disbelief at various times. Finally, she said we should go to bed.

"There is one thing your brother said which we should not dismiss."

"What's that?"

"What he said about Vindex. If Larry is afraid of this man, we should be terrified."

19

The next day, Rosalie and I were up early and went for a short walk in Green Park. The rolling, grassy hillocks and the huge, leafy old trees were still in shadow, although the sun was penetrating their canopy with long shafts of light.

We went back to the hotel and went straight to the restaurant for breakfast. I ordered the classic eggs Benedict, made with English muffins, cured ham and Hollandaise sauce. Rosalie had the Loch Duart smoked salmon with scrambled eggs, and toasted sourdough. Everything was delicious and satisfying.

A few minutes after we returned to our suite, the phone rang. It was the desk, calling to tell us that a 'strange man' was wanting to see us in the lobby.

"What do you mean 'strange'?" I asked.

"I can't really go into it," the desk manager whispered.

"Well, did he give a name?"

"Just one moment, sir. I'll ask."

"Who is it, Marc?" Rosalie called from the bathroom.

"Don't know. Sounds weird."

"Excuse me, sir," the desk manager said, "He says his name is Robbie."

"Oh, okay. Send him up."

"Are you sure, sir?"

"Yes, it's quite alright."

Soon there was a rap at the door and I opened it.

At first, I thought there must be some mistake, because in front of me stood a rather disreputable, unshaven fellow dressed in dirty pants and a sweater which had seen better days. I was about to quickly slam the door, but he put his foot in the way.

"Let me in, Marc. It's me."

"Good grief. What on earth happened to you?"

"Nothing, old chap, just dressing for the occasion. You should, too." He looked around. "Very nice. It must be a comfort to be able to afford this luxury."

He came into the room as Rosalie came out of the bathroom, wearing a lovely lilac summer dress.

"I'm afraid neither of you will do," said Callister, "We will be visiting some places today where we don't want to stand out. Do you have any-thing...ordinary...with you? Preferably something with a bit of wear on it."

Rosalie and I looked at each and immediately started rummaging around to find articles of clothing which did not announce wealth or privilege. Judging by the look on Callister's face, we were not very suc-cessful, but he had no alternative but to accept us in jeans and sports shirts.

"But before you put them on," he said, "can you crumple them up and roll them around the carpet for a few minutes? Just to take the edge of af-fluence off them."

Reluctantly, we did as he instructed, feeling quite ridiculous. But when we were done, he nodded.

"Now, then. You are serious environmentalists visiting from Canada, taking advantage of your vacation to see how things are done this side of the pond."

"Okay."

"We have a lot to do and not much time in which to do it, so we will have to move as fast as we can between locations, but whenever we ar-rive we must slow down, giving the impression that we have all the time in the world. This is important, because the people I hope we will meet will be on the alert for anything which looks like on-the-run information gathering."

"We understand," said Rosalie.

"I hope you do. If we put a foot wrong we could find ourselves being roughed up in an alley."

"Surely not?"

"Please don't argue," said Callister. "I know these people. You do not. Let me do the talking. Do not speak unless you are spoken to. Is that clear?"

"Yes."

"If I sense we could be in serious trouble at any point, I shall start vig-orously rubbing the back of my neck. If that happens, just get out as fast as you can. Before we go into any pub, make a careful note of where the Underground station is. If there is trouble, head for the station and wait there, preferably mingling with crowds of travellers."

"You make this sound like a very dangerous mission behind enemy lines in World War II," said Rosalie shakily.

"We probably won't run into difficulties, but it is wise to be prepared."

He reached into his pocket and produced two pieces of thin, pink cardboard, which he handed to us. "These are your daily travel cards for the Underground. When you go into the station, put your ticket in the machine and make sure you pick it up again when you are through the barrier. You will be able to go anywhere in the London area until 4:30 am, at which time the machine will retain your ticket. Any questions?"

"If by any chance we get separated, how will we know how to find the rest of our party?"

"Good question. First, directions on signs and walls in the Underground are logical and well-organized. If you keep your wits about you, it is impossible to get lost. Second, make a note of the places we are going to visit, in the order in which we shall be visiting them. At a rough estimate we shall spend about half an hour travelling between locations and maybe an hour at each. The whole operation should take about six plus hours."

"Rosalie, you have a little notebook in your purse. I can't remember where I put mine."

"I'll look in your suitcase, I think I saw it in a pocket in the lining."

She walked into the bedroom and rummaged in my case. Callister was impatiently tapping his knee with his ticket.

"Here it is," she said, handing it to me.

"Aright. Stop Number One: The Prince, corner of Lillie Road and Empress Place. Underground Station: West Brompton. Stop Number Two. The Culpepper, Commercial Street, Spitalfields. Underground: Aldgate East. Stop Number three: The Three Stags, corner of Lambeth and Kennington Roads. Underground: Lambeth North. Last stop: The Windmill, Blenheim Gardens, Clapham. Underground: Brixton. Have you got all that?"

"Yes," I said. "I get the impression we are travelling in a sort of circle. Is there any significance to that?"

"No, but we go from west to east, then south, then west again, then north. I've planned it this way because at the end we'll have a direct run from Brixton to Green Park without having to change lines."

He stood and hitched up his trousers. They were old corduroys in a colour somewhere between yellow and brown. "Also, if we're delayed somewhere and have to hit the Underground at rush hour, we'll be on our way into Central London, which shouldn't be too bad. Going the other way at that time would be murder. Come on, let's go."

Callister hurried us out of the hotel, up Half Moon Street, and across Piccadilly to the Green Park Underground station. We did as he instructed us, and no sooner had we inserted our tickets at one end of the machine than the barrier let us in and the ticket shot up to be retrieved at the other side.

We then descended into the earth on an alarmingly-steep escalator. Every few feet on the wall on the way down was a colourful advertisement, passing too fast to really take in.

"How deep will we be going?" Rosalie asked.

"Of the eleven different Underground lines, seven are deep," Callister answered. "This is one of them, but it is not the deepest."

"Which line is?"

"The Northern Line. We may be going on that line later today. The deepest station on that line is at Hampstead, 58 metres below the surface. In Central London the deepest station is Bank, also on the Northern line. That is about 41 metres below street level."

When we got to the bottom we followed the signs saying 'Piccadilly Line Westbound'. We waited on the platform while strangely-warm air blew out of the tunnel along with a faint booming sound. Signs above the platform told us that a train for Uxbridge would be arriving in three minutes and one for Heathrow Airport in eight minutes.

"Which one shall we take?" Rosalie inquired.

"It doesn't matter," Callister said. "Either one will do for us, because we get off long before Acton, which is where the lines branch off."

Soon a train came rumbling into sight and stopped. A voice from the loudspeakers intoned, "Mind the gap. Mind the gap," to warn us that there was an appreciable space between the platform and the train.

Rosalie and I took seats, but Callister remained standing. Along the wall, above the windows, was a diagram of the line with each of its stations marked, and the address system announced each station as it approached. Callister said we would be changing lines at Earl's Court and I counted off four stations before that one: Hyde Park Corner, Knightsbridge, South Kensington, and Gloucester Road.

As we rumbled along, Callister gave us a potted history of the Underground. He told us that it began as the Metropolitan Railway in 1863, which was the world's first underground passenger railway. Electric underground trains were introduced in 1890.

"The system covers over 400 kilometres," he said, "carrying five million passengers a day, and there are over 200 stations."

"Is London's underground the biggest in the world?" Rosalie asked.

"It depends what measure you use. Shanghai has the longest route length, and the highest annual ridership. New York City has the most stations. The London Underground is the oldest metro system, and is roughly the same size as New York."

"Does it serve all areas of the city?"

"It serves some areas which are right out in the country," said Callister, "but, on the other hand, London south of the Thames is not nearly as well served as north of the river. There are 239 stations north of the river, but only 33 south of the Thames."

"Why is that?"

"The main reason is that, before the Underground lines were built, south London already had lots of regular, above-ground railway lines in operation, so when the first private Tube companies began around 1863, they targeted north London, where there were more potential customers."

"Were the tunnels always as deep as they are now?"

"No, the first tunnels were just below the ground. They dug big trenches then put roofs over them. Then, at much deeper levels, they used roughly circular tunnels—which gave is the nickname, the Tube"

"One last question, then I'll shut up," Rosalie said with a laugh. "How fast do the trains go?"

"I think the average speed is somewhere around 30 kilometres an hour, but outside the tunnels some trains go about 60 kph. When they get out into the suburbs, where there is more distance between stations, the Northern and the Metropolitan lines can get up to 100 kph."

When we got to our stop, we disembarked and followed signs to the District Line, which meant going up an escalator. We went to District Line South and very quickly climbed onto a train going to Wimbledon.

However, only one stop later, at West Brompton, Callister said, "This is us."

We came up into the daylight and to what seemed a comfortable, middle-class neighbourhood. Less than a block away was a huge, blue-painted pub, The Prince.

Before we entered, Callister said, "Here I'm Bob or Robert. Please don't forget. But as I said before, let me do all the talking as far as possible. You'll hear a lot you don't understand, but if you see me nodding, nod, too, to show you agree."

"These people, whoever they are, what do they think you are?" I asked.

"They think I am a freelance reporter who gets pro-environmental material into several national newspapers. I say I get paid but I don't get a byline."

"If we absolutely have to say something, what should we say?"

"As little as possible. But variations on, 'We have to kill pollution, or it will kill us.' 'Go green; breathe clean', 'We must wipe out pollution before it wipes us out', and 'Keep the oceans blue, the planet green and the animals safe' are part of the mantra."

"Okay, we'll try to remember."

Inside, The Prince was spacious and apparently quite chic, not at all the dark dive I had expected Callister's contacts to frequent. There were a number of rooms for drinking and eating, including a massive beer garden, and it was into this that we were led.

At a table in the far corner were two women and a man, all in their mid-thirties and, at first glance, middle-class professional types. We fought our way through the throng and sat down.

"These are comrades from Canada," said Callister, "Rose and Marc. They're in the movement there, and are here to learn how we do things on this side. This is Caroline, Valerie and Cyril."

The women gave us forced smiles, while Cyril offered a haughty stare bordering on hostile.

"How do you know Bob?" he asked me.

"Friends of friends," said Callister. "Like I say, they're here to listen and learn. Where they come from they're still at the level of writing letters to their MPs."

"Christ!" Valerie exploded. "Fucking children!"

"Writing fucking MPs." Caroline's face contorted with derision and contempt.

"We all have to start somewhere," said Callister with a disarming smile. "Tell me, what's going on?"

There was not much of the following conversation, or the three subsequent discussions, that either Rosalie or I fully comprehended, or even found interesting, so after a while our eyes glazed over and we sat there like vegetables while their words washed over us.

Cyril explained something about what he called a "demo" which they had recently held at some official's home, and how they had forced him and his family to evacuate their house and flee into the night. This narrative was punctuated by one or other of the women interjecting with, "Fucking right!" or, "Good enough for the fucking plonker!" and, "We put the bugger's fucking windows in too!"

The rest of the conversation seemed like a miasma of irritable discontent, liberally sprinkled with terms like biodegradable, biodiversity, carbon footprint, carbon balanced print, abiotic components, carbon balance, autotrophs, bioaccumulation, carbon sinks, closed-loop circular economy ecotone, composting, ex situ conservation, volatile organic compounds, and thermochemical technologies.

Our ears finally tuned in when we heard Callister's voice become more serious and drop to almost a whisper. He leaned forward across the table. "Anything big coming up?"

"Where?"

"Here. Anywhere?"

"Maybe." Cyril looked suspiciously at us. "I've heard something, but no details."

"Is Vindex involved?"

"So they say." Cyril was starting to look nervous. "You'll have to talk to Marga."

"Okay. I'm seeing her later." Callister polished off his beer and stood up. "Thanks, guys. It's happening!"

"It's real!" Cyril replied.

~

Once outside, we headed back to the West Brompton Underground. The sign above the platform told us that a train for Edgware Road was expected in two minutes and one for Upminster in four minutes.

"Which one is ours?" Rosalie asked.

"Upminster," Callister replied. "The other one would take us to northwest London. We want to go to the east end. We'll get off at Aldgate East."

"Will that officially put us in Cockney territory?"

"It's less than two miles from there to Bow. If you were born within the sound of Bow bells you would be a cockney."

"Bow bells! How romantic."

"The great bell at Bow was smashed by the Nazis in an air raid of 1941. In 1961 as part of the repair programme after the war, twelve new bells were hung."

"St. Mary le Bow. That's one of Wren's churches isn't it?" I asked, showing off a little.

"Yes, one of over 50 he designed in London." Callister said. "The original St. Mary le Bow was destroyed in the Great Fire of 1666. Wren was commissioned to rebuild the church, and it was finished in 1680. He considered it the most important after St. Paul's"

We clambered onto the train and I counted twelve stops before we arrived at our destination. Among them were some of London's most iconic place names, including South Kensington, Sloane Square, Victoria, St, James Park, Westminster, Embankment, Temple, Monument and Tower Hill. It took almost 45 minutes to make the journey, during which Callister regaled us with tales of mysterious happenings which were alleged to have occurred on the Underground.

"The first curious story concerns the station we just left, West Brompton, where a man dressed in old, dark working clothes is seen early in the morning and late at night. He walks to the end of the platform, then completely disappears."

"Who was he? A ghost?"

"Nobody knows. On some of the lines, Bakerloo in particular, Northbound passengers can sometimes see the reflection in the window of someone sitting next to them, even though the seat is empty."

"That's very creepy!' Rosalie said.

"At Aldgate, where we're going, there is the story of the 'Elderly Angel'."

"What's that all about?"

"Years ago, an electrician fell onto a live rail, knocking himself unconscious and taking something like 600 volts. Amazingly, apart from a few bruises, he was unhurt. The interesting thing is that the men he was working with say that, just before the fall, they saw the luminous figure of an old lady kneeling next to the stricken worker, stroking his hair."

"That's hard to believe."

"I'm not saying it's true," said Callister with a grin, "I'm merely passing it along. But Aldgate station has so many ghostly stories about it, they have an official 'ghost log book'."

"You're joking."

"No. The station was built on the site of a pit in where, Daniel Defoe says, in his *A Journal of the Plague Year*, 1,000 bodies were buried in only two weeks during the plague of 1665."

"Uggh!"

"Now at Bank station, which we shall be coming very near to soon, there have been many sightings of a spectral figure ever since the 1890s. A spirit which is dressed in black, known as 'the Black Nun', goes up to people and whispers, 'Have you seen my brother?', then disappears. Whenever this occurs there are unexplained foul stenches in the tunnels."

"Does anyone know who she was supposed to be?"

"They say she could be Sarah Whitehead, who was overcome with grief when her brother Phillip was executed in 1811 for forgery."

"Were there many of these plague pits following 1665?"

"Oh yes. At one point the Piccadilly line goes around a pit so thick with human remains that it couldn't be tunnelled through. The same thing happened in 1960, when the Victoria Line was being built and a tunnel boring machine bored straight into a forgotten plague pit at Green Park, which is where we started our journey today."

"That can't have been pleasant for the construction workers on site," I said.

"Indeed not. Another interesting legend concerns a girl with coal-black pits for eye sockets. Apparently she was first seen in the 1980s and is now on the loose again. A man and his wife were waiting for a train when they heard the eerie sound of a little girl giggling in the tunnel. Then she appeared on the track in front of them, and quickly disappeared."

"Any more weird stories?" Rosalie asked.

"Just two, then we should be close to our stop. One is about The Page's Walk under the Thames, where people say they have heard and seen doors in the tunnel opening and shutting by themselves, and that they feel watched by unseen eyes."

"Are there any *pleasant* stories?" she asked.

"Not many," Callister replied, laughing. "We're coming up to Tower Hill, so the next stop after that is ours. Here's a quick story. Underneath Buckingham Palace there is a branch line to a station just for the Royal Family, in the event of war or civil uprising. It is said the King, his family and retinue can escape to their Royal Tube Train and leave London."

At Aldgate East station we got out, emerging into daylight on Whitechapel High Street. We crossed the road and walked four blocks up Commercial Street to The Culpepper, an interesting, wedge-shaped pub adorned with shiny ceramic tiles on the walls and stacks of barrels on the sidewalk. We were now in the East End, and the difference in atmosphere between here and Brompton was palpable.

"You're now in the heart of Jack the Ripper country," Callister said.

"Yes, I guessed," said Rosalie with a laugh. "I saw a sign back there for a fish and chip shop called Jack the Chipper!"

The pub was open, airy and well-lit, with an abundance of tables as well as chairs at the bar and around the perimeter.

Callister looked around and, seeing two men at the end of the bar, led us to them. "Hello Ralph, Maurice."

"Hello, Bob, what brings you to the mysterious east?"

"Showing friends from Canada around. This is Rose and Marc."

"It's happening," said Maurice to us.

"It's real!" Rosalie and I answered in unison.

"Draw up a pew," Ralph said. "What are you drinking?"

"White wine please," Rosalie said, "Do they have organic?"

"I think so," Ralph said, looking at her strangely. "How about you, Marc?"

"Half of bitter, please."

The barman noted the orders and moved away to get the drinks.

The others started to talk and, as in the previous encounter, Rosalie and I were left out of the discussion. Again, we heard the mantra of solar and wind repeated often, along with terms we had barely heard of let alone understood. Auto ecology, climax carnivores, biogeochemical cycles, co-extinctions, biome, biospheres, biotic component, brood parasitism, and many other abstruse designations and appellations thickened the air.

Then they spoke in glowing terms about people who apparently were their heroes. Mariano Abarca, a Mexican activist who was assassinated in 2009, was mentioned, along with Edward Abbey, David Bellamy, and a man whose name sounded like Ngo Cho Nam.

Eventually, the conversations changed gears.

"Have you seen anything of Marga?" Callister asked.

"Not in over a week. Why?"

"I thought Rose and Marc should meet her. She seems to know everything that's going on."

"I suppose she does," said Ralph.

"What kind of stuff did you have in mind?" Maurice asked.

"Heavy stuff. My Canadian friends want to learn how to carry off big stuff. Have you heard if anything's happening?"

"Maybe."

"Around here?"

"Nah. Not for a while, anyway. Something big abroad. Don't know where."

"Know what?"

"No, but serious."

"Who's involved?"

"Can't you guess?" Maurice looked back over his shoulder to see if anyone was listening.

"I sometimes think he's out to lunch," Ralph whispered. "He's got lots of guts and is committed to the cause, but I wonder if he's all there...you know, in the head."

"We need people like him," Maurice said.

"We have to go," said Callister, standing up. "I'll give your regards to Marga, if we run into her."

20

We left The Culpepper, and when we were half way back to the Underground station, Callister grabbed my arm.

"Look Marc, I think it's high time you told me what this is all about. Why are you really here? I need to know in order to be able to conduct myself strategically in the presence of these activists. You see that, don't you?"

"That sounds fair, Marc," Rosalie said. "If Robbie doesn't know everything, he might say the wrong thing and put his foot in it."

"Okay," I said. "Let's go and sit down."

We walked into a small roadside park called Mallon Gardens. Facing an old building, where blue plaques announced that it had been the residence of poet Edwin Arnold and social reformer Jimmy Mallon, were several wooden benches.

When we were seated, I told Robbie the whole story as I had received it from the premier and Tom Aldridge.

"I see," Callister said thoughtfully. "Nothing definite. Just threats. Why did you come to Britain?"

"The language in the threats contained British colloquialisms, not commonly employed in Canada."

"So, you're here to pick up any indication of the identity of the person making the threats, and, if they are serious, when such an attempt might be made upon the premier's life."

"Exactly."

"Alright, now we know where we stand, let us proceed. On to Lambeth!"

At Aldgate East, we took the District Line West back to Embankment and changed there to the Bakerloo Line South, which has its terminus at Elephant and Castle. However we were only two stops away from our destination of Lambeth North.

"Isn't this the line where you said people can see a reflection of a stranger in the seat next to them?" Rosalie asked excitedly.

"Yes," said Callister, "but that only happens to north-bound passengers. We are south-bound."

"Boo. That's not fair!" she exclaimed. "Will we come back this way?"

"Sorry, no, but there is something which occurs on this very line which is supposed to terrify the train drivers. As the train approaches Elephant and Castle, the drivers report seeing a young woman getting on the train. They don't see her after that but they hear running footsteps, tapping noises and the slamming of doors."

"Shall we see her?"

"Alas, we have to disembark before Elephant and Castle this time, but we shall be doing that stretch briefly on our way back."

"Oh, good!"

After we alighted at Lambeth North, we found ourselves in Kennington Road, looking at a very pleasant, open-air district with a large park containing the Imperial War Museum. Occupying the corner of Kennington with Lambeth Road was a three story, early nineteenth century building. The upper stories were of brick but the ground floor was painted an attractive dark green.

This was The Three Stags, which, although looking old-fashioned on the outside, was more like a modern restaurant inside.

On one side of the entrance was a table occupied by five people. Two were rather scruffy women, and none of the company looked particularly appealing, as several of them appeared to be the worse for drink.

"It's happening!' Callister called as we walked over.

"It's real!' three of them replied, but the other two seemed hostile and suspicious from the outset.

"If it isn't good old Bob, the snob," slurred a short man with a Scottish accent. "What the fuck have we done to deserve this honour?"

"Hello, Gordon," Callister said cheerily. "Glad to see you, as always. Hello, boys and girls."

"Hi, Bob," a few said, without much feeling.

"I'm doing the rounds with some comrades from Canada. I was hoping to see Marga here."

"We haven't seen that fucking bitch today," said a large, bearded man, breathing spittle.

"Hello, Swithin," said Callister. "Nice to see you in good cheer."

"Fuck you," said Swithin, swaying as he started to stand up.

"We'll not disturb you any further," said Callister, furiously rubbing the back of his neck. "Good bye to all."

"Fuck off! Fucking spies!" Gordon shouted, coming round the table.

I hastily pushed Rosalie towards the door, and as I started to follow, Swithin also left the table. I ran and could hear Callister breathing heavily behind me.

We raced up some way up Kennington Road, when Callister suddenly dove into the traffic and across the road and down the small Cosser Street. We followed and he pulled us under an arch of the building, which turned out to be a hotel. From there we peered around the corner at The Three Stags.

We saw Gordon and Swithin stagger out of the pub and stand, staring around. Not seeing us, they kicked at some outside tables, then went back inside.

"Not a wholly successful interlude," said Callister. "Sorry about that."

"What now?" I asked.

"Onward and upward. Next stop, Brixton."

We retraced our steps to Lambeth North station, where we took the Bakerloo line south to Elephant and Castle. Unfortunately for Rosalie, we did not see the apparition of the mysterious young woman, nor did we hear the footsteps or the tapping.

"Not everybody witnesses the apparition," Callister said consolingly.

We took the Northern line two stations to Stockwell, then changed again to the Victoria Line south to Brixton.

Even though I had lived in London for many years, I had never been to Brixton and, cognizant of the troubles associated with the area, expected it to be seedy, seething with violence and full of black people. Therefore, I was surprised to see that it looked like a fairly nice and normal place. I was not surprised when I looked up the demography on my phone, and discovered that Brixton was only 6% black.

If one believed the media, there had been furious riots in Brixton in 1981, in the predominantly Caribbean community. The police launched an operation aimed at reducing crime and large numbers of plain clothes police officers were dispatched into Brixton.

Naturally, this caused local indignation, as most of those stopped by the police were young black men. The riot resulted in almost 279 injuries to police and 56 police cars were burned, resulting in 82 arrests.

Again in 1995, there were more riots, and later, in 1999, Brixton was the site of the first of three attacks known as the London Nail Bombings, in which 48 people were injured.

As I looked around, none of this sordid history was evident, and I was reminded of my recent visit to North Preston, where media sensationalism had also prejudiced my view of a community.

We had a long walk from the station to Blenheim Gardens, where we saw some of the many inhuman housing estates, some of them towering blocks of concrete. In close proximity to the estates was the pub we were to visit next.

The Windmill was a low, modern, unimpressive, concrete affair with bright, garish murals and paintings across the front.

"Be very careful what you say here," Callister warned us. "If Marga is here, you need to know she is very well connected in the movement and is one of the leading advocates of 'non-peaceful' methods."

"Is she connected with Vindex?" I asked.

"Keep your voice down, Marc! I'm not exactly sure of their relationship, but they're close. If we are going to discover anything which might help you, this is the place we'll find it."

"Good."

The pub was heaving with patrons, crammed into a number of not-very-well-lit rooms. My immediate impression was that this was very much a working-class establishment, but I wondered what these people did for a living, if indeed they did anything, because it was now mid-afternoon on a weekday.

"Ah, there's Marga!" Callister almost had to shout as he heaved his way through the standing people, all with pint glasses in their hands.

When we reached Marga's table, she got up and hugged Callister affectionately.

Having been told that Marga was an environmentalist of the violent kind and a confidante of the dreaded Vindex, I expected to see an immensely tall, well-built woman with a ferocious expression and piercing eyes. I also expected her to be dressed in a kind of all-black cat suit.

Contrary to my conjectures, she was little more than five feet and painfully thin, with a pale, drawn face. She wore a flowered dress and a faded pink cardigan. Callister introduced us.

"Greetings dear comrades," she said, her soft, soothing voice matching her appearance. "Any friend of Robert's is a friend of mine."

Callister left us to fight his way to the bar to get drinks. Strangely, Marga put a hand on each of our arms.

"You're a long way from home."

"Yes, we are," said Rosalie.

"But wherever we are, the eternal battle continues to save this precious earth."

"Yes, indeed," I said.

"You're a believer," she said, staring into my eyes.

"Yes, I am."

"So am I," Rosalie said.

"And you are brave."

"We try to be. But we are still learning."

"We want to be of service to humanity."

"And the animals," Marga said as if correcting a child.

"Yes, and the animals."

I was praying for Callister to come back soon. Rosalie and I were wildly ad-libbing, desperately hoping we would not say the wrong thing. I cannot describe the degree of relief I felt when he put the drinks down on the table and began to talk to Marga.

As before, most of their discourse went over our heads. The initial part of their conversation was about people we didn't know and could only speculate on who they were. The names of a Wendy Bowman and Stewart Brand were bandied about by Marga, and Callister spoke of one Ansel Adams. Then they went off into the veritable litany of terms like commensalism cryosphere, thermodynamic modules, ecotypes, sensitivity analysis, particulate matter, polar vortex, ecocline, mesoscale, ecological niches, ecophene, mitigation potential, ecological efficiency, urban interface, and thermochemical technologies.

"Where are you from?" Marga asked us after she had taken a swig of her pint.

"Canada."

"Yes, yes, yes, but where in Canada?"

"Nova Scotia."

"No!" Her eyes lit up. She stared at us as if bells were ringing in her head.

"Yes, really."

"Robert, this is extraordinary."

"Why, Marga?"

"I can't spell it out."

"You mean...?"

"Yes. Is Marc *really* someone we can trust?"

"Yes, certainly. Why?"

"We may need help soon. In Nova Scotia."

"I'm available," I said quickly, not knowing for what I might be volunteering.

"This is a great blessing," she said. "Give me your contact details. Someone may be in touch with you when you go home."

"Okay."

I scribbled down my phone numbers on the back of a beer mat and handed it to her. She carefully tucked it into her bra.

"When do you go?"

"Any day now."

"Oh, good."

"Marga," Callister said, "is anyone we know going to Nova Scotia by any chance? A certain, special someone?"

"Oh no, my dear," she replied. "He's already gone."

I had never really believed the expression about one's blood running cold, but at that moment mine certainly did. I glanced at Rosalie and saw she was as stricken as I was with what we had just heard.

"Do you understand, my dear?" Marga asked me.

"Yes." My mouth was dry.

"And you really want to help us?"

"I do," I barely whispered.

"Let's have a drink on it," she said, as she rose and headed to the bar.

"Stay cool," Callister said in a low voice. "Whatever happens, we must not rush out of here. Give it at least another twenty minutes before we make the move. Then, I'll look at my watch and say we have to be some-where."

They were some of the longest twenty minutes of my life, not least be-cause Marga was getting quite intoxicated and insisted on stroking my arm and breathing in my face. I was extremely grateful when Callister looked at his watch, stood up and made our excuses.

Before we left, Marga kissed me on the lips, and said, "Go. You are the chosen one."

"You'd better get home as fast as you can," said Callister as we walked back to the Underground station. "You have what you were looking for."

"Yes, we'll leave tomorrow."

"That was Vindex she was talking about, wasn't it?" Rosalie asked.

"No question about it, I should say," Callister answered.

We were very quiet during the four stops from Brixton to Green Park on the Victoria line. When we arrived, we thanked Callister for all his help.

"You will receive my account by email, old chap. It's been a pleasure doing business with you."

"Are you going all the way back to Fawley this evening?" Rosalie asked.

"Oh no. I'm staying with a friend and will get the train back in the morning. So I'll say goodbye, then. Good luck."

He disappeared into the crowds, heading north up Piccadilly.

"What a strange man," said Rosalie, "Where do you suppose he's going?"

"I wondered about that. Do you think he might have a girlfriend in town?"

"Or a boyfriend."

"Either way, I wonder if Dolly knows."

"A man who can live the kind of double life he does must be capable of great deception."

"In any event, we were right to choose him. He got us our man."

"We don't have him yet."

We walked back to our hotel, feeling excited and worried. Immediately I contacted Air Canada and changed our return flights. This time we would not be going via Toronto and would have a direct flight to Halifax, but there was no Business Class so we had to get Premium Economy. The flight left at 9 am so we would have to be up and about early.

Then I called Tom Aldridge.

"Marc. What news?"

"We're coming back tomorrow. I should get to the office sometime in the afternoon."

"Anything to report?"

"Yes, by God. We know who it is. I'll tell you about him when I see you."

"Well done."

"Tom, you're going to have to involve the police now."

"Why?"

"We think the guy is already there."

"Where?"

"There. Halifax."

"Christ!"

"Yes. Why don't you contact the RCMP? Maybe we can get Superintendent Kennedy on the case."

"Okay. I'll probably have to get HRMP involved too."

"Wendell won't like that."

"He'll be as mad as a hornet."

"Can't be helped. The gloves are off. See you tomorrow."

In view of the time constraints, Rosalie and I decided to dine at the hotel again. So after we had washed off the grime of travelling all day and changed into some clean clothes, we went down.

We ordered a bottle of 1998 Nyetimber *Blanc De Blancs* to sip while we studied the menu. This was a Champagne-style wine from Sussex in

England, about which I heard great things. Unknown to most, England has been making world class sparkling wine for some decades and it is getting better and better as well as expanding its production by planting new vineyards.

It did not let us down and, while nothing is quite like Champagne except more Champagne, we were quite impressed with it. We also drank the Nyetimber with our starters of Scottish Langoustine and Iberico ham jelly.

For our main courses we ordered the roast guinea fowl—an old favourite of mine—which we matched with a bottle of 2011 *Volnay Domaine Michel LaFarge.*

This was not a wise move. Although the wine had some of the fine characteristics I expect from a Volnay, such as aromas of violets and cherries and a certain sappiness, this was not up to standard. It was thin and a little pale, and I thought it was seriously overpriced. It was only after the bottle had been opened and poured that I remember that 2011 was not a good year in the Côte de Beaune.

However, the food was fine and we particularly enjoyed the sumptuous guinea fowl, but our minds were on other things, which still swirled around in our heads when we were trying to get some rest.

We booked a wakeup call for 5:30 am and a taxi for 6:30. There would be little sleep that night.

21

We got back to Halifax around 12:30, having been delayed by strong head winds over the North Atlantic which made for an unpleasant, bumpy ride. We took a taxi back to the premier's home, where I extricated the Bugatti from his rear garage.

I left Rosalie at the house, arranging to pick her up in a few hours' time in order to head home to Grand Pre. It had been a long time since we were there and we needed to check on a number of matters, not least among them any developments in the Father Mike affair.

When I pulled into Province House to park in my usual spot, the place was crawling with police and I was stopped at the gate. I had to wait for the officer to summon the commissionaire to confirm that I was legitimate.

As usual, I walked through the building to get to the premier's office on the opposite street, and at once noticed that there was a high police presence, and that the security system had been completely restructured so that now every individual seeking access had to produce ID and go through the metal detectors. There were even two policemen covering the west door, which could only be accessed by Members of the Legislature.

Across the street the security was, if anything, even tighter, and I had to go through two more checks before I got as far as Susan's desk. Whether to try my patience or test my sense of humour, she demanded to see my ID, but I played along and produced it.

She examined it dubiously, then reluctantly, said I could go in. "They're waiting for you," she added.

I wondered who 'they' were. When I opened Tom's door, his office was empty. I went in and spent a few minutes gazing out of the window before the inner door burst open and Tom appeared.

"What the hell are you doing, Marc? Get your ass in here, for God's sake."

"I didn't think it polite just to barge in on the premier."

"This is a fucking emergency. Don't fart about!"

I entered, closing the thick padded door behind me, and saw that every chair but one was occupied. Wendell was behind his desk, Tom was sitting next to him, then Superintendent Kennedy and four others, two of them women.

"Come in, Marc," The Premier said. "You know Superintendent Kennedy, I think?"

I nodded.

"This is Chief Simmons of the Halifax Police."

A big man with iron grey hair inclined his head.

"Then we have Deputy Chief Agnes MacKillop."

She smiled at me.

"And these people are from the Security Division of the RCMP. I can't tell you their names because I wasn't even told them myself."

The people to whom he had referred stared at me with slightly disgusted looks. I had met them before and I did not like them one iota. The first, a stout, sixtyish man wearing a herring bone suit was flanked by a stern, middle-aged woman who looked like a librarian.

"We know Mr. LeBlanc," Herringbone said dryly.

"How was your trip?" asked the premier.

"Interesting, thank you Wendell," I said.

Under any other circumstances, I would not have referred to the premier by his Christian name in public, but I wanted to let the security division people know I was connected and was not to be kicked around by them. I had had quite enough of that kind of treatment from them on the Ray Bland case, and did not intend to take any more.

"Tell us your story, Marc," the premier said. "From the beginning."

So, I explained how I had decided that the threats came from Britain, how Tom and I decided on Robson Callister as the right contact in the UK, how Rosalie and I had spent two complete days with him, and how we had a 'pub crawl' around the London, culminating with our meeting with Marga.

"Tell us about this Marga," Herringbone said.

"She is a non-descript, middle aged woman about forty. She seems to be held in awe by the other activists in the city, and Callister is convinced she is our best hope of getting close to Vindex."

"Vindex?" Agnes MacKillop asked.

"The pseudonym of, apparently, the most violent, and most unbalanced, of the environmental activists in Britain."

"What's his real name?" Kennedy asked.

"I don't know. Neither did Callister, but apparently he is a former SAS member who went wobbly in the head."

"SAS?"

"Strategic Air Services. The British top line emergency combat troops."

"I don't like the sound of that," Herringbone said.

"Do we have a photograph of this Vindex?" the Librarian asked icily.

"I don't," I said. "Tom, you could email Callister to see if he could provide something. I have the impression that if he had something worthwhile he would have given it to me."

"Tom, will you get on to that?" The premier ordered, whereupon Tom quickly left the room.

"Now then," said Herringbone, leaning forward, "describe, in detail, your meeting with this Marga. Leave nothing out. Give us the dialogue exactly as it occurred."

I did as he asked. He stopped me twice, once to repeat the conversation about Vindex having left, and again her final words to me.

"Let me be clear. Callister asked if a certain someone—meaning Vindex—was going to Nova Scotia and she said 'Oh no my dear, he's already gone'?"

"Yes."

"And she asked for your contact details?"

"Yes."

"And you gave them. The genuine ones. Not ones you made up."

"Yes. No."

"Yes? No?"

"Yes, I did give her genuine contact numbers. No, I did not make them up."

"After which she said: 'Go, you are the chosen one.'"

"Yes."

"What did she mean by that?"

"Presumably, that she thought Vindex would contact me and that I was chosen to help him if he needed assistance."

"And what do you propose to do now?"

"That's for you guys to tell me."

"Exactly," said Herringbone.

"But I thought I should play along with him in the hope he might reveal his whereabouts."

"We'll have to think about that," said the Librarian curtly.

"Indeed we will," said Herringbone. "We have to consider whether Mr. LeBlanc might inadvertently tip off Vindex if they spoke. And we have to consider whether Mr. LeBlanc might have to be sacrificed in order to achieve our object."

"Now wait a minute!" The premier jumped up.

"Don't worry, premier, just a little gallows humour." Herringbone smiled thinly.

"I should hope so."

Tom came back into the room and handed a sheet of paper to the premier.

"This is no good. It could be anyone. Any white male under fifty, that is."

"May I see that please, premier?"

The paper was passed to Herringbone, who examined it, then showed it to the Librarian. "Useless for identification purposes. We'll be on to Air Canada to get a list of all passengers who came here in the last two weeks to see if there is anyone there who might fit the bill."

"He might not have come direct," I said. "He could have got flight via Toronto, Ottawa, Montreal or even Boston."

"We none of us thought of that!" Herringbone said in mock amazement.

The Librarian, the Chief, and the Deputy Chief all had a good chuckle. I was grateful to the premier and Patrick Kennedy that they did not laugh, but I still felt like a prize chump.

"Well, Premier," Herringbone said stuffily, "there's not much more we can do now. Superintendent Kennedy will let you know of any developments you need to know. He will be the contact point for all three law enforcement agencies represented."

He and the Librarian rose simultaneously and marched out of the office without further word.

"Pompous ass!" The premier said.

The Chief and Deputy Chief looked distinctly uncomfortable, made their excuses, and hastily left.

"Who the hell does that guy think he is? 'Let us know any developments we need to know.' What the hell is his name anyway?" The premier said angrily when they had gone.

"I can't tell you, Premier," Patrick Kennedy said quietly.

"Can't or won't?"

"Both, Premier."

"Damn him! Well, what do we do now, Superintendent?"

"I'm afraid all we can do is wait. We don't know his real name, so we can't check against arrivals; we don't know what he looks like, so we can't put out an all-points bulletin for him; we don't know where he is staying or if he has friends here, so the local police can't arrest him."

"Meantime, he's got me in his sights."

"It occurs to me," said Patrick, "that if you announced a reversal of your policy, Vindex might back off."

"I'd look like a complete fool if I did that."

"Couldn't you just *pretend* to reverse your position? It would buy us more time."

"Wendell, don't even consider it," Tom interposed. "Imagine trying to explain that you did a massive policy flip-flop because you were scared."

"You're right, Tom. Sorry, Superintendent, it's out of the question."

"Just an idea," Patrick said. "Marc, where will you be for the next little while?"

"Rosalie and I have to go home to Grand Pre for a few days. Then I'll come back here. Rosalie has to go back to work at the university."

"If you hear from Vindex, let me know immediately," Patrick said.

"What if I do hear from him and he asks for my help, what do I say? I can't very well say I need time to think about it. That would give the game away."

"Agree to whatever he asks. We'll figure out what to do as soon as we know what we're dealing with."

"Okay. I won't have to report to Herringbone, will I?"

They all laughed, instantly knowing to whom I referred.

"No, leave him to me."

Patrick got up, shook the premier's hand, then said to me, "Marc, why don't you walk with me to my car?"

I said my goodbyes to Wendell and Tom, and followed Patrick. We left via the Barrington Street entrance and stood there watching traffic go by.

"I don't suppose there've been any developments on my father's murder?"

"It's been over two years. I won't say the case is closed, but until we get an extradition treaty with Russia there isn't a hope of anything happening. And, to be honest with you, even then I wouldn't give much for our chances of finding the perpetrator."

"That's pretty much what I was thinking too," I said. "Apart from that, how is it going at 'H' Division?"

"Not bad, although some days I'd rather be driving that than doing desk work."

He pointed to a passing Harbour Hopper, its guide reeling off a rehearsed commentary about the city's history over a loudspeaker system. These big vehicles had become a commonplace sight in Halifax over the past twenty years or so. They were originally LARC-V (Lighter, Amphibious Resupply, Cargo, 5 ton) military vehicles with aluminum hulls, developed in the United States during the 1950s for use in a variety of roles. The LARC-Vs were used in Argentina's 1982 invasion of the Falkland Islands, and of the thousand manufactured, half were scuttled during the U.S. withdrawal from Vietnam. I read in the newspaper that each one weighs almost 10 tons, and has a top land speed of almost 50km/hr and a water speed of about 8.68 knots.

Carrying forty or so passengers, the Harbour Hoppers wound their way around the city and could go into the waters of the harbour. Tourists seemed to enjoy the experience of the hour's ride, for which they paid over $50.

"I think I'd rather be behind a desk than drive one of those," I said. "It must be hard work, slinging ten tons around some of the bends and corners we have in Halifax."

"Yeah, I guess so. I just miss the detective work I used to do when I was a sergeant and inspector. Don't get to do much of that anymore."

"Maybe you should have turned down promotion."

"Mrs. Kennedy wouldn't have agreed to that."

"Well, It's been good seeing you, Patrick. I have go and pick up Rosalie and get on the road. I'll be seeing you in a few days."

"Right. You know, Marc, you're just like a magnet."

"Magnet? For what?"

"Trouble."

I picked up Rosalie at the Proctors' house, but before we set off for home, I called Frank Wilberforce to see if he could come to dinner the following evening. It happened that he was going to be in the Valley area, so was glad to accept.

"What are we having to eat, Marc? Poached thrushes in aspic, followed by sturgeon *en croute*?"

"Very funny. If you're not careful, you'll get moldy cheese sandwiches."

"Sorry."

"If we can get some nice fresh cod or haddock, why don't we have fish and chips?"

"Wonderful! But isn't that a little down-market for you?"

"Rosalie's battered fish is magical," I said, "and I'll do the chips. We might be able to find a modest wine to go with it."

"What time?"

"About six."

We had a good run back to Grand Pre, the Bugatti performing perfectly.

It was well into the evening when we arrived and there was not much in the fridge, so we just had bacon and eggs with baked beans and coffee and, since we were quite jet-lagged, went straight to bed.

22

The next day, though not fully recovered, we felt a great deal better for a long sleep. Like me, Rosalie had experienced drifting dreams about London pubs and meeting weird people. She also had a dream in which Robson Callister appeared as her long lost uncle from Australia!

We did not rise until after nine, which was one o'clock London time. Over a leisurely breakfast of Blue Mountain coffee, scrambled eggs, home-made sausages, somewhat stale croissants, and honey, we discussed the case.

"It's not like we will think of anything the police haven't," Rosalie said.

"I know, but wouldn't it be one in the eye for Herringbone if we did?"

"Yes. I think he is what is referred to as 'the deep state'. Governments come and go, but Herringbone is always in charge."

"Unless they can find out who Vindex is, they won't be able to discover if he knows anybody over here whom he could shack up with."

"I guess not."

"Sweetheart, assuming you were Vindex and he didn't have any contacts here—apart from me—what would you do? Where would you go?"

"If he thinks it's better to hide in a crowd, he would likely get a hotel room—or a boarding house room—in Halifax. He might need to be somewhere in and around the premier to make observations and work out how he could pull it off."

"That makes sense. But if he's waiting for something—I don't know what—he might head for the hills, so to speak, and hole up in some remote cabin."

"Wait a minute," said Rosalie sharply. "What was that you said about waiting for something?"

"Ah! I see what you're driving at. We should check with Tom to see if Wendell has any outdoor public events coming up where an assassination might take place."

"Call him now."

Tom was in meetings when I called, but he phoned me back an hour later. No, he told me, Wendell had no outdoor functions until Remembrance Day, which was months away. There had been a number of party barbecues in the previous weeks, but no more were planned as summer was winding down.

"What about indoor events in public places, say in the next month and a half?" I asked.

"Just one—well, two, if you count the reconvening of the House—and that is a speech to the Federation of Agriculture in Truro on September 7."

"Where is it being held?"

"At the Dalhousie Agricultural College. It's actually in Bible Hill, just outside Truro."

"Does it have an assembly hall or something like that?"

"Let me check…Um…yeah. There's Jenkins' Hall, where there is a large dining hall, and the Langille Athletic Centre, which is centred on a fair-sized gym."

"That should be checked out from the security standpoint," I said. "Will you call Kennedy, or shall I?"

"I'll do it."

"And you say the Legislature is coming back into session?"

"Yes, that's right."

"When?"

"September 10. That's a Tuesday."

"At least Province House should be easier to secure. There were cops all over it yesterday, like ugly on an ape."

"I know. I 'm getting tired of having to show my ID. Leave it with me, Marc."

"Are you going into Wolfville today?" Rosalie asked when I had hung up.

"Yes, I need to check with Louise at the wine store. She should have received a small shipment of 2010 *Morgon* from Beaujolais. If she has, I'll pick some up."

"2010? That's getting a little old for Beaujolais, isn't it?"

"Not for *Morgon,* and it was a great year for the top wines, but you're right, the *villages* wines will not likely have lasted."

"I'm not familiar with *Morgon.*" Said Rosalie. "I like the silky Beaujolais like *Fleurie* and *Chirouble*s."

"I'll see if she has any of them, too. And I want to get some nice run-of-the-mill Chablis to go with our fish and chips."

"God, yes! Frank is coming tonight. I almost forgot. I'd better come in, too, and see what fresh fish I can find."

"Do you want me to drop you off at the supermarket, or would you rather take the Fiat?"

"I'll take the Fiat because neither of us know how long we'll be."

"Fine. What will you get for the first course?"

"I fancy a salad, but I don't think that would be Frank's choice."

"No, you're right!" I said with a laugh.

"So I thought I'd get some smoked salmon and capers with a little fresh brown bread."

"Sounds good. I'll see you here later."

My visit to the wine store was very satisfying, not only because I loved being there among the shelves of gleaming bottles, but because I was so proud of what my partner, Louise, had done with the place. I looked around to see if I could find any small matter on which I could make a suggestion for improvement, but I could not. I knew full well that I could not have done better, no matter how hard I tried, and that I had made the right decision to give her a minority share in the business.

She had no *Fleurie* or *Chiroubles,* but the *Morgon* had just arrived, so I paid her for six bottles of that along with four bottles of Chablis, and stowed them in the Bugatti.

I was driving along Main Street when I noticed two young women strolling by. As I drew alongside them I realized that one of the girls was Jennifer Bryson, the daughter of my lawyer, and one of those implicated in the case against Father Mike.

I pulled up and put down the window. "Hi Jennifer. It'll be a squeeze but can I give you girls a lift?"

"Oh, it's you. Mr. LeBlanc." she said. "Can we really fit in that one seat?"

"You can try. One of you will have to sit on the other's lap."

"Okay. Tracey is coming back to my house anyway."

With considerable difficulty they piled in. Then I pulled out into the traffic.

"How are your Mom and Dad, Jennifer?"

"They're fine."

"And how are *you* doing?"

There was an awkward silence in which the girls looked at each other.

"We're feeling some pressure," she finally said. "You know the court case has been brought forward?"

"No, I didn't know. When is it?"

"In two weeks."

"Are you prepared?" Again silence, so I said, "*Really* prepared? You know they could ask you some tough questions."

"They wouldn't—you know—grill us like you see on television, would they?"

"Father Mike's lawyer will have the right to cross examine you, and if he thinks it's necessary to be tough to represent his client, he will."

They fidgeted for a minute, then Tracey burst out, "Oh fuck it!. Let's ask him, Jenny."

"Ask me what?"

"If telling the truth is more important than keeping your friends."

"I would say 'yes', it is. Especially in court, because to lie there is a crime. It's called perjury."

"Look, can you pull over before we get home?" Jenifer asked. "We need to talk, but we can't do it sitting like sardines in a can."

I did as she asked and we all got out and sat on a stone wall at the side of the road. I had the sense to say nothing until they had spoken again.

They looked down at their feet for a few seconds, scuffing them against the wall.

"It's just that we didn't see anything happen," said Tracey. "I mean anything, you know, sexual."

"Catherine asked us to say we saw it, but we didn't see anything like that."

"Do you think anything did happen?"

"No."

"No way."

"Then why would she lie?"

"She's like that. She's always boasting that she can lure any man she wants because she's so sexy-looking. Then when the priest wouldn't play ball, she invented the story"

"We did it because she's a friend. If we told the court that would he get off?" Tracey asked.

"I'm not sure. I'm not a lawyer. Your dad would know better than I do," I said carefully. "But I think that if you both went with your father to see the prosecutor, he would likely drop the charges."

"Shall we do that, Jenny?"

"Let's talk to Dad when we get in."

"I'm sure you're doing the right thing, girls. If you ruined an innocent man's life, I don't think you'd ever forgive yourselves."

"I think you're right," Tracey said.

"You want a ride the rest of the way?"

"No, thanks, Mr. LeBlanc, it's only just around the corner."

As I drove home, it occurred to me that my conversation with Jennifer and Tracey might be construed as witness tampering, and I experienced a cold, sinking feeling in my belly.

Was that what I intended, I asked myself. Was I really trying to influence the testimony they should give? At the time I thought I was just trying to do the right thing, but now I recognized that my regard for Father Mike may have affected my judgment.

I now regretted what I did, but mostly because it might result in Walter turning away from me, and my losing him as a good friend and maybe also as my lawyer.

Rosalie's Fiat was already in the yard when I pulled in, and when I went into the kitchen she was preparing the batter for her fish, which was drying on paper towel on the side bench. I was pleased to see she had been able to find big, thick filets of beautiful, fresh cod.

"Hi, Darling, I'll get to work on the chips right away."

"Hey. What kept you? Frank will be here in half an hour."

"I ran into Jennifer and her friend and gave them a ride home."

"Jennifer who?"

"Jennifer Dryden. Walter and Joyce's daughter. You remember."

"I never actually met her. Just saw her from across the street."

"Oh, right. I may have put my foot in it. I talked to them about the trial."

"Oh, Marc. Was that wise?"

"I thought so at the time, but now I'm not so sure."

"Should you call Walter and explain?"

"I think I'd better let sleeping dogs lie. When they wake up of their own accord, I may be in trouble."

I got out the potatoes. They were Yukon Gold, being the best we could get. When I lived in London I used to buy Maris Piper potatoes, which were perfect for French fries due to their high, dry matter and low reducing sugars. The variety came highly recommended by chefs Heston Blumenthal and Tom Kerridge, but, alas, I could not obtain them in Nova Scotia.

My method was to cut the chips and soak them in cold water, then, in fresh water, bring them to a boil. When the chips were just starting to get soft, I drained them and dried them on paper towels. When they were dry, I would deep-fry them at a low temperature until they just started to take on colour, and then drain them again. When Rosalie was almost finished cooking the fish in her amazing batter, I would plunge the chips into oil which was at very high heat, then turn them out on a platter and sprinkle them with sea salt.

Rosalie said her batter was a closely-guarded family secret, passed down from generation to generation, and would not give it to me; but I had watched her make it and noticed that she used flour, sugar, salt, baking powder and water, with no eggs or other additions. Knowing the ingredients was one thing, but I never could determine the quantities of each.

Playing the game, in turn, I refused to give her my recipe for tartar sauce, which was a perfect accompaniment to the fish. I mixed finely-chopped dill pickles with Worcestershire sauce, equal quantities of English and Dijon mustard, chopped dill weed, and mayonnaise.

"Oh, I almost forgot," Rosalie said, her apron covered in flour. "I looked in at the University to get some papers, and guess who I saw?"

"Who?"

"Betty Ponister."

"Am I supposed to know who that is?"

"I was at Memorial with her, in St. John's."

"I didn't even know you went to Memorial."

"Yes, just for a year. Researching my thesis."

"You learn something new every day. Okay, who is Betty Poninster?"

"She works at the Nova Scotia archives in Halifax."

"So?"

Rosalie dusted off her hands and came over to where I was working. Something about her made me stop what I was doing and pay attention.

"What is it?"

"I don't know," she said. "Betty told me that the other day a strange-looking man came in, wanting very old architects' drawings of Halifax buildings."

"Yes?" My interest was certainly aroused now.

"She told me he had an accent."

Suddenly I was alert. "A British accent?"

"She said she thought it was Australian, but she could have been mistaken."

"Certain educated Australian accents sound a bit like English home counties. Did she get his name?"

"She said it sounded like Dagaltus. And it looked something like that on a form he filled out, but it was kind of scribbled."

"Dagaltus?"

"Yes."

"Means nothing to me. Did he give an address?"

"He gave the Lord Nelson Hotel. He said he was a tourist."

"Call them up now." I said, reaching for the laptop and looking up the number. "The number is 902-423-6331."

She picked up the phone and dialed.

"Hello, Could you connect me with Mr. Dagaltus's room please? I think it's spelled D-A-G-A-L-T-U-S. What's that? You don't have anyone staying in the hotel by that name? Anything close? I see. Well, thank you very much. Goodbye."

"I wonder if he's our man?"

"Vindex?"

"Yes."

"Should you call Patrick, or Tom?"

"I don't see how it would help them. The guy is in the wind."

Just then the phone rang.

"Do you think this could be him? Vindex?"

"I don't know, but keep quiet, just in case."

It was not Vindex, but Walter Bryson. I thought he might be calling to tell me off for talking to Jennifer without his permission.

"Hello, Walter. How are you?"

"I'm alright, Marc. You?"

"Fine, thanks. If this is about my talking to Jennifer—"

"Yes it is. I wanted to tell you that I think you were right. I've been worried about her for some time. There was obviously something troubling her, but I wasn't sure what it was. Now I know."

"I'm glad you feel that way It seems clear that Father Mike was falsely accused because he wouldn't respond to Catherine Morton's advances."

"Yes, there's no doubt about that. Contrary to my expectations, I'm not involved in the case, either in a magisterial or advocacy role, so my hands are no longer tied."

"Does the trial have to go ahead?"

"I don't think so. I'll talk to Prescott, who's prosecuting. He's a very sensible sort of guy. I'm pretty sure that when I have Jenifer and Tracey tell him their side of things, he'll decide he can't get a conviction and won't proceed with a trial."

"Walter, that's great news. Father Mike is a really good guy. I never doubted his innocence."

"I'll let you know if I'm successful. Please don't say anything to the priest until then."

Rosalie was thrilled with this development, but before we could discuss it further, Frank Wilberforce was at the door.

He came in beaming, larger than life, and his arms were full of cans of beer.

"Greetings dears!" he cried, "Marc, I know you go in for Chateau Nose in the Air, but I brought some of the people's drink to warm up with."

We laughed. Frank was one of our favourite people. I first met him about two years ago in an official capacity. He was investigating my father's nefarious business activities, and asked me to meet him on Evangeline Beach, where he was wearing shorts. It was a sight I will never forget, because Frank weighed at least 350 pounds.

Since then we had become friends, and Rosalie and I derived great pleasure from watching him eat enormous quantities of food, and from the fascinating stories he told about the art world.

Within minutes, Frank had downed four cans of beer. When the food was ready, we put it on large platters in the centre of the table so he could help himself. I had cooked two huge pans of chips and Rosalie had battered and cooked twelve filets of cod.

We would have two each, and we had taken bets on how many Frank would devour. I bet he would have six, but she was betting on eight because she said Frank could not bear to see a plate with leftover food on it.

Frank showed remarkable restraint with the smoked salmon, only taking about as much as Rosalie and me combined. For this, he abandoned his beer and drank Chablis with us, consuming about half a bottle.

The main course was delicious, largely due to Rosalie's battered fish, but my tartar sauce was also a great success. We ate in silence for about twenty minutes, as Frank seriously, methodically attacked the food as if he were conducting a military campaign.

We finished before he did and, some while later, he put down his knife and fork. I gave Rosalie a gentle kick under the table to indicate that I would win the bet, but then Frank looked at the remaining filet on the platter and sighed.

"It would be a shame to let it go to waste," he said, and scraped it onto his plate. Now it was Rosalie's turn to kick me.

Frank polished off the piece of fish, sat back and wiped his face and head with a big red handkerchief. "Excellent!" He proclaimed. "Absolutely marvellous! What's for dessert?"

Rosalie and I collapsed, laughing hilariously. We managed to find some frozen cheesecake, which we placed in front of him. He looked longingly at the plate as he anticipated the cake's thawing.

"While you're waiting, Frank, why don't you tell us some of your stories?" Rosalie said. "You're such a fund of good tales."

"Okay," he said, pushing the plate to one side and pouring himself another glass of wine. "Have you heard of Tony Tetro?"

"No."

"Tony was one of the most talented painters who ever lived."

"Was he a forger?"

"No, not according to him, at least not an ordinary forger. He thought that a forger would copy a painting simply because the original already exists. But he saw no fun in that, because anyone could prove the copy was fake by pointing to the original in a gallery. He believed that he had to make a painting which never existed, pretend it had been discovered, and give it a history and a provenance.

"He also learned to forge the marks, or stamps, of famous dealers like Nicolaes Flinck, who collected many Rembrandt prints and etchings. Tony would get antique paper from a three-hundred-year-old book. It was yellowed and even had a watermark which could be found in northern Europe in the 1600s."

"Did he fool anyone?" Rosalie asked.

"Oh yes, lots of experts. For quite a while. His 'Rembrandts' are quite beautiful. He also did very convincing paintings allegedly by Dali, Rockwell and Rubens. But, for him, the documented history of the painting—the provenance—was more important than the work itself."

"Would you say he was one of the greatest?"

"I would. He's up there with Van Meegeren, who everybody's heard of for forging excellent Vermeers."

"Who else is on your list?"

"Well, I think Wolfgang Beltracchi has to be on it."

"I've never heard of him," I said.

"No, most people haven't. He was painting in the styles of famous artists when he was a boy, but instead of making copies of existing works, he did new works and sold them at flea markets.

"In the 1970s and 80s, Beltracchi did 'Campendonks' and even fooled the leading scholar, Andrea Firmenich, who featured some of Beltracchi's paintings in his Campendonk catalogue."

"Did he get much money for those?"

"Sure. In auctions. Huge prices. The most famous was *Landscape with Horses*. Steve Martin paid $860,000 for it in 2004. He also sold an 'Ernst' in Paris for $7 million."

"Was he caught?"

"Yeah. In 2008, after some of his paintings were found by a forensic specialist to have pigments which didn't match the dates. They were too recent."

"Frank, I've heard of John Myatt and Tom Keating," I said. "What can you tell us about them?"

"Scotland Yard said Myatt pulled off 'the biggest art fraud of the 20th century'. The guy painted something like 200 forgeries, some of them being sold at Sotheby's. He forged stuff by Matisse, Chagall, and Giacometti. He was arrested in 1993 but only got a year in jail."

"And Keating?"

"Oh, Keating! He was a weird one," said Frank, polishing off his cheesecake. "He said he had faked over 2,000 paintings by more than 100 different artists. He said he didn't do it for money but because the capitalist system was rotten and because so many artists had lived and died in poverty. He was arrested in 1979, but never got any time because he was badly injured in a motorcycle accident. Even though his stuff is all fake, it sells for between $20,000 and $80,000."

"Incredible!' said Rosalie.

"Look, I must go and leave you good people in peace. Thanks for a lovely feed."

"It's always a pleasure to see you, Frank."

He hauled his bulk up and, tightening his belt, started to make for the door.

"Oh, before you go, does the name Dagaltus, D-a-g-a-l-t-u-s, mean anything to you?"

"Not spelled like that, it doesn't."

"What are you saying?"

"If you spell it Dìoghaltas, it's Scottish Gaelic."

"What does that mean?"

"It means 'avenger'."

Frank had been gone for about fifteen minutes, and Rosalie and I were clearing up and putting the plates and glasses into the dishwasher when my phone rang.

"Hello."

"It's happening," said a quiet voice in an English accent.

Even though I was expecting the call, it still took me by surprise.

"It's real," I said.

"Mark?"

"Yes."

"You still on for this?"

"Yes."

"I may not need you, but if I do, can I count on you?"

"Absolutely." My mouth was dry and I was shaking like a leaf.

"We're going to shake 'em up first. Maybe I can turn the motherfucker without killing him."

"What will you do?"

"You'll find out. No names, no pack drill."

"Okay. How can I reach you?"

"Don't be a fucking numpty. You can't. I'll call you."

"Where are you?"

"You ask a lot of fucking questions. Too many. I'll be in touch. Maybe. 'Bye, Mark."

23

As soon as I got up the next morning, I phoned Patrick Kennedy.

"Contact has been made."

"With Vindex? When?"

"Last night, I didn't want to disturb you at home so late."

"Maybe you should have. Repeat the whole conversation to me, word for word."

When I had done as he instructed, he paused and I could hear him take a deep breath, followed by a heavy sigh.

"Why did you ask him those questions? You're not a rank amateur anymore. You should have known they would raise his suspicions."

"I thought you wanted to know where he was and how I might reach him."

I was stung by Patrick's tone because I knew he was right. I had known at the time I asked them that the questions were a stupid mistake.

"I'm sorry, Patrick, but the call was like getting an electric shock. It completely unnerved me and threw me off-balance. Do you think he'll call again?"

"If he's the man I think he is, he won't go near you again. But in desperation, he might have no option. What did you think he meant by 'shaking things up'?"

"No idea."

"I guess it could be anything from a carefully planned operation to an opportunistic action," Patrick said. "And then again, it could have just been talk to impress you."

"I was impressed alright," I said disconsolately. "Should I call Aldridge, or will you?"

"For the moment, let's leave him out of it. Let's confine this information to the professionals."

Rosalie and I had our breakfast under a pall of gloom. My appetite had disappeared and I despondently pushed the ham and eggs around my plate. My condition seemed also to have infected my wife, as she sat glumly nursing her coffee.

"Shall you go up to Halifax today?"

"Yes, I pretty much have to go."

"You know I have to stay here? I've got a lot to do at the university."

"Yes, I know. I'll miss you."

"Please stay in touch, Marc."

"I will."

"And don't go haring off with Vindex if he asks you to."

"He's not likely to now."

On the way up in the Bugatti, my mind was filled with a jumble of information, little of which was taking any useful form. The whole conversation with Vindex and its aftermath had shaken my self-confidence. I felt rather like a small child whose teacher had just scolded him for wetting his pants.

To make matters worse, the sky clouded over and the stretch of the 101 between Ellershouse and Upper Sackville seemed more than ever soulless and boring.

Vindex had said *We're going to shake 'em up first. Maybe I can turn the motherfucker without killing him.* What did that mean?

My best guess was that it probably meant some kind of scare was in store for Wendell, but there was no way of really knowing.

Then I cast my mind back to the other threats he had made in emails before I went to London. I remembered *Idiot! If you don't reverse you position, you are dead man.* and *You have really lost the plot. Better call the undertaker.*

What came after that? Oh yes, it was *In the countdown. Measure your coffin, moron.*

Then there was a time lapse before we received the final message. I struggled to recall the precise wording. I thought it was something like *You want a cock-up. You'll get one that will really have you hopping. Next time it will be you.*

Yes, that was it. Now, what the hell did that mean?

I drove along in a daze, thinking that I preferred a different kind of case from this one, a case where its possible culmination was not of such critical importance, especially not one of life and death.

A truck towing a Cape Island boat on its trailer sped past me on its way to the Annapolis Valley. The hull of the boat was a bright blue, while the superstructure was painted green, a combination of colours not often seen in fishing boats. It was a composite of hues I had seen somewhere recently.

Then it hit me like a sledge hammer. Of course! I braked sharply, and pulled the car over onto the shoulder amid blaring horns from other vehicles.

You'll get one that will really have you hopping. The damn Harbour Hopper!

I tugged my phone from my jacket and hastily scrolled down, looking for Patrick Kennedy's number. Despite my saying it was very, *very* important, they told me he was not available. So I called Tom.

"Adridge."

"Tom, it's Marc."

"Hey, Marc, what's up?"

"Marc, listen carefully. I know what Vindex is going to do—"

I was interrupted by an ear-splitting boom followed by a loud roar.

For several minutes I could not communicate with Tom because of the noise, in which I could hear people shouting.

Then he came back on the line. "Marc, there's been some kind of explosion. It seems to have come from west of here. There's a lot of smoke and some windows appear to have been blown in."

"The waterfront."

"What?"

"It came from the harbour."

"How do you know? Where *are* you?"

"I'm on the road. That's what I was trying to tell you when it happened. Remember the threat in the email: *You'll get one that will really have you hopping?* It's Vindex. The bastard has struck. It's the Harbour Hopper. The Harbour Hopper has been blown up."

"*What?* Holy shit!"

"That bang sounded loud enough to cause some serious damage so I'm guessing the vessel has been sunk."

"Jesus! You were too late. If only you had called earlier."

"Even had I got to you ten, fifteen minutes earlier you wouldn't have had time to stop it," I said stiffly. I was in no mood to be lectured twice in one day.

"I guess not. *Fuck!* I'm going to call Kennedy and tell him what you said. When will you be here?"

"About half an hour, I reckon."

"Alright. I imagine we'll have to get those stuffy bastards from RCMP Security in again."

"I don't want to see them."

"You may have no choice. Look, buddy, the place is crawling with cops now so I better go."

"Is Wendell okay?"

"I think so. Oh he just came out of his office...You okay, boss? Good. Yes, he's fine. Get in here as fast as you can!"

~

When I got into Halifax I found I could not get close to Province House or Tom's office because the police had closed all roads leading to, and surrounding, the site of the explosion. As far as I could tell, it occurred somewhere near the Maritime Museum of the Atlantic.

I drove around for some minutes, then, not finding anywhere to park, drove to the premier's house, left the Bugatti there, and called a taxi.

When I got to the police cordon closest to One Government Place, I tried to tell the officers there that I had an appointment with the premier, but they ignored me. When I edged closer and asked them to call Superintendent Kennedy or Chief Simmons, they turned nasty, telling me to stand back and get away from the cordon.

I called Tom and explained my dilemma. He suggested I hand the phone to one of the policemen so he could talk to them, but when I tried to do that, the officer shouted at me that I was causing an obstruction and would be arrested if I did not go away.

Tom said he would ask Deputy Chief Agnes McKillop, who was there in the office, to come and get me.

Soon she arrived and lifted the tape for me to enter. I gave the policeman a long stare before following Agnes into the building, but it was not nearly as hostile as the one he gave me.

She led me to the elevator and soon we were rising to the 7th floor.

"I'm sorry to have bothered you, Deputy Chief, but the guys wouldn't let me in."

"They are doing their jobs," she said curtly, "For all they knew, you could have been the bomber trying to get in to finish the job."

"Was it the Harbour Hopper?"

"Yes."

"Was it sunk?"

"Partially. Some of it is still sticking above water."

"Anyone get hurt?"

"No final number yet, but it looks like two elderly people were killed, and seven, including kids, in hospital."

"Do you know the cause?"

"Some kind of bomb." She looked at me as if I were a psychiatric case. "Why, what were you expecting?"

"I'm not sure, but he would have to have obtained the explosive materials here. And in that case, I wondered where he would get them."

"How do you figure that?"

"He could hardly have brought them in on the plane." It was my turn to be condescending.

She did not respond, except to put her nose in the air and ignore me until we reached our floor. Then she quickly disappeared.

I checked in with Susan and then went straight to Tom's office. He looked like hell; his face was white and he was in his shirt sleeves with his tie hanging loose.

"Hey, Marc. We'd better go in. They're all here."

I headed for the inner door to the premier's office, but he stopped me.

"No, we're meeting in the cabinet room. Wendell thought the time had come to put the cabinet in the picture. Some of them will be guessing that there's more to this explosion than meets the eye."

When we entered the room, I saw that the whole cabinet had been assembled, but that they were not sitting in the same places they occupied when I last attended a cabinet meeting. Today, apart from the premier's, the seats at the top of the table were occupied by Herringbone, the Librarian, Patrick, Chief Simmons and Agnes MacKillop.

Members of the cabinet were crammed uncomfortably into the remaining space around the table, with Tom and myself standing in the corner.

Somewhat to my surprise, when the premier called the meeting to order, Patrick took the floor. I had expected Herringbone to take charge and lord it over everyone, but he seemed content to sprawl in his chair, looking at the ceiling.

"Ladies and gentlemen," said Patrick. "I'm Superintendent Kennedy from H Division of the RCMP. You probably recognize Chief Simmons and Deputy Chief MacKillop from Halifax Regional Police. These are some colleagues from the National Security Division."

The police smiled wanly and nodded their heads, but neither the Librarian nor Herringbone moved a muscle, remaining transfixed on the ceiling.

"For some weeks the premier has been receiving death threats"—There was a chorus of gasps around the table—"And after considerable investigation by police, and by Mr. Marc LeBlanc, it has been concluded that the would-be assassin is a member of a violent, extremist group of environmentalists.

"In one of his communications, the would-be assassin threatened to provide a shock to the premier by way of trying to persuade him to reverse his policies on environmental matters.

"Without offering any opinion on the wisdom thereof, I have to inform you that the premier decided to adhere to those policies, refusing to be intimidated."

Again, there were gasps and mutterings among the cabinet.

"The incident today appears to have been the assassin's response. One of the fleet of Harbour Hoppers was sunk near the Maritime Museum of the Atlantic as it was southbound on its regular tour. Two persons were killed and we now know that nine more were injured, two seriously."

"Excuse me." Angus MacKinnon spoke up from the far end of the table.

"Yes?"

"What was responsible for the sinking?"

"All we are prepared to say at this juncture is that it was caused by 'an explosive device'."

"No chance it was an accident?"

"None at all."

"And you're sure the two are connected?"

"Not *certain,* but it seems wise to assume so."

"Thank you."

"We don't know where or when the assassin proposes to strike," Patrick continued, "or, indeed, how many attempts he might make, but we intend to take all reasonable precautions to protect the premier's life.

"Now. So far, none of the threats has mentioned anyone other than the premier, but I want to advise you that you are all potential targets—"

The table erupted, and as the uproar subsided, Ernest Maddingly rose.

"I'm sorry, Premier, but I have to leave. Gladys and I have a house guest and we have arranged to take him down to Chester for dinner. I'm as sure that the meeting can manage without me, as I am that the assassin will have no desire to dispatch a man already in his ninth decade."

There was good-natured laughter as Maddingly squeezed his slender frame behind the chairs to get to the door.

"Good old Ernie," said someone.

"One of the great minds of the nineteenth century," said someone else with a snigger.

"As I was saying," Patrick continued, "we have no indication that any of you are also targets, but we cannot rule it out, so we advise you to be on your guard at all times. Please do not go out alone, or go into open spaces, if you can avoid it. And stay away from public transport."

"Do we need to cancel all public engagements?" asked Angela Staples, the Minister of Justice.

"In so far as it is possible, I think you should," said Patrick. "Larger events which have been planned for some time can go ahead, but please let us know about them in advance."

"Would it help if we wrote that down now and gave it to you before we leave?" Joan Howard, Deputy Premier, inquired.

"Excellent idea!" grunted Herringbone, aroused from his silence.

"Perhaps you could all do that now and pass them around to Superintendent Kennedy," The Librarian said, following her colleague's emergence into the land of the living.

For several minutes the sound of scribbling was interrupted only by the ticking of the wall clock and by the premier's pen tapping impatiently on the table.

"Are there any other questions?" Patrick asked, and, hearing none, announced that the meeting was adjourned.

When cabinet members had filed out, Patrick wandered over to Tom and me in our corner.

"I'm one short," he said, riffling through the papers.

"Short?" Tom asked.

"Yes. There are eighteen in the cabinet. I only have seventeen."

"That would be Ernie. He left before the end of the meeting."

"Yes, of course. Would he be home by now?"

"He lives in the South End, so if he's not home yet, he will be soon."

"Yes, that's right," I said.

"Marc, I have to go to Wendell. Can you call Ernie and get his list of engagements? It's not likely he has any, but we'd better make sure."

"Okay," I said.

I walked out to Susan's desk, sat down and waited ten minutes before dialing Maddingly's number. It was answered, and a voice said, "Maddingly residence."

Immediately I slammed down the phone. I knew that voice. It belonged to Vindex!

24

"Tom!" I shouted at the top of my lungs.

"What is it?" He was standing in the doorway of the cabinet room.

"Get Patrick here, right away!"

They rushed over to Susan's desk where I was sitting, still shaking from my discovery.

"What is it, Marc? You're as white as a sheet."

"Vindex is at Maddingly's house."

"*What*?"

"I just called there to get Maddingly's list of public public events, and Vindex answered the phone."

"Are you sure?"

"Of course, I'm sure," I said irritably. "I know that voice."

"What did you say to him?" Patrick demanded.

"Nothing. I hung up right away."

"Thank God for that." He pulled out his phone and dialed. "What's Maddingly's address?"

"I don't know. Somewhere in the South End, I think."

"Tom, do you know?"

"Give me a second."

He rummaged in Susan's desk and found a black notebook. "It's 6252 Regina Terrace."

"Janet? This is Superintendent Kennedy. Call HRP immediately and ask for a red alert. Armed Response to 6252 Regina Terrace. Suspect to be detained is...how old is Vindex, Marc?"

"I think, late thirties."

"Male. Late thirties. English accent. Be aware two elderly people, Ernest and Gladys Maddingly, may be hostages. And, Janet, have HRP send a car to pick us up at the corner of Granville and George streets. Go!"

He thrust his phone into his pocket and charged out of the room. Tom and I followed. Once downstairs, we made for the corner, but had to wait a full five minutes before a cruiser, lights flashing, pulled alongside. We piled in, went down George Street, onto Hollis, roared down to the end, then up South, west to Robie, then west again on Oakland and came screeching to a halt at the end of Regina. There were already two police vehicles in place and we could hear more coming behind us.

"Tom, Marc, I want no heroics from you. Stay in the car."

Patrick got out and, flashing his ID, went up to speak with the sergeant closest to the house.

It was an old, white-painted place with a large lawn and a gravel driveway. There were no lights on in the building and no cars in the forecourt. I noticed that the garage door was open and that there was no vehicle inside.

In a few moments a team approached the house, bashed in the front door and scrambled inside. Some minutes later, they re-emerged, shaking their heads. Patrick came over to us.

"Place is deserted. Where did Maddingly say they were going for dinner? Do you recall?"

"Chester," I said.

"That's right," Said Tom.

"What's the best place to eat in Chester?"

"I don't know," Tom said.

"Marc?"

"There isn't one, but I'm guessing Maddingly would go to the Sunroom on Pleasant Street."

"You get a description of Maddingly's car," he said to the officer driving our car. "His first name is Ernest. The address is 6252 Regina Terrace I'll call our detachment in Chester to get to the restaurant."

Patrick came back and climbed in beside the driver. "Let's go to Chester. And step on it."

"It's out of my jurisdiction."

"Fuck the jurisdiction. Just go!"

~

Having received official blessing for operating outside the municipality, our driver now seemed to be pleased with his assignment and gunned the car down the leafy street past dozens of residents who were looking on from their windows, yards and gateways. At least one police vehicle got away ahead of us, so we followed it until we were out on the highway.

Then our driver, who was called Len, overtook the other car, waving cheerfully at his colleague as he did so.

I was used to driving at high speeds in the Bugatti, but my car was built for it, and you hardly noticed when you were going 140 kph. But I was terrified with Len at the wheel of the Ford Taurus as he drove like the wind, taking exactly 42 minutes to get to Pleasant Street in Chester.

We pulled up outside the restaurant and Patrick hopped out.

"What is the vehicle we're looking for?" he asked Len.

"A 2013, dark green, Lincoln Sedan."

"There's no car fitting that description anywhere around here," said Patrick. "Maybe they didn't come to this restaurant."

"Or maybe we passed them on the highway," I said with a grin.

Patrick gave me a dirty look. "Just for that you come in with me. Let me know if you spot Maddingly. I've only seen him once. Len, sneak around the side and cover us if anything happens."

We walked quietly to the restaurant and gently pushed the door open. Instantly, I saw Ernest Maddingly with an old woman at a table near the window. They were alone, so Patrick told me to approach the table while he checked out the washrooms.

"Hello, Minister."

"Why, Mr. LeBlanc are you dining here, too?"

"Are you and Mrs. Maddingly dining by yourselves?"

"Why, no, otherwise you'd be welcome to join us. We have a guest, but he wasn't feeling well. I was just about to go and check on him."

"Where did you park your car, Minister?"

"Right outside. Look, what's this all about?"

Patrick came back from the washrooms, shaking his head.

"I'm sorry but it looks as if your car has been stolen." I said.

"Stolen? That can't be."

Patrick sat down at the table and showed his identification to Mrs. Maddingly. "Please excuse me, madam, sir."

"I remember you, Superintendent, from the cabinet meeting. Now please explain yourselves!"

"If you will give me two minutes to make a report, I shall be glad to oblige."

"What is this all about, LeBlanc?" Understandably, Maddingly was starting to get annoyed.

"There's no easy way to say this, Minister, but I think your dinner guest has taken your Lincoln."

"But he's in the washroom. I told you he wasn't feeling well."

"There's nobody in the washroom."

"Ernie," said his wife, "I have a feeling we've been swindled."

"Great Scott! This is outrageous!"

"Might I ask who your guest was, Minister?" I asked as Patrick returned and resumed his seat.

"He's a visitor to the province. His name is Jonathan Smith."

"How do you know him, sir?" Patrick inquired.

"He's a young man I met in London when I was over there for the Commonwealth Parliamentary Association meeting. He was such a nice fellow that I told him to look me up if ever he was on this side of the Atlantic."

"I'm afraid your Mr. Smith may be the man who has been planning to assassinate the premier."

At this news, Mrs. Maddingly almost passed out, and her husband's eyes widened. His hand shaking, he reached for his glass of wine and downed it in one.

"Bless my soul," he said hoarsely, "What about my car? It's by no means new but we have come to like it a great deal."

"I've put out an alert to look out for the car on all roads surrounding this area, but I strongly suspect we'll find it abandoned somewhere."

"Will it be damaged, Superintendent?" Mrs. Maddingly asked weakly.

"I doubt it, madam. Meanwhile, I have sent for a police car to drive you home. But please finish your meals first."

"I don't think I could, Ernie."

"Me neither, Gladys. We'll go whenever you're ready, Superintendent."

They got up and shambled towards the door. As they were too confused, I paid their bill on my way out.

As we stood outside waiting for the car, a slight breeze was blowing off the sea and the evening was gradually darkening. About fifty feet away, some seagulls were having an argument over a cardboard box.

"Excuse me, Minister," I said. "How long has Mr. Smith been staying with you?"

"Just a few days."

"What did you talk about most of the time?"

"Knowing Ernie, it was probably about himself," Mrs. Maddingly said with a weak laugh.

"Now, Gladys, don't be unkind. If you must know, it was mostly about the old days."

"The old days?" Patrick asked.

"Yes, you know, the early days. You know, I've been in the legislature for more than half a century."

"Yes I did know. It is a remarkable record of public service."

"Thank you."

"You must have been elected at the same time as Akerman," I said.

"Oh, that fellow! Yes, I remember him. Never knew when to shut up. Always up on his hind legs, making a nuisance of himself. Yes, we came in after the same election. I imagine the fellow must be dead now. Probably arguing with the Devil."

"Here's your ride," said Patrick. "We'll let you know when we find your car, sir. Goodnight to you both."

Len drove us back to the city in silence. All of us were absorbed by our thoughts and nobody felt like volunteering opinions.

As we pulled up outside the office building on Granville Street, a message came through on the radio. Maddingly's car had been found. It was apparently unharmed and was sitting in the driveway when he and Gladys returned. The key was in the ignition and the tank had been refilled.

"Saucy fucker, isn't he?" Tom ventured.

"Well, at least we know he's back in Halifax," Patrick said.

"But he might not stay here," said Tom.

"Why do you say that?"

"Because the Federation of Agriculture meeting in Truro is the day after tomorrow."

"Shit, you're right. I had forgotten! Marc, you and I had better get up there tomorrow and check the place out."

"Okay by me."

"I'm afraid we'll have to share the experience with our friends from National Security."

"Herringbone and Librarian."

"Is that what you call them?" Patrick laughed heartily.

"If they won't let us know their names, we have to call them something."

"But, please, Marc, not to their faces."

25

When I went down the next morning, the premier was having his bowl of cereal.

He looked up with a grin. "Hey, Marc. I hear you had some adventures yesterday."

"Yes, but we didn't catch the bastard."

"Maybe you frightened him off."

"I wouldn't even hope for that. This guy is smarter than any of us thought. He'll make another try, that's for sure."

"Imagine old Ernie harbouring an assassin!" He laughed. "You don't think the old buzzard knew who his house guest was, do you?"

"No, I'm pretty sure he is not a co-conspirator, but I'd like to know the details of his conversations with Vindex. What the hell was he pumping Maddingly to find out?"

"Whatever he was hoping to hear, you can be sure Ernie told him all about the glory days when he was premier—for five minutes!"

"He likes to talk about that. He gave me an earful on that subject when I met with him a few weeks ago."

"What's your next move?"

"Patrick Kennedy and I are going to Truro today—apparently with the National Security spooks—to check out the Agricultural College campus."

"Oh yes. I'm speaking there tomorrow, aren't I?"

"Yes, you are. And we don't want Vindex taking any potshots at you."

"I hope I don't have to wear a special vest. I can't stand that nonsense."

"I'm afraid you will have to, Wendell. The cops will insist on it."

"Fuck! Can I get a normal shirt and tie over it, I wonder. That wouldn't be so bad if it wasn't visible."

"Sorry, that's not my department."

"Where will you be staying?"

"I don't know yet. We should be able to find somewhere in Truro."

"Just a minute." He pulled out his phone and pressed a number.

"Susan, book a room each for LeBlanc and Kennedy in Truro. Don't take any crap about them being full for the convention. Pull rank. Okay. Thanks."

He hung up and beamed at me. "By the time you get to the office, Susan will have it worked out."

"Thanks. I should have done it last night, but I forgot."

"Well, I've gotta go. Good hunting."

Sure enough, Susan had booked us into the Willow Bend Motel, not far from the town centre and from the site of the meeting.

When Patrick arrived, he suggested we go up in the Bugatti. He reminded me of the first time he saw, and admired, it several years ago, at the site of my father's murder.

"I must say, it stands the test of time. It's still a beautiful machine. Does it still run well?"

"Perfectly. The engineering is out of this world, and the craftsmanship is astounding."

"What can she do?"

"Top recorded speed was 408.84 kph. At the time, it broke the world record."

"Holy shit! And how much did it cost?"

"New, it was $2.4 million, but I got it second-hand from an Arabian sheik."

"What did you pay for it?"

"Less than half the book price, but I had done some favours for the sheik."

"Could...no...I guess not."

"What is it Patrick?"

"Could I drive it?"

"I'm not insured for other drivers."

"Oh, I see." I have seldom seen such disappointment on a man's face.

"But if we can find an open space which is not officially a provincial road, you can have a try."

"Thanks. You don't suppose they would close the airport for an hour?"

"Not a chance. Okay, let's get going."

We got to Truro in fifty-four minutes, which involved speeds greatly in excess of the 110 kph limit on the 102, but since I had a Superintendent of the RCMP as my passenger, I figured I was safe from the Mounties' speed traps.

As it happened, we did not encounter any, so Patrick's influence was not put to the test. But I could tell from his face that he was thrilled to be in a vehicle capable of such speeds yet maintain perfect stability. It also has incredible braking ability, the car being able to go from 400 km/h to a standstill in less than 10 seconds.

We checked into the Willow Bend, and then went to the campus, which covered a larger area than I expected. It contained a rather pleasant mixture of modern and old buildings, one of which I was later informed dated from 1904.

We went straight to the administration building, where we were to meet a Dr. Dajan, who would conduct us around, but we were told he was already over at the centre with 'the people from Ottawa'.

The Langille Athletic Centre, where the Federation of Agriculture would be meeting, was one of the very modern buildings, a low-lying concrete spread with narrow strip windows. Before going in, we wandered around the building, checking the entrances and exits, and making notes as to which should be completely sealed on the day.

Then we strolled into the centre and found the gymnasium, where Herringbone and Librarian were standing on the highly polished floor, talking to a man who we deduced was Dr. Dajan.

We introduced ourselves to Dajan, and offered minimal greetings to 'the people from Ottawa'.

"You here too, LeBlanc?" Herringbone asked in his most insulting tone. "Was that necessary, Kennedy?"

"Yes, I thought so," said Patrick coldly.

"Oh, very well. We were about to get the Royal Tour. So, Dr. Dajan: please continue."

There was not a lot to see. The gym floor would have some 200 chairs, a head table and a sound system. There were no particularly dangerous blind spots, and even I could calculate that as few as twenty officers could secure the premises.

"Alright, then," said Herringbone, "we'll need to inspect the place again when you have it set up for the meeting. So let us know when that is done."

"Yes, of course, sir," Dr Dajan said. "Where?"

"Where what?"

"Where will you be? Where will I contact you?"

"Oh yes. Where are we Marjorie?" he asked Librarian.

"The Best Western Glengarry. On Willow Street."

"There you go, then. Where are you Kennedy?"

"At the Willow Bend. Also on Willow Street."

"Golly gee wilikers, we're going to be neighbours," said Herringbone with a mocking, artificial heartiness.

We returned to our motel, fully understanding that we were not to be included in the final inspection at the athletic centre, so we directed our thoughts towards dinner. The Willow Bend, it transpired, was a B&B so, after a wash and brush up, we strolled into town.

On Prince Street we found the Nook and Cranny and decided that we might walk all night and find nothing better, so went in and secured a table.

Patrick had seafood chowder, followed by something called Tuna Poke Stack and wontons, whose description of ingredients scared me half to death, being ginger, tuna, cucumber, avocado, sweet soy glaze, toasted sesame seeds and crispy wontons.

I ordered steamed mussels in garlic and white wine, and then the pan-fried haddock. We washed it all down with an Argentinian Sauvignon Blanc, which was quite the best part of the meal.

We strolled around town for about an hour and, finding little excitement, went back to the motel and said good night.

~

The next morning we had breakfast and then headed up to the campus. The place was already buzzing with police, mostly RCMP, but also some people wearing plain black uniforms and driving black SUVs. These, we thought, must be associated with Herringbone and Librarian, something which was later confirmed when we saw them taking orders from the latter.

The gymnasium was unremarkable, the addition of chairs and a table not altering the risks involved with the premier's attendance. It seemed the event would mainly be confined to members of the federation and a handful of others, including government officials and media. We could not see anywhere in particular from which an assassin could wage an attack on a man at the head table, or, if he did, how he could escape afterwards.

Patrick and I went outside to watch the delegates arrive. Most had singularly un-sinister appearances, being down to earth farmers in checked shirts and sports jackets. Among the arrivals, I was surprised to see John Dempster, my partner in a winery in the Gaspereau Valley, who also used to be a friend before he betrayed me in a particularly foul manner. It occurred to me that wine growing was also agriculture and that vignerons could be members of the federation, too. John looked quizzically in my direction, but he knew better than to speak to me.

It started to rain, so we went back inside.

For hours we listened to debates on sugar beets, the price of milk, and the breeding qualities of different types of livestock. There were very few people around the walls, most being on chairs in the middle of the floor.

Eventually, there was a bustle at the door and the premier entered, accompanied by Tom and several RCMP officers. I was again struck by his handsome appearance: very tall, very upright and very black. I took undeserved pride in his being my friend.

As always he spoke extremely well, barely even using scribbled notes, and was surprisingly eloquent on the problems of the land.

Early on in his speech, there was a kind of cracking sound and some commotion from the side of the gym. Instantly, the black garbed men leapt on a poor woman who was merely closing her umbrella. Indignantly, she brushed herself off.

The men made no attempt to apologize for their mistake and imperiously moved away.

"I'm so sorry, Madam," Wendell called out from the dais. "These guys are here to protect me. That's why I have to wear this monstrosity,"

Here he opened his jacket to reveal the bullet-proof vest. "Hideous, isn't it? They're just doing their job. I hope you will forgive them."

"That's alright, Premier," the woman replied. "It's nice to know there's at least one gentleman here."

The speech concluded, he received a warm reception and was soon hustled out of the building and into his car.

"So, that's that," said Patrick. "The bastard is still keeping us guessing."

26

After the fruitless episode at Bible Hill, I dropped Patrick off at H-Division and drove on to Grand Pre. I missed Rosalie, and told myself I would be very glad when the Vindex affair was concluded, hopefully by catching him before he could do any damage.

I was late getting in, so I tip-toed upstairs and slid into bed, where my wife was sleeping. I drifted off to sleep and had recurring dreams about the woman with the umbrella being pounced on and mauled by Herringbone's gorillas.

Despite being dog-tired, I was up and about early the next morning. I had to call Walter Bryson to see if there were any developments in the Father Mike affair, but it was too early to because he would still be in bed, so I decided to put in a call to Robson Callister, as the UK was four hours in advance of us.

Dolly answered the phone and, after we exchanged pleasantries, I heard her bellowing up the stairs for Robbie, followed by his heavy footfalls on the creaky staircase.

"Hello, old chap. This is a pleasant surprise. What can I do you for?"

I explained everything that had happened since I last saw him. He asked me to repeat a number of things I said, and when I had finished, I heard him take a large breath, followed by a sigh.

"So, again, what can I do you for?"

"I need your advice."

"Is it free advice you want? If so, it's only fair to say that it might not be as sound as the advice you pay for."

"I'm sorry, I hadn't thought. I'll only keep you for fifteen minutes. Shall we say fifty pounds?"

"How about a hundred?"

"Alright, a hundred. I want you to rack your brain for any small detail which might help me find Vindex and neutralize him."

"Alright, but I think I've told you pretty much all I know about the man. You know that I've never met him, and all my info comes second-hand?"

"Yes, I know that."

"Is there anything specific?"

"Yes, have you ever heard of an Ernest Maddingly in connection with Vindex?"

"No, I'm sure I haven't."

"Or his befriending any old man from Canada?"

"Sorry, no."

"Does he have an MO—modus operandi—when embarking on his escapades?"

"Only that he's an ex-SAS man and is physically equipped for tough action."

"Do you think you might be able to get more info out of Marga? We'll pay, of course."

"I would, but she hasn't been around lately. I haven't seen her at the usual haunts. She may be sick."

"When you do run into her next, could you do a little fishing?"

"Will do, old chap. Similar sort of fee if I do?"

"Yes, of course. Can you give me an idea whether Vindex is so fanatical that he wouldn't mind getting caught if he had achieved his goal?"

"You mean, 'go down with the ship' sort of thing?"

"Yes."

"I can't be sure, but until recently I would have said he would be committed to doing the deed—whatever it was—but only if he had a reasonable assurance of getting away with it."

"You said 'until recently'. What's changed?"

"Well, from what I hear, he's becoming more loony lately. You know, gone off the deep end. If that's true, it might mean he's more reckless,"

"More willing to take chances?"

"Precisely."

"Thank you Robbie. You'll let me know as soon as you get anything else?"

"Will do, old chap. Keep your pecker up."

I wasn't at all sure if the information I got from Robbie carried a hundred pounds' value, but I liked talking to him, and something might conceivably come of it. On that score, I had no authority to incur expenses of that nature on behalf of the province, so I would pay Robbie privately. It might be worth it, and I could easily afford it.

Then the phone rang. It was Robbie.

"I say, old chap, I completely forgot the most important piece of info of all. Dolly says I am entering my dotage. She says I'd forget my noggin if it wasn't screwed on."

"Most important? What is it?"

"The chap's name. I found out Vindex's real name."

"That's fantastic. What is it?"

"William Howard Cummings."

"Date of birth?"

"That's all I have, sorry."

"Okay, thanks very much, Robbie."

"TTFN."

"TTFN?"

"Ta Ta For Now."

Immediately, I called Patrick to pass on the information about Vindex's identity. He said it would be widely circulated, but that it might not do much good because we still did not know what he looked like. He said he would have the airlines check to see if any passengers travelled under the name Cummings, but said that if Vindex had access to forged documents, he could have used an alias.

Then I called Walter Bryson. I caught him while he was shaving, so he said he would call me back.

While I was waiting I scoured the fridge to see what could be procured for breakfast, and found some bacon and lambs' kidneys. With a very sharp knife I cut each kidney in half, carefully removed the renal veins, arteries and pelves, and then set them aside. Then I put the bacon in the pan, knowing that as soon as it started to cook, Rosalie would magically wake up and come down.

She did, just as the phone rang. I turned the stove down and sat in the window.

"Walter?"

"Yeah. How are you, Marc?"

"Not bad. What news of Father Mike?"

"All good. The prosecutor has agreed not to prefer charges. After hearing Jennifer and Tracey's version of events, apparently he confronted Catherine Morton, who broke down and confessed that it was all a big lie."

"That's good. Thanks for your help, Walter."

"No worries."

I held and kissed my lovely wife, then, while I was cooking the breakfast, told her everything which had transpired.

While I was frying the kidneys, Rosalie heated some croissants and made some Kopi Luwak coffee. This latter, from the Tagalog region of the Philippines, was a particular favourite of mine and was guaranteed to put me in a good mood. Or so I thought.

While we were finishing up breakfast, we heard a key in the door, and in walked Mrs Bezanson for her weekly cleaning.

"Morning Mrs. LeBlanc," she called. "You're back, are you, Mr. LeBlanc? Lord knows what you get up to in that old Halifax. Chasing women, I shouldn't wonder."

"Mrs. Bezanson!" Rosalie was sharp with her. "That's is entirely un-called for. Please go about your chores."

"Alright, alright, there's no need for you to lose your rag."

"As a matter of fact, I'm glad to be here when you arrived, Mrs. B," I said. "I guess you've heard that the charges against Father Michael have been dropped?"

"I have. It's a scandal. The mucky-mucks are sticking together again!"

"Not at all, Mrs. B. The girl confessed to the prosecutor that she lied."

"Brow-beaten into it no doubt."

"No, it was confirmed by Catherine's two friends."

"Friends! Traitors, more like!"

"Mrs. Bezanson." I was getting seriously annoyed with the woman. "Can you not see, and admit, that your prejudices have been laid bare and proven incorrect?"

"I know what I know," she said in a surly fashion. "And I know that there priest interfered with an innocent young girl."

At that moment the phone rang. It was Father Mike.

"Marc, you know the charges have been dropped?"

"Yes, Walter told me. It's great news."

"I wanted to thank you and Rosalie for everything you have done for me."

"Don't mention it, Father. I have someone here who wants to talk to you. Hold on a moment please..." I turned to Mrs. Bezanson and smiled. "Mrs. B., I have Father Michael on the line. He'd like to hear why you still think he's guilty."

Mrs. Bezanson cowered like a frightened rat, squirming this way and that. "No. I won't speak to a pedolophile!"

"Do you mean pedophile?"

"Tell him I will not speak to a servant of Rome!"

"It's no good, Father Mike. Mrs. Bezanson is too shy," I said with con-siderable satisfaction. "Anyway, congratulations. You must come round for dinner tonight. Come about six-thirty."

"It's disgraceful for you to be maligning yourselves with such a sinner!" shouted Mrs. Bezanson.

"Have you any evidence to support your assertions?" Rosalie demanded.

"I know what I know," Mrs Bezanson repeated.

"Mrs. Bezanson!" My temper was at boiling point. "Come here!"

The woman was quaking in her shoes and shuffled towards me. I pulled out a fifty dollar bill and thrust it into her hand.

"Now get the fuck out of here before I kick you all the way to Main Street. And don't ever come back!"

She scurried out, throwing her key to our house on the table as she went. We watched her scrambling into her ramshackle car and disappearing down the lane.

"Well done, you!" Rosalie said.

"Thank you."

"Just one thing, Marc."

"What's that?"

"You'll have to do the cleaning until we find someone else."

27

Father Mike arrived a little earlier than expected, but that was not a problem because he was not one to stand on ceremony, and we left him happily leafing through a magazine while Rosalie and I were preparing dinner. He asked for a beer and I have him a glass of Schorschbock 57.

We planned to start with my shrimp soup (which Rosalie teases me by calling *soupe de crevettes aux légumes finement coupés*), which I made with small cooked shrimp, onions, carrots, celery, tomato, fish stock, and sherry. First I sliced the vegetables as finely as possible and put them to sweat in a large pot with olive oil and butter. It is surprising how much flavour can be obtained from such simple ingredients if they are reduced to tiny slivers first.

When the vegetables were soft, I added the stock and three tablespoons of Tio Pepe dry *fino* sherry, together with a teaspoon of minced garlic, a handful each of chopped parsley and dill, salt and pepper to taste, and one spoonful of curry powder. I then let it simmer gently for about twenty minutes.

Only at the very last minute did I put in 300 grams of shrimp and then served right away.

For our main course we were serving ham with scalloped potatoes (again, Rosalie's sense of humour dubs it *Jambon aux pommes de terre gratinées*), but with some serious differences from the regular way the dish is made.

The skipper of a Spanish ship which occasionally puts into Nova Scotia ports smuggles in for me *jamon Iberico de bellota*, a gorgeous ham from acorn-fed pigs in the high mountain meadows of western and southwestern Spain along the Portuguese border, and in parts of Andalucía. Because of the methods used in its curing and because Spain does not have any slaughterhouses which conform to North American regulations, it is illegal to import it into Canada or the United States. But the taste is incomparable, especially when I gently heat it up in a weak solution of water, white wine, brown sugar, nutmeg and clove before carving.

For the accompaniment, I thinly slice Yukon Gold potatoes, onions, mushrooms, carrots, season liberally then add butter and half a cup of heavy cream. Sometimes I grate Parmigiano cheese on top. This I bake for about 40 minutes until the top is golden brown and bubbling.

For dessert, Rosalie was making her justly-famous Almond Galette, a dish which looks like nothing, but tastes like heaven. Because this is another or her family secrets, I do not have the exact amounts, but she mixes a lot of ground almonds, a lot of butter, plenty of sugar, some flour and masses of egg yolks, and bakes it at a moderate temperature until you can stick in a knife and pull it out cleanly.

All courses were a great hit with Father Mike, who confessed to us that he seldom had a decent meal as neither he nor Abbé Mystère, his landlord, could boil an egg properly. They ate mainly prepared foods or the contents of cans. He also said they almost never had wine, and then only the Abbe's favourite Mateus Rose, a cheap Portuguese wine I loathed.

I decided to serve a *Chateau Fouisse* 2016 with the soup and a hearty *Mayacamus* Cabernet Sauvignon 2000 with the main course. I thought the dessert would be too rich and sweet for any but the top wines, so decided to forgo it and have coffee with our last course.

We described Mrs. Bezanson's extraordinary intransigence to Father Mike, and my less than rational response to it.

"Marc, I wouldn't want to be the cause of Mrs. Bezanson losing her job. Couldn't you relent and offer to take her back?"

"I doubt she would come even if we did," Rosalie said. "And, quite frankly, Michael, I wouldn't want Marc to do it. I was absolutely furious with her."

"It is not as if her opinion has been formed by the passage of time and the unfolding of events," I said. "She had her mind made up from the very beginning. As soon as the alleged incident was known, she said, 'I know what I know,' when it was clear that she knew nothing."

"I think the Bezansons are not Catholics."

"No, Baptists."

"That might have something to do with it, although I suspect it had more to do with all the publicity about priests and young boys."

"Maybe, but it was my impression that—as old as she is—it was more about her idea of feminism."

"Ah," Father Mike said. "All men are rapists. Women must be believed.

170

That sort of thing."

"Exactly that sort of thing."

"You know, Mrs. Bezanson is almost an exemplar for our times," said Rosalie. "People seem to be rigidly wedded to certain beliefs on a variety of topics these days."

"And moreover, they are wedded to those opinions from an early age, or from the origin of the issue," said Father Mike. "I guess we are all guilty of this to some extent, but there are so many now who not only fervently believe a certain thing but do not want to hear any argument to the contrary."

"Yes, we found that when we were over in England recently."

"You were in England? I didn't know. Business or pleasure?"

"It's a very long story, Michael. We'll tell you about it some other time."

"Alright."

"The point is that we were in contact with some environmentalists who, I'm sure, would have physically attacked us if we disagreed with them. They actually tried to beat us up at one pub we went to."

"No! Did they catch you?"

"No, we ran away and hid," said Rosalie.

"Good thing!"

"Yes, nasty brutes," I said. "It was not only the glazing-over of the eyes as they chanted their mantra 'wind, solar, earth's temperatures, rising sea levels, extinct species, *et cetera, et cetera*', but the sheer viciousness they displayed when speaking of those they deemed to be responsible for these alleged crimes."

"Alas, some people—a good many, I fear—firmly, devoutly, hold opinions even when they are completely contrary to the facts." Father Mike frowned. "A case in point is Israel. A very sad case in point."

"Yes, our friend Rachel Bland has educated us on that subject. Do you know her?"

"No. I've heard of her, but we've not met."

"Well, before I met her, I was utterly convinced I knew the whole history of the Middle East and had formed fast and solid opinions based on that understanding."

"She disabused you?"

"I'll say so! She showed me that my opinions were based on nothing but lies and propaganda. To a large extent, what I believed to be true was exactly the reverse of the truth."

"Anti-Semitism is rife," said Rosalie, "although nobody who isn't a Jew wants to admit it."

"Yes, indeed," said Father Mike, "We can never forgive the Jews for the Holocaust."

"That's an extraordinary thing to say."

"Well, think about it. Gentiles are furious with the Jews for being so persecuted that they made us feel guilty. That makes us uncomfortable, not to mention irritable, in our skins. So we have to come up with reasons why we shouldn't feel guilty. So some say it never really happened. Some say it may have happened but wasn't as bad as reported. Some say the Jews could have prevented it if only they had stood up for themselves. Others say the Jews deserved it because they are strange-looking people with weird customs. Still others say they had it coming because they committed horrific crimes throughout history, such as stealing babies. And some point to totally fictitious books like *The Protocols of the Elders of Zion* to 'prove' their bigotry."

"Do you think that is why, after last year's brutal, obscene, inhumane massacre by Hamas, the world's emphasis switched within twenty-four hours to pitying the 'poor Palestinians', most of whom voted for and still support Hamas?"

"Undoubtedly. We can't allow ourselves to be suckered again into feeling guilty, not even by babies being roasted in ovens, fetuses being ripped from mothers' bellies and children being beheaded."

"It also has to do with the so-called 'progressives' having been invested in the Palestinian mythology for so long," Rosalie said. "To admit that nothing under the sun could justify or mitigate the loathsomeness of the massacre would be to admit their beliefs have been founded on lies."

"The phenomenon we have been describing also explains Trump Derangement Syndrome," said Father Mike, "where a personal dislike has been conflated with absolutely every thought, action, policy, opinion or intent of the man. This has escalated to the point where his opponents are pathologically incapable of allowing him to possess any qualities which are not utterly diabolical and demonic."

"I never thought of that," said Rosalie. "Would you like some more coffee, Michael, or a glass of Cognac?"

"No thanks. I must be off. Thank you both for a splendid meal."

"And thank you, Father Mike, for a stimulating conversation."

28

The next day I had to go back to Halifax for the opening of the Legislature. The premier had prorogued the previous session, which meant that there would be a fresh session starting today with a new Speech from the Throne. This entailed quite a bit of hoopla, fanfare and tradition, with the Lieutenant Governor wearing a cocked hat and a special uniform dripping with gold braid.

Today the Lieutenant Governor was accompanied by his aide de camp, a military guard of honour, a band and a flag party. On arrival, he stood on a saluting platform on the steps of Province House.

The band played the Royal Salute, whereupon a 15-gun salute fired from Citadel Hill. The Lieutenant Governor then inspected the band and entered Province House through a guard of honour formed by the official escort.

Meanwhile, inside the legislature chamber, MLAs took their allocated seats. The Supreme Court justices had a special block of seats between the government and opposition benches.

The trumpet sounded and the Sergeant-at-Arms shouted, "Mr. Speaker, the Lieutenant Governor is without!"

He came in and was escorted to the Speaker's chair, where he read the Speech from the Throne, which was a general outline of the government's proposed business. Then the Governor left the chair and tramped out with his honour guard and ADC.

I have outlined all this to indicate what an absolute nightmare it was for the Security Services, the RCMP and the Halifax Police. The extra people crowded into the ancient building, and the comings and goings, rendered perfect security impossible. With all the commotion taking place, and provided he was equipped with a non-metallic, plastic gun made on a 3D printer, Vindex could easily get in to execute the deed.

All manner of fanciful scenarios flew through my mind. Could the assassin have had plastic surgery to now resemble a Supreme Court judge?

If so he would have a perfect shot at the premier, only a matter of feet away. Could he somehow have contrived to be a member of the band? Maybe he could hide his face behind a tuba? Maybe his trumpet had a propelled poisoned dart hidden inside.

So, in this state of excited expectation, Patrick and I joined about 25 RCMP and Halifax police officers in patrolling the halls and galleries of Province House, on the lookout for any suspicious activities. In the crush I did not see Herringbone and Librarian, but had no doubt they were ensconced somewhere in the building.

Then the debate on the Speech from the Throne began. A government member moved what is called the Address in Reply to the Speech from the Throne, in which she described the government's plans as heralding a new Utopia. Another government member then got up and said the province would soon be an absolute paradise.

The Leader of the Opposition jumped up a delivered a few impromptu remarks and adjourned the debate. Then the House rose and Members and spectators scrambled out in a mad rush.

During all this time, Patrick and I constantly roved around, closely examining all persons in the gallery passages and, as far as we could, every person crammed into the gallery benches. Only once did we see anything out of the ordinary, when Wendell's head suddenly jerked back on its shoulders. We thought he had been hit by some projectile, but to our great relief he was only sneezing.

Apart from that incident, there was nothing; no person mysteriously reaching to an inside pocket, nobody bending down to extract a weapon from a sock, no one taking off a steel-brimmed hat to hurl at the premier, no lady strangely pointing a bulky handbag. And, except for his sneezing fit, Wendell sat upright throughout it all, dignified and showing not the slightest sign of fear.

Patrick and I walked out to the parking lot, to where I had been required to move the Bugatti to make space for the Lieutenant Governor's band and honour guard. We leaned against the car and breathed easily for the first time that day.

"We may have underestimated this bastard," said Patrick grimly. "He's still got us guessing."

"Maybe we haven't been thinking outside the box."

"How do you mean?"

"We've been thinking of the obvious opportunities he might have for an attack."

"You mean public events?""

"Precisely. Perhaps we should be strengthening his protection at home. Do more thorough checks on his car to make sure there isn't a bomb underneath. Stop him from walking in the street. That sort of thing."

"You could be right. I'll pass this along to the Chief and to your pal, Herringbone."

"He's no pal of mine!"

"Nor anyone else, as far as I know."

"What should you and I be doing next?" I asked.

"For a few days, anyway, I think we should continue our watch in the Legislature. The guard will be reduced there after today, so it might not be a bad idea."

"Okay. What time does the House sit tomorrow?"

"One in the afternoon," Patrick read from the Order Paper.

"Until when?"

"Ten o'clock."

"Ugh. I don't fancy listening to all that stuff for nine hours."

"We do it for King and Country!"

"What's on the agenda?"

"It shouldn't be too bad. First up is the Leader of the Opposition replying to the Throne Speech, then the Premier gives his speech."

"That should be good. As you know, he's an excellent speaker."

"So I gathered from our useless journey to Bible Hill."

"If you come back to his place with me after the House rises, you might get to meet Wendell at close quarters. He's a really nice guy."

"I'd like that. You sure he wouldn't mind?"

"I don't see why. Sometimes his house is like a marketplace."

"Right. Let's go get a bite to eat. Where do you recommend?"

"Let's stroll up to Gio at the Prince George. They usually make good food."

Patrick and I enjoyed a leisurely dinner, he having the shrimp and snow crab starter, while I went for half a dozen oysters.

Then he chose the Arctic Char, Almonds, Green Beans, Spruce Beurre Blanc. I had the seared Scallops, Kataifa Shrimp, Farro, Seasonal Vegetables and Sea Parsley Chimichurri. Since we felt some degree of accomplishment at having come this far without Vindex striking, we ordered a bottle of Veuve Clicquot Ponsardin Brut. Tonight we could relax, but we both knew it might be the calm before the storm. The problem was that we had idea when the storm would arrive.

29

I woke about four the next morning in a cold sweat. I had been haunted by dreams of Vindex assuming a protean quality and coming at me from different directions. There were crowds of people, all looking exactly alike, and suddenly he would leap out, throwing off his disguise and screaming in my face.

Another dream had Wendell walking along, being joined by many others who looked exactly like him, and then one of the Wendells tore off his mask and lobbed a bomb at the premier, which I caught, but then I lost my arm in the explosion.

Rosalie not being with me gave rise to yet another nightmare, even more frightening because it seemed more probable, which had Vindex going to our home in Grand Pre and tearing Rosalie limb from limb.

Knowing that further sleep was impossible, I tiptoed downstairs, only to find the premier poring over a mass of documents which were strewn over the kitchen table. He looked up and grinned.

"Your friend Patrick is an interesting guy. I'm glad I met him close up."

"I wasn't sure if it would be alright to bring him back last night, but he was keen to meet you."

"Not a problem. I've seen him several times at meetings, of course, but if he's in charge of the investigation, I should have spent some face time with him before."

"I've known him for a few years now. I first met him when my father was murdered—"

"Your old man was murdered? I didn't know that."

"Yes, it's a long story."

"Did they get the killer?"

"No. He's safely hidden in Russia."

"Too bad. I guess there's no way you can get at him there?"

"Not legally."

"Tough."

"Anyway, when I first met Patrick, he was a sergeant with the City Police, and now he's a superintendent."

"Remarkable progress in such a short time. The Mounties must think highly of him."

"I guess they must. I know I do."

"Any progress on my case?"

"Insofar as we have eliminated a number of possibilities when Vindex could strike, you could say that, but we have no idea when he might try in the future."

"Not very encouraging."

"I want to talk to you about today, because Patrick and I think he might try to get to you while you are giving your speech."

"You thought he would strike yesterday."

"That's the point. Every day must be viewed as a potential target day."

"Well, I guess I must trust that you guys know what you're doing. I can't change my entire character and habits because some lunatic is out there. I have to rely on my protection."

"The guard will be less today because—"

"Less! What the fuck!"

"That level of protection can't be maintained indefinitely. Yesterday the cops also had to consider the safety of the Lieutenant Governor, and they needed that amount of manpower because there was so much going on and so many people milling about."

"Yeah, I guess I can see that. You'll be there today."

"Certainly, I wouldn't miss your speech."

"Huh. Where will you be?"

"Patrick and I will probably be roaming at the back of the galleries. If we pick a spot to settle, it'll be in the Speaker's Gallery."

"That way you can see everything in both the east and west galleries?"

"Exactly. And if—God forbid—something should happen, we'd be in the best position to catch the guy when he tries to escape."

"Yeah, you go catch the guy. Don't worry about me. I'll be lying there in a pool of blood!"

"Glad to see you haven't lost your sense of humour, Wendell."

"You'll be seeing more of that, Marc. Guess what the title of my speech is."

"'These Stirring Times'?"

"No, 'We Must Not Live in Fear'." He roared with laughter.

I told Wendell to call Jack and say he didn't need the car, and that I would drive him downtown in the Bugatti.

His six feet three inches did not fit easily into the passenger seat, but he seemed to get a kick out of sitting in what was until recently the fastest road model in the world.

"Is there somewhere you can take her where I can feel her at high speed?"

"I guess so. Do you have time?"

"Sure, it's only 5:35. There won't be cops around at this hour. And if there are, I'll take my chances."

"I intoned a fake headline: 'Premier arrested as accessory in reckless breaking of speed limit'."

"Let's hope not." Wendell laughed. "Get going!"

We went over the bridge to the 102, and drove as far as Elmsdale before turning back. At Wendell's repeated urging, I took the Bugatti to 160 kph, which produced not the slightest tremor or rattle. I resisted his wish to go faster because traffic was just starting to increase.

Later, when we pulled into Province House, he turned to me, grinning like a kid. "I haven't had that much fun since I won the leadership. Thanks, Marc."

"You're welcome. Don't get out yet. Wait until I am out and have a look around."

"Okay."

I summoned the policeman at the door and explained I had the premier in my car. He peered in and Wendell waved to him. He radioed and two more officers came out and scanned the area. Then they clustered around Wendell as he left the car and walked into the building.

The House did not meet until one, and I did not expect Patrick until after nine, so I went across with the premier and sat in Tom Aldridge's office, reading the paper.

When Susan arrived I went to her desk, regaling her with accounts of my previous two cases, *Holy Grail, Sacred Blood* and *Unspeakable Evil* both of which are now published. It may have been wishful thinking, but I got the impression that she now regarded me with more respect than before. Previously I had sometimes thought she saw me as a lightweight who had no business dealing with a threat against her beloved boss.

Tom arrived about 30 minutes later, so I went back into his office with him.

I could see that the last few weeks had aged him badly. Whereas Wendell did not seem to have been unduly bothered by the situation, and often made a joke of it, Tom was lined, rather grey, and now looked fully fifty. His job was a thankless task, as he was regularly expected to accomplish the impossible, mediate between squabbling ministers, and take the blame when things went wrong.

Everything Tom did, everything he ordered, was in the premier's name, but it was always done in such a way that if things did not work out as the premier anticipated, or too many people were offended, Wendell could escape responsibility by saying that Tom had misunderstood his instructions.

Seeing him like this, I was very glad he had a wife like Heidi, whose love for him was boundless and unconditional. I had no doubt she would see him through this rough patch, no matter how long it lasted. I also thanked my lucky stars that I had a similarly devoted wife in Rosalie.

"So, what do you think?" Tom asked, running his hands over his face. "Is the boss going to get killed, or what?"

"Not if I have anything to do with it. The problem is we don't know what Vindex looks like."

"Can't we ask the British Army to go through their graduates at SAS HQ in Hereford?"

"How could they? There must be dozens and dozens of former SAS soldiers in the world. How would the Brits know which of them had gone looney?"

"I guess so." Tom put his head in his hands. "I couldn't bear it if anything happened to Wendell. He's not only my boss, he's my best friend."

"I know."

"Do you have any special measures in place?"

"Like what?"

"I don't know. Measures to anticipate what the attacker might do."

"But we have no idea what that might be or where he might decide to strike."

"No further word from Callister? God knows we're paying him enough!"

"No. Nothing. Besides, what could he really provide which would be of any use to us, other than a photograph?"

"I guess you're right. I have to go into the boss now. Check with me later."

I was left alone in Tom's office, feeling lonely and useless, and wishing I was back with Rosalie at home or with Louise at the wine store.

Shortly, Susan came and told me that Patrick had arrived. There was not much either of us could do except constantly patrol the area, looking for weaknesses in security.

At 12.45 we duly took up our positions in the galleries of Province

House, Patrick in the east gallery and I in the west. There were also two police officers in each gallery, one in the Speaker's Gallery, and two legislature pages.

After the Orders of the Day had been read, the clerk called for Government motions, and the Address in Reply to the Speech from the Throne.

The Leader of the Opposition got up and continued the speech he had started the day before. In view of the situation, he was wise to give a somewhat circumspect speech in which he commiserated with the government for the inconvenience caused by the heightened security, even though he said he did not personally know what had given rise to it.

When Wendell rose to speak, he surprised everyone, first by taking the House into his confidence and explaining that the increased police presence was occasioned by the fact that he was under threat of assassination. Then he surprised everyone further by taking an entirely jocular approach, cracking jokes and delivering funny one-liners. He had the House in the palm of his hand, the Opposition benches laughing and applauding as much as his own troops.

That day I felt proud to know him as a friend, so impressive was his performance. I doubt many could have done as well with a sentence of death hanging over them.

Contrary to expectations, there were relatively few visitors in the galleries, so it was not difficult to keep them all under surveillance. But nothing untoward occurred. Not a twitch, not a stretch, not an expression out of place. Nobody looked in the slightest degree suspicious.

Eventually, the House rose, the occupants fanned out to their homes and offices, and the police and commissionaires locked the place down for the night.

30

The next day was very much like the day before. Patrick and I maintained our watch over the Legislature's proceedings, but found we were invigilating an even smaller crowd in the galleries. The police presence, now reduced to three upstairs, seemed so bored as to be on the verge of sleep.

The premier was in his seat for Question Period, but left after an hour to go to his office, and did not return.

Patrick and I, bored to tears, wandered into a bar and ordered drinks.

"I'm thinking you were correct," he said. "We have to think outside the box."

"We need to find the most unlikely place and unlikely time for an assassination attempt."

"What are the possibilities? Number one, his car. That can be dealt with by increased inspections. The bomb squad will have to check it out every time he gets into it. No exceptions."

"Right. Number two would be while he's in his office. Is that covered?"

"We've two officers there now. One up, one down. I guess if the building was rushed, the guy downstairs could be overcome. But then the attacker would have to come up in the elevator. I'll get the downstairs guard doubled. Does he leave the office to take a piss?"

"No, he has his own bathroom in the office."

"Good."

"How about the fire escape?"

"I'll get that looked into right away. I'm sure we already got it covered. Whatever it is, I'll double it."

He took out his phone and gave instructions. "That's done. What next?"

"While he's sleeping," I said. "Not that he gets a lot of sleep."

"How come? Nightmares?"

"No, the guy is always working. Yesterday I came down round four and he was already beavering away at his papers."

"We've got a car with two officers outside the front of the house at all times, and another on the street behind, because his garden can be accessed via a small door in the wall. What else could we do?"

"For God's sake don't put officers inside the house," I said. "Both he and Cynthia would hate that. So would I, for that matter."

"We may not be able to avoid it, Marc. Maybe only one."

"Good luck telling him about that."

"We've put a stop to his walking anywhere, apart from going from the car to the house or office. Is there any way we can cut down that distance?"

"I don't see how. It's already only a few feet."

"Yeah, I guess so. That covers all the bases. Let's get something to eat. Where do you want to go?"

"I fancy seafood with fries. How about MacKelvie's?"

"Sure."

"Will we still do the routine at the Legislature?"

"Yes, for a few days, anyway."

"That was too obvious all along."

"Yeah. We should have known he wouldn't make it that easy for us."

31

The next day, being a Friday, the Legislature would be convening at nine in the morning and rising at 2 pm in order to let the MLAs get home in good time for the weekend. This time-honoured custom had been restored by Wendell Proctor after having been breached in recent years by ruthless and inconsiderate premiers, who believed that a legislative session was an inconvenience which had to be got through as quickly as possible. To that end they often had the House sitting from nine in the morning until midnight, which not only meant that the Members had no time to take calls from constituents and go to various departments with constituents' problems, but also that they were beaten into submission by sheer exhaustion and boredom.

Wearily patrolling the galleries for the fourth day, Patrick and I found our task more than a little tedious, as did the two police officers, judging by their yawns. The police presence had now been reduced to two in the galleries, one at the west door, and two at the main entrance.

This was in addition to several commissionaires who conducted the electronic searches and admitted people through a carefully channelled system. Now everyone, including staff, had to undergo the checks on entering. Only the city police and the MLAs had free access, even Patrick and I having to be treated like members of the public.

"Where are Herringbone and Librarian? I haven't seen them for days," I asked Patrick. "Have they gone back to Ottawa?"

"No, they're doing the thinking. I have to report to them every night."

"You didn't tell me that. What kind of thinking are they doing?"

"Thinking at a level that you and I could not possibly comprehend."

"Huh. And have they come up with any answers which you and I have not already thought of?"

"Not that I have heard. They're holed up at the Muir Hotel."

"Not bad. The cheapest room there is $500 a night. I presume they are staying there at taxpayers' expense."

"Of course," said Patrick with obvious distaste. "If they come up with any bright ideas, I presume I shall be summoned and informed of their Excellencies' decisions."

An opposition backbencher was droning on about a constituency problem in which only the person directly concerned could be interested. A look around the Chamber told me that I was not alone in my utter boredom, because it appeared that nobody else was listening to him. Almost all of the Ministers were elsewhere, and the Members who remained in the House were on their laptops or surreptitiously reading newspapers or magazines.

"God, I am so tired," I said. "I can't wait to get back to Grand Pre."

"Wish I was going with you."

The House rose at 2 pm and, after saying goodbye to Patrick, I went out to the Bugatti and headed out.

I was overjoyed to be back on the open road and going home to see my lovely wife. She had told me that she had invited Walter and Joyce over for dinner, so that would make a nice change. So would the fact that Rosalie would be doing all the cooking and wine selection. All I would have to do would be to shower and relax.

The Bugatti was gently roaring along, overtaking all vehicles with ease and eating up the miles. For the first time in weeks, my mind was not on Vindex and the assassination plot, if indeed it existed, but instead on the wonderful rows of grapes in the *Romanee Conti* vineyards in the *Côtes des Nuits* in Burgundy.

My phone ringing startled me.

"Yes."

"Marc?"

It was Vindex! I cautiously pulled the car onto the shoulder of the road.

"You still up for the big one?"

"Yes."

"I suppose you've been aware of some of my antics?"

"Yes."

"What do you think?"

"Daring."

"Haha! I've got one more up my sleeve before the main deal."

"What is it?"

"Marc, Marc, Marc. You should know better than that by now."

"Yes, of course."

"Now, listen carefully. You know Spring Garden Road, where the entrance to the Public Gardens is?"

"Yes, of course."

"Be there next Monday."

"Is that this coming Monday?"

"Yes, dopey, of course it is."

"What time should I be there?"

"I don't know. But be in the near vicinity all day."

"All day?"

"Why? You have better things to do?"

"No."

"Okay. Say from about ten in the morning till midnight. Be somewhere so that you can pull up by that gate at a moment's notice."

"It won't be easy, but I'll try."

"You're going to have to do better than try." There was menace in his voice.

"Okay."

"What will you be driving?"

"A blue Bugatti." My mind was in a whirl. I could not think of anything else to say

"You're joking, right."

"No."

"Jesus. Well, that should get us away fast enough."

"Where will we be heading?"

"The airport."

"Okay, I'll have the quickest route worked out."

"Good lad. Be there. Be ready."

"It's happening."

"It's real."

I called Patrick immediately and told him what had happened.

"What the hell is on Spring Garden Road? Is the premier planning a visit to that area of the city?"

"Not that I've heard. I can call Tom and find out."

"And what did he mean when he said he had one more trick up his sleeve."

"I shudder to speculate."

"Okay, you call Aldridge and call me back."

~

"Aldridge."

"Tom, it's me, Marc."

"What's up Marc?"

"Is Wendell planning to be anywhere on Spring Garden Road on Monday?"

"Hell, no. He's got wall-to-wall meetings until the House sits at four. Then he'll be there and in his office, depending on how the Opposition is behaving."

"Will you be with him?"

"Can be."

"Okay. Tom, make sure both you and the police officers are with him when he crosses the street from office to House, and *vice versa*."

"Will do. Why? What's going on?"

"Just extra precautions until we've caught this bastard."

~

"Kennedy."

"Patrick, I just spoke to Tom. He says Wendell isn't going to be anywhere near Spring Garden Road on Monday."

"Then what the hell is Vindex playing at?"

"Don't know. Can't think what it could be."

"Son of a bitch! I'll have to report this to Herringbone and Librarian right away. Knowing them, they'll come up with orders we won't like."

"Let me know."

~

"Marc?"

"Yes. Patrick?"

"Yeah. I just spoke to Librarian. Herringbone wasn't available. Probably in the bar or having a shit."

"What did she say?"

"She says she'll have the location staked out. Forces will be concentrated in that general area."

"I guess that makes sense."

"One thing she said you're not going to like."

"What's that?"

"She said you're to stay well away from the location."

"But…."

"I know what you're thinking. You'll have to give the Bugatti to a designated cop to drive."

"Damn! What if he damages it?"

"It'll be your contribution to the public welfare. Have a nice weekend."

~

I pulled back onto the highway and drove on, possessed by agitated thoughts. I had visions of some ham-handed plod grinding the gears, having a heavily-booted foot on the accelerator, and misjudging braking distances. He would likely total the car, and when I tried to get compensated, the city would say it was the RCMP's problem, and they would tell me it was a matter of national security and could not discuss it. Since I did not know Herringbone's name, they could not refer the complaint to him, so I would be out in the cold and over a million dollars lighter.

I got to Grand Pre just before 4:30, trundled in, kissed Rosalie, and went up and stood in the shower for about twenty minutes, punching the walls, which I christened Herringbone and Librarian. My knuckles became red and sore but I felt better.

I put on fresh clothes and wandered downstairs to see what my wife had in store for dinner.

"What's the menu, my darling?"

"Hello, grumpy. Are you feeling better?"

"Somewhat. I'll tell you the whole story later. I'm afraid we're no further ahead."

"That's too bad. I thought we'd just have tomato soup and cheese on toast, followed by Ben and Jerry's vanilla."

My face fell. I had had a hell of a week and was really looking forward to something a little special tonight.

Rosalie looked at me seriously for a second, then burst into laughter. "Marc, you chump! You don't think I'd serve cheese on toast to guests? If it was just you, yes, but not guests."

She darted away to avoid the tea towel I was flicking at her.

"If you must know, sorehead, we are going to start with *Potage St. Germain* and then we're having *Melanzane alla parmigiana,* or eggplant parmesan."

"What, no meat?"

"Apparently Joyce is experimenting with vegetarianism."

"That will be an interesting conversation!"

"Now, Marc, be careful. I don't want you insulting her."

"No I won't insult her, but I will mention that two Nobel prize-winners have found that plants cry out in pain when they are harvested."

"Is that true?"

"Certainly it's true. And that for every plant we eat we are destroying or damaging the natural habitat of several species, including insects and worms."

"She won't care about worms."

"Why not? They're flesh, and they're God's creatures."

"So, what you're saying is that to live a principled life you have to die of starvation?"

"That's about the size of it. If you look at it logically, those who lecture us about what we eat on the grounds that we're taking life are a bunch of canting hypocrites."

"Now I'm certain I don't want you to say *anything* about vegetarianism while Joyce is here!"

"For you, my darling, I will keep *schtum*."

"Thank you. I've got some fresh mint to put in the *potage* with some heavy cream."

"Yum. Did you find fresh peas for the soup?"

"Yes, but they looked too old. Little frozen ones will be best. Will you blend them for me when they're cooked?"

"Sure. What will you put in the *Parmigiana*?"

"Sliced eggplant layered with different types of cheese and tomato sauce, then I bake it."

"Sounds lovely, despite there being no meat."

"I think I'll serve some lightly-toasted bread on the side, with some *rouille*. I'm making that by mixing breadcrumbs, garlic, saffron, roasted red peppers and mayo."

"That's daring. I've never seen those two served together."

"If Joyce is allowed to experiment, so am I."

"You are a treasure beyond compare, my angel. Experiment away!"

"I hear their car," said Rosalie. "Let them in and give them some drinks. And, Marc..."

"Yes, my love?"

"Absolutely *no* lectures about dietary hypocrisy!"

~

The evening started smoothly and stayed that way throughout. Rosalie had chosen the wines well: A nice, lively New Zealand Sauvignon Blanc with the *potage*, and a beautiful, rich *Barolo* from the 1996 vintage from Giacomo Fonterna.

Walter and Joyce were old friends, if you call three years' acquaintanceship old, and we always enjoyed their company. Right up front, Rosalie and I made it clear how grateful we were to him for helping Father Mike.

"That was a tricky one," said Walter. "I must admit that, at first, I thought you were barking up the wrong tree. I guess that was because I didn't want to believe anything dishonourable about my daughter."

"Walter!" Rosalie said. "Jennifer didn't do anything dishonourable. She was scared, and was torn between helping a friend and maybe hurting someone she didn't know."

"It's kind of you to put it that way," said Joyce, "but she's been brought up to tell the truth no matter who it hurts."

"She did the right thing in the end. That's what counts." I said.

"I'm glad it's over anyway," said Walter. "I guess you heard that the accuser, Catherine Morton, has moved away?"

"Gone to live with relatives in New Brunswick," Joyce added.

"No, I didn't know. We've both been away quite a bit in Halifax recently."

"Oh? I wondered where you'd got to. Any particular reason?"

Rosalie and I exchanged glances. We were not sure what we could safely say and what we could not. The Brysons looked at us pointedly.

After a good deal of hemming and hawing, we gave in and told them the whole story. They were stunned.

"I don't know what to say," said Joyce. "You've certainly become first-class sleuths since we met. I'm impressed."

"Me, too," said Walter. "But may I make an observation?"

"Certainly."

"Don't put all your eggs in one basket. This Vindex fellow may be on to you and may have given you a bum steer."

"To divert our attention?"

"Precisely," said Walter.

32

It was good to be home, to wake up in my own house and be able to go anywhere I pleased. I certainly was made very welcome at Wendell and Cynthia's, but I always feel a little awkward in somebody else's home.

After breakfast, I called Patrick to pass on what Walter had said, although I thought it better to tell him the notion had come from Rosalie.

"She has a point, now I think about it," Patrick said.

"What will you do about it?"

"If the Spring Garden Road contingency is a diversion, the difficulty comes in deciding what it's a diversion from: his home, his office, the Legislature, or something else."

"Yes, that's true enough. Will you at least pass it on to Herringbone and Librarian?"

"Sure. But since Vindex called you they have the bit between their teeth. They are gung-ho for Spring Garden Road. I don't know what they think he's going to do there."

"All we can do is suggest. And pass on ideas, which is what I've done."

"Yeah, thanks Marc. When will you be back in Halifax?"

"Monday morning. Is that Okay?"

"Yes, I guess so."

Then I drove into Wolfville to pick up some supplies. I found some lovely-looking lamb cutlets, some baby gem potatoes, a nice cauliflower and some Bermuda onions to make onion sauce with.

I thought we would have the cutlets tonight with a Chateau Palmer 1985. This wine, though powerful and velvety, with both complexity and elegance on the palate, was better known for its incredible perfume.

After that, I went to Herbin's on Main Street and bought a tasteful five-carat diamond bracelet for Rosalie because I loved her so much, and because I thought she deserved something special.

Then I had to see Louise at the wine store, to ask if she could acquire some rare, older Burgundies at auction for my personal use. As always,

she was obliging and efficient, and made meticulous notes on the proper-
ties and vintages in which I was interested and the prices I was prepared
to pay.

She told me business at the store was very brisk and she might have
to hire an assistant, for which she asked for my approval. I told her she
was almost an equal partner and did not need my consent. She was the
manager and had a free hand to do what she thought necessary.

I left more than ever convinced that starting the store was one of my
best decisions, and that choosing Louise as a partner was equally wise.

After I had seen Louise, I crossed the street to look in on Gerald at the
bookstore. He had become more eccentric since assuming ownership of
the shop, something I put down to his new-found security allowing him
to more freely express his sexuality. Always a little foppish, he was now
extravagantly effete, displaying a lot of silk and plenty of colour.

"Marc, how delightful to see you."

"How are things, Gerald?"

"Very good. Business is fine. It's all thanks to you. I will never be able
to tell you how much I appreciate what you did for me."

"It was my pleasure, Gerald. I just looked in to say hello, Must dash."

"Love to Rosalie," he said, blowing a kiss into the air.

~

We had an excellent meal that evening, and the Chateau Palmer was sub-
lime. I remembered being at the Chateau once when the owner had first
served the 1966, a renowned year, and then followed it with a wine
which we all thought was even better. Naturally, we figured it must have
been the legendary 1961, but it was revealed as the 1967.

That was an eye-opener for me, and taught me that bad wines can be
made in great years and very good ones produced in bad years.

For the first time in weeks I went to bed and slept soundly without
once dreaming of Vindex and his villainous plans.

33

On Sunday, Rosalie and I had a late, leisurely breakfast of warm croissants, yellow butter from Parson's farm, beautiful pink ham from Ben Wilson's pig, and fresh eggs from the lady next door.

Then we lazed around the house, following which we went out and wandered around the field and up the hill as far as the woods. From the top we could see the Acadian National Historic Site, Evangeline Beach, and Kingsport and, beyond that, Blomidon bathed in sunlight.

Both near and far, the air was filled with birds, which we attempted to identify. I had come to know a few species, but Rosalie was something of an amateur expert. Between us we managed to recognize herring gulls, black-backed gulls, a sandpiper, cormorants, guillemots, a northern gannet, a northern shoveler and, of course, the ubiquitous Canada geese.

We had breakfast so late, we decided to skip lunch, and to drive and see if we could find some fresh fish for dinner. Rosalie decided she would like to have bouillabaisse and that we would make it with whatever we could find.

In the event, we obtained some cod, halibut, lobster, tomatoes, fennel and onions, and thought that, using frozen tiger shrimp we had at home, we could fashion a delicious meal.

It was such a lovely day, we took our time going home, and drove slowly around, visiting the area's many beauty spots and stretching our legs frequently. We got back about four to the sound of the phone ringing.

In order to get some peace and quiet, I had not taken my mobile with me, so I opened the door and picked it up from the kitchen table.

"Where the fuck have you been?"

"Who is this?"

"Wendell. Who do you think it is? Where are you when you're needed?"

"I'm in Grand Pre."

"Grand Pre? What the hell are you doing down there when you should be up here?"

"Why? Has something happened?"

"You better believe something's happened. My sister's house was burgled this afternoon, and on his way out the bastard shot out the windows! In broad daylight, for God's sake!"

"Jesus! Grace's place?"

"Yeah, Grace and Mathew's. On Creighton Street."

"Was anybody hurt?"

"No, just shook up. Obviously, he intended them to know that he could have killed them if he wanted to."

"This was really a message to you, though."

"Yeah, that much was clear to me."

"What did he take?"

"A glass ornament of some kind. Grace collects them. The house is crawling with the things."

"Was it valuable?"

"Hell no. I think she paid something like $30 for it."

"The theft was symbolic. The whole exercise was to tell you that if he can get to your family, he can get to you."

"Brilliant deduction! Of course it was. I just called Kennedy. You'd better get back here."

"When?"

"Now! When do you think? Get up here and catch this son of a bitch fast! This cat and mouse game is starting to piss me off!"

I was annoyed to have to leave home again so soon, and especially because I would miss out on the Bouillabaisse. I would have to get something to eat in a restaurant in Halifax or, if I was lucky, might be in time for Cynthia's cooking Chez Proctor. As I was throwing my travel bag into the car, Patrick called.

"Big news, Marc. Bad news."

"I know. Wendell just called and ordered me back to base."

"Oh, right. Are you on the road now?"

"No, just starting out."

"Where shall I meet you?"

"At the Proctors'."

"Okay. See you in about an hour."

"Patrick, why don't you call Cynthia, tell her we're going to rendezvous at their place? If she invites us to Sunday dinner, say 'yes'."

"Good thinking. See you soon."

~

The drive along the 101 was even more boring and soulless than usual, and I headed back possessed by an ominous feeling that terrible events would soon occur, and that, more than ever, I was clueless and out of my depth.

Patrick had been successful in wangling a dinner invitation, so, soon after I arrived, we sat down to roast beef, horseradish, gravy and four vegetables. What was more, we were able to get the story first-hand from Matthew and Grace, who ate with us.

As usual, Grace did most of the talking. "I was upstairs making the bed. Lord knows where Matt was."

"I told you twice, I was in the bathroom, taking a—"

"When I heard these bangs going off. There were four of them—maybe five—*bang, bang, bang, bang*. Loud enough to wake the dead."

"Yeah, I thought maybe the boiler had blown or—"

"And when I got downstairs I saw we had no windows. They were all smashed, with glass lying everywhere."

"He must have shot them from the outside—"

"And when I looked at the wall, I seen the holes where the bullets went in. Matt, you're gonna have to put new wallpaper up right away. I can't be having my wall full of bullet holes!"

"I guess not—"

"And then when I went to pick up some of the ornaments that had been knocked over, that's when I seen that my hand-blown Bahamian fisherman was missing."

"So what now?" Wendell asked, clearly thinking that we had had enough of Grace's narrative. I am sure he thought she would dine out on this drama for weeks and her friends would all become tired of hearing it. He looked pointedly at Patrick, as if to suggest there was little point asking me.

"Premier, I wish I knew," Patrick said solemnly, putting down his fork. "I did get a bit of goodish news just before I came here."

"About time. Let's hear it."

"When we got Vindex's real name, my superiors applied to the Metropolitan Police in London to give us his picture. But, for reasons best known to themselves, the Department of Defence didn't reply."

"Why, for God's sake?"

"It later became clear that, when they contacted SAS Headquarters in Hereford, they met a flat refusal."

"So, what's the good news?"

"Eventually, the Minister of Defence became involved and finally SAS coughed up."

"Good. Do you have it with you?"

Patrick took a folder from his briefcase, extracted a photograph and handed it to Wendell, who studied it and then passed it to me. The photograph, which did not have the feel of being recent, showed a young man in the uniform of a captain, with a square jaw, grey eyes and a thin, set mouth. It was so undistinguished that it could have been any one of thousands of men.

"He doesn't look so scary," Wendell said.

"I wish that were true," said Patrick. "Of course, you realize, Premier, that we can distribute this widely, asking the public to call in if they have seen him, but it doesn't necessarily help us."

"Why do you say that?"

"If he's disguised in any way, this photograph is worthless. The only photograph which could help us is one we don't have."

"What's that?"

"His passport photograph."

34

The following morning we were summoned to another round-table meeting convened by Herringbone and Librarian. As before, it was held in the cabinet room, but this time the Halifax Regional Police chief and deputy chief, the premier, Patrick and I were joined by H-Division's boss, Chief Superintendent Roland Clarkson, Deputy Premier Joan Howard, and Justice Minister Angela Staples.

It was early for a meeting in government offices, being only just past six when it got started. Herringbone silenced the buzz by hitting his pen against his water glass, an action which cracked the vessel and allowed the liquid to run all over the table.

"Damn and blast!" he cried.

I looked around the table, noting that a number present were suppressing smiles. I was glad to observe that Patrick and I were not the only ones to dislike the great man from Ottawa.

"I guess you have all heard about the recent wrinkle," Herringbone spoke as if he were addressing a public meeting. "But for the benefit of those who have not, yesterday the house of the premier's sister and brother-in-law was broken into, an item was stolen, and shots were fired, breaking a number of windows. Does anyone not think it is reasonable to assume this was the work of Vindex?"

Many heads shook and some people muttered.

"I thought not. The problem this presents is that we must now deploy some resources to the house on Creighton Street, meaning that we have to take some away from other presumed target areas. It's not likely that Vindex would return to the same residence, but we cannot be sure, so we must allocate some, if minimal, manpower."

"It better not be too minimal," the premier butted in hastily. "If Grace doesn't see at least two cops and a cruiser outside the house, there'll be hell to pay."

"Yes, yes, of course," said Herringbone impatiently. "Chief, you'll take care of that?"

"Sure."

"Now, at the office here, we currently have...how many is it?"

"Four."

"Hmm. It was three, wasn't it?"

"Yes, but we added one to cover the fire escape," Patrick said.

"Yes, alright, alright. What about the legislature?"

"At one point we had seven, but lately that has been reduced to five. Plus Superintendent Kennedy and Mr. LeBlanc," the chief said.

"How are they deployed?"

"Two at the main entrance, one at the west door, which only MLAs can use, and one in each of the galleries."

"I see. Premier, will you be spending much time in the House over the next little while?"

"Sure. I have to attend Question Period and if there are any votes. I also need to show my face from time to time."

"Hmm. I propose that Kennedy and LeBlanc continue there, reduce to one at the east door and deploy the main contingent of our resources in the Spring Garden Road area."

There was general agreement to this, but I knew Patrick shared my reservations.

"May I speak?" I asked.

"What is it?" Herringbone barked.

"We know, or assume, Vindex will be at Spring Garden Road, sometime during the day..."

"Well?"

"But we don't know what he is planning to do before he goes there."

"I don't see that as being relevant," said Herringbone dismissively. "Chief, who'll be driving LeBlanc's Bugatti?"

"Sergeant Sullivan is the man we have chosen. Been on the force for 13 years."

"Is he familiar with the vehicle?"

"He will be. I'm sure he won't have a problem."

"It's not like ordinary cars," I said. "It has an 8 litre engine which has nearly 2,000 horsepower. If you're not used to it, it can easily get away from you. I really think I should be driving it."

"Out of the question," Herringbone snapped. "For all kinds of reasons, it has to be a police officer."

There was so much muttered agreement and nodding of heads that I knew it was senseless to continue to argue, so, with a glance at Patrick, I sat back in my seat and let them get on with it.

"Chief, what forces will be at Spring Garden?" asked Librarian, looking down her nose.

"Apart from Sullivan, we'll have three cars in the area, each with two men; two plain clothes officers on the street; and, of course, ourselves and yourselves. You have to understand that HRP is doing everything we can, but we still have to carry on with normal policing throughout our remit."

"Yes, yes, I'm sure we all understand that. Right. Let's get on with it." Herringbone rose, buttoning his jacket. "Meeting adjourned."

When we were outside, I turned to Patrick.

"I know, I know," he said. "Save your breath. When the bandwagon is rolling, all you can do is get out of the way."

"I'm not a policeman," I said, "but that all seemed a bit haphazard to me."

"They're all intimidated by Herringbone, and he isn't a cop."

"But he's RCMP."

"Yes, but he was seconded from CSIS."

"Oh, I didn't know that. What about Librarian? Is she a cop?"

"I think they came as a package deal."

We stood watching the traffic and groups of tourists meandering about the streets.

"So what now?" I said.

"Let's go over to the House and check it out in minute detail."

"For the twentieth time?"

"We may have overlooked something."

"And we have hours ahead of us, listening to those politicians ramble on."

"Yeah, but it may not be that bad. I gather the Premier is giving another speech today."

"Oh, good. At least he makes himself heard, which is more than some of them do. They mumble, or read their speeches, which is worse."

"It beats me how someone can run for politics and not be able to give a public speech in a half-decent fashion. You would have thought that would be the primary requisite."

"You would," I said. "And if they really knew and understood their constituents' problems, they should be able to speak without reading from a text."

"I noticed that the Premier just has a few notes scribbled on the back of an envelope. He refers to them from time to time, but other than that, he's completely spontaneous."

"So, that should be something to look forward to amid the dross."

We walked up Granville Street, down George and along Hollis and turned into the Legislature grounds, which were presided over by statues of Joseph Howe and a soldier from the Boer War.

The Bugatti, normally parked outside, was presumably at Police Headquarters, where Sergeant Sullivan was, no doubt mercilessly grinding its gears. In its place was a police cruiser, with another parked nearby.

We walked up the steps where so many famous (and infamous) Nova Scotians have trodden for over 200 years, and went into the security funnel. Even though Edgar, the senior commissionaire, greeted us by name, we still had to produce our IDs and go through the metal detector.

We stopped to talk at length with Robert and Wayne, the drivers of the police cars, who were the officers on duty at the main entrance; with Kevin, who was on guard at the west door; and with Cliff and Reid, who were in the galleries. They had heard our litany of precautions so many times, their eyes almost glazed over.

Yet again, we walked the hallways, lobbies, galleries and even the floor of the House, looking for—we were not even sure what—and eventually settled in the Speaker's gallery, awaiting the opening of the proceedings.

There were a few empty desks down on the floor, including the premier's, and the galleries were only about a quarter full. The Orders of the Day were read, then a government bill received its second reading.

It was introduced by Angela Staples and was an Act to amend the Judicature Act. As far as I could understand, the legislation was reorganizing the Family Courts, adding a judge, and tightening up the wording of some eight or nine sections. It was heavy stuff for laymen like us and we almost fell asleep as the MLAs who were lawyers droned on for hours.

I glanced at both galleries and noticed that Cliff and Reid were apparently as somnolent as we were, and one of the commissionaires also seemed to be half asleep.

The galleries were filling up on both sides. The back rows were almost full and there were people standing behind in the gangways. A group of a dozen women from the Speaker's constituency, bustling and muttering, filed into the seats behind and alongside Patrick and me.

About eight, to applause from the government benches and murmurs from the galleries, Wendell entered the chamber and took his seat. He looked handsome and dignified in a dark-blue, pinstripe suit, a dazzling-white shirt and a polka dot tie. He looked around then leaned over and whispered something to Joan Howard.

A vote on the Judicature Act took place and it was referred to the Law Amendments committee. Then Joan rose.

"Will you please call Bill number 17?"

"Bill 17, an Act to amend the Executive Council Act," intoned the clerk.

"The Honourable the Premier," the Speaker announced.

Wendell rose, explaining that the proposed legislation would clarify a situation in which the Government Chief Whip could also be a minister without portfolio. He spoke clearly but had a little trouble making himself heard above the loud heckling from the Opposition. Their cat calls only seemed to encourage him to respond in kind, so he raised his voice and, arms waving, laid into the opposite benches with taunts of hypocrisy and charges of deceit.

At one point he noticed that his water glass was empty, so reached over to Joan's desk to take hers.

That's when it happened. We saw Bill Marshall, who was sitting directly behind Wendell, collapse onto his desk and, half a split second later, we heard the shot.

It took a minute for what had occurred to register with Patrick and me, then, deducing that the shot must have come from the Opposition side, our eyes swept over the west gallery.

Seeing nothing, we knew the shooter had already left, so we tried to exit as fast as we could, but the women were in the way and valuable time was taken up by them moving into the aisle to let us through.

When we burst out on the landing we saw no one, so ran down the stairs.

"Anyone go out that door?" Patrick demanded of Kevin.

"No. Why?"

But we were moving on down the stairs.

"Anyone go past you?" he shouted at Robert and Wayne.

"No, Superintendent. Nobody."

We stood there in a daze. Then suddenly it hit me. I pulled out my phone and pressed Akerman's number.

"Hello."

"It's Marc LeBlanc. Remember the tunnel you told me about at Province House?"

"Yes."

"Who else knew about it?"

"Well, apart from me, the guys who had meetings in the adjacent room."

"Was Ernest Maddingly one of those guys?"

"Yes, he would have known."

"Thanks."

Quickly I turned to Wayne and Robert. "Anyone go down to the basement in the last five minutes?"

"Only one of Edgar's lot."

"A commissionaire?"

"Yeah."

"Edgar," I called out to where the metal detection unit was. "Any of your colleagues around here just now?"

"I guess, but I don't know him. I figured he was a new guy sent by the Corps."

"What is it, Marc?" Patrick asked. The policemen were crowding around us.

"The fucker got in and out by tunnel." I said. "Robert, get down to the basement, go through the door on the south side and at the far end there's a tunnel. Take Kevin and get after the shooter. You'll need flashlights if possible."

They looked at me as if I had two heads, and glanced at Patrick to confirm that I was not out of my mind.

"Go!" Patrick barked. "What do we do?"

"Wayne, take us down to the Provincial bank in your cruiser. Now!"

We rushed out and piled into the car.

I hauled out my phone. "Heidi?"

"Yes, is that you, Marc?"

"Yes. This is an emergency. I'm with the police. We're coming down and need to get into that tunnel right away."

"Right. Okay. I'll meet you by the front door."

In the few minutes we had, I explained to Patrick that, if we got into the bank's tunnel soon enough, we might be able to get to the main tunnel and confront Vindex on his way south from the Legislature.

Heidi was waiting for us and took us down to the lower level. She had a flashlight ready, but no protective clothing.

"We're going to get filthy," I said, "but it can't be helped. In we go!"

It was a lot darker, rougher and wetter than I remembered it. The going was so slow that I was sure we would be able to intercept Vindex before he reached the junction, but when we came out into the main tunnel we could hear his footfalls echoing to the south of us.

Behind us, to the north, we could hear Robert and Kevin scrambling along and could just see flickers from their flashlights.

We set off in pursuit of Vindex as fast as we could. After about fifteen minutes—it could have been longer—we came to another junction, one tunnel leading southwest and the other to the east.

"Which one?" Patrick asked, but I could not provide the answer.

Then I had an idea.

"Vindex, you bastard, we're going to nail you to the cross!" I bellowed at the top of my lungs.

As I hoped he would, he responded by firing off a round at us, which told us to take the easterly tunnel.

I quickly fashioned an arrow on the ground out of loose rocks to let Robert and Kevin know which way to go, then we set off again.

"Where d'you think this comes out?" Patrick wheezed as we struggled forward.

"Take a guess."

"Somewhere near Spring Garden Road?"

"First prize for you."

The tunnel began to climb upwards, becoming even harder to negotiate, and after what seemed like an eternity of our elbows being grazed and our lungs bursting, we came to a wider space with an opening directly above it.

"He's out," Patrick said. "The question is, has he left or is he lying in wait to kill us both?"

"We have no choice," I said. "I'll go first, and if he shoots me, you'll still be able to take your revenge."

"That's hilarious," said Patrick grimly. "You sure?"

"Yes."

I gingerly poked my nose into the fresh air, and through a mass of stems and foliage. Instantly I realized that the tunnel had come up in the Public Gardens, in the middle of a clump of rhododendron bushes some yards from the south gate.

I could just see Vindex moving out onto the grass. He was limping badly, suggesting he must have torn a muscle or sprained his ankle somewhere in the tunnel, and could barely drag himself across the ground.

Feeling Patrick right behind me, I climbed out and gave chase.

He was heading towards the south gate at such a painfully slow pace that I could have caught up with him, but knowing he was armed, I hung back, thinking the police trap would get him once he was out on the street.

As we approached the gate, I was astonished to see that Sergeant Sullivan had parked the Bugatti on the opposite side of the street. He was gunning the engine in order to attract Vindex's attention, which it did as soon as the latter staggered through the gate.

At that moment, the lights changed at South Park Street and, asVindex stumbled towards the Bugatti, a Number One bus smashed into him, sending his body flying several metres in the air.

There was a screech of brakes from the bus, and from the police vehicles which were madly converging on the site. Police were every-where and, as I approached Vindex, I saw the Chief, Herringbone and Librarian, pushing through the crowd.

Patrick and I got to Vindex first, turned him over and took a look. It was obvious he was dead, as half his face was missing and ribs were sticking out of his chest.

"Kennedy, LeBlanc, what the hell are you doing here?" said Herring-bone, sounding hurt that he was not first on the scene. "How did you get here?"

"Forward thinking, sir," said Patrick with a noticeable sneer. "And we had to come a lot further than you."

"But how did you get here?" The chief sounded flabbergasted.

"We came underground," I said.

35

The following night, Wendell took us out for a celebratory dinner in the private room at Gio. Rosalie came up from Grand Pre and Patrick brought his wife, Ruth.

Of course, Cynthia was there. So also were Tom and Heidi; Joan Howard and her husband, Harold Nickerson; Susan and her husband, Archie. Conspicuous by their absence were Herringbone and Librarian, whom we devoutly hoped were on their way back to Ottawa.

The food was excellent, the service pleasant and rather good wine flowed freely.

"Be upstanding," said Wendell. "I want you to raise your glasses to Patrick, Marc and Rosalie, who it would seem, may have saved my life. Good work, guys."

"Just doing my job, Premier" said Patrick humbly.

"I'm glad you did. And I have to say that the LeBlancs are turning out to be a formidable detective team. Marc, will you send your final account to Tom, please?"

"There will be no charge," I said, "and I shall be returning the honorarium to the Province."

"Then we are doubly in your debt."

"Hear, hear," said Tom.

"Have they confirmed that the guy who was killed was Vindex?" Rosalie asked.

"As far as we know," Patrick said. "We've taken DNA samples and asked Scotland Yard to check with the British army to make sure, but there doesn't seem any reason to doubt his identity."

"If it's not him," I said, "who else would it be?"

"No, that's him, alright," said Wendell. "Now, folks, tomorrow I'd like the pleasure of your company at the legislature to take a photograph of this group. I'd like to remember you all in the years to come. I've got a photographer coming in at eleven, if that's okay. I thought we'd take it in front of Joe Howe."

36

The next day was warm and sunny when we gathered at Joseph Howe's statue in the grounds of Province House, and we were all in a good mood. Robert and Kevin were still on duty, but the others had been recalled now that the assassin had been apprehended. Wendell insisted that they join us for the photograph to acknowledge their efforts, and getting filthy in the tunnels. Grace had heard about the photo shoot and had badgered Matthew into becoming part of it, so they were there, she loudly and prominently, he shyly and partly hidden behind others.

Angus MacKinnon was walking by, saw the gathering and decided that he, too, would like to be in the picture.

Not that Wendell minded, saying, "Come on! The more the merrier."

A bus-load of tourists who were visiting the legislature milled around us, thinking this event was part of their tour, and several of them joined the line-up. Wendell laughed, saying that the sudden growth of participants from 16 to 25 was attributable to his animal charisma.

The poor camera man was getting into a state because the size of the tableau kept changing, as did the places of some people like Grace, who jockeyed for a better position. One change Wendell would not permit was that Rosalie and I should be on one side of him, and Patrick and Ruth on the other.

Finally, the group settled down and the snapping began. Then the photographer asked us to stay still while he changed the position of his tripod.

"Big smiles," he cried, and somebody yelled, "Say cheese!"

We all obliged, especially Grace, who showed almost every tooth she possessed.

Then, without warning, a woman brandishing a large knife rushed forward and lunged at Wendell.

When the knife was only millimetres away from him, a shot rang out and she dropped like a stone.

There was a cacophony of cries and shouting as the group dissolved in disorder, the tourists running away as fast as they could.

Robert and Kevin rushed forward to secure the woman, but quickly looked up and pronounced her dead.

I stepped forward and looked down at her face.

It was Marga.

I remembered her last words to me: *You are the chosen one.*

It struck me that whatever trust she had reposed in me had certainly not been repaid in any way she could have approved or understood.

"You know her, Marc?" Patrick asked.

"Yes, her name was Marga. I don't think I ever knew her last name. I thought she was still in London. She was a close associate of Vindex, maybe his lover."

"Well, she can join him now," Patrick said. He looked at Kevin and Robert. "That was good work. Which of you got her?

"Not me," said Kevin. "Well done, Bob."

"My gun never left my holster," Robert said, a dazed look on his face.

"Anyone see a gun in the crowd?" Patrick shouted to those who were left. "Anything suspicious? Anyone?"

All present shook their heads.

"Okay. Call it in, Kevin, and get the body out of here ASAP. Premier, unless you need anyone to stay around, I suggest you all disperse and go about your business."

"Will do, Patrick, and gladly. Come on friends, let's go."

He came over to where Rosalie and I were standing. "Thanks again. I won't forget this in a hurry. Oh, by the way, Tom has a present for you. Just take it and don't ask how it was done."

Tom handed me a manila envelope. Inside was my private investigator's licence.

I thanked them both, and my wife and I walked away up Hollis Street, on our way to Police Headquarters to pick up the Bugatti. We both were glad to be going home and getting back to normality.

There were a lot of people about and a number of them were bunched together at the crosswalks at the Brunswick and Duke traffic lights. As we were waiting for the lights to change, I said to Rosalie, "Where the hell did that shot come from? It's a damn good thing, whoever did it. Otherwise our premier would be dead now."

A low voice came from right behind me. "Always glad to be of service, little brother."

I whirled around, but he was gone. Larry had disappeared into the tide of humanity.

Acknowledgements

Grateful thanks are due to my wife, Caroll Anne, and my editor, Andrew Wetmore, for their assistance and forbearance during the writing and preparation of this book.

About the author

Jeremy Akerman is an adoptive Nova Scotian who has lived in the province since 1964. In that time he has been an archaeologist, a radio announcer, a politician, a senior civil servant, a newspaper editor and a film actor.

He is painter of landscapes and portraits, a singer of Irish folk songs, a lover of wine, and a devotee of history, especially of the British Labour Party.